THE
VANISHING
MAN

Center Point
Large Print

Also by Charles Finch and available from Center Point Large Print:

The Last Enchantments
Home by Nightfall
The Inheritance
The Woman in the Water
The Laws of Murder
An Old Betrayal

THE VANISHING MAN

CHARLES FINCH

CENTER POINT LARGE PRINT
THORNDIKE, MAINE

This Center Point Large Print edition
is published in the year 2019 by arrangement with
St. Martin's Press.

Copyright © 2019 by Charles Finch.

The text of this Large Print edition is unabridged.
In other aspects, this book may vary
from the original edition.
Printed in the United States of America
on permanent paper.
Set in 16-point Times New Roman type.

ISBN: 978-1-64358-164-4

Library of Congress Cataloging-in-Publication Data

Names: Finch, Charles (Charles B.), author.
Title: The vanishing man / Charles Finch.
Description: Center Point Large Print edition. | Thorndike, Maine :
    Center Point Large Print, 2019. | Series: A Charles Lenox mystery
Identifiers: LCCN 2019002805 | ISBN 9781643581644 (hardcover :
    alk. paper)
Subjects: LCSH: Lenox, Charles (Fictitious character)—Fiction. |
    Private investigators—England—London—Fiction. | Murder—
    Investigation—Fiction. | Large type books.
Classification: LCC PS3606.I526 V36 2019b | DDC 813/.6—dc23
LC record available at https://lccn.loc.gov/2019002805

For Emily, with greatest love

ACKNOWLEDGMENTS

With every book I write, I seem to wind up thanking the same people, and yet my debt to them continues to grow. Should I give up and just start selling these spots? Watch this space. In the meanwhile, I am, as ever, grateful foremost to my inimitably generous and wonderful editor, Charles Spicer, and to my agent, Elisabeth Weed, whose calm, intelligent, and affectionate guidance is what every writer deserves but too few have. I know how fortunate I am.

Neither works alone: at Minotaur, Andy Martin leads a spectacular team, including Sarah Melnyk, Hector DeJean, Sarah Grill, Paul Hochman, and David Rotstein, while Elisabeth has in her corner at The Book Group the kind and capable Hallie Schaeffer.

I want to give special thanks to Martin Quinn, whose ingenuity and enthusiasm and great cheer have turned him from an acquaintance into a valued friend and an invaluable colleague as we've worked more closely together.

In my personal life, I'm again overrun with people I should name. But let me just use this occasion to point out some of the amazing people I've met during my time in Chicago's literary community: Rebecca Makkai, Kim Brooks,

Sasha Hemon and Teri Boyd, Rebecca George, Elizabeth Taylor, Jennifer Day, and of course everyone who was at Ragdale, along with the people who run it. Each of you is extremely dear to me.

Readers, you've given me a career. I don't think I deserve it, and I don't know how I ended up here. But you are in my heart as I write these books, truly. Plus, without talking to you on Facebook I might go crazy.

Finally, to my family, near and far: I love you so much.

THE
VANISHING
MAN

CHAPTER ONE

Once a month or so, just to keep his hand in the game, Charles Lenox liked to go shopping with his friend Lady Jane Grey.

On this occasion it was a warm, windy day in early June of 1853, quiet, the gently sunny hour of late morning before the clerks would fill the streets on their way to take lunch. The two friends were next-door neighbors on tiny Hampden Lane, in the heart of London, and he was waiting on her steps at ten o'clock precisely. At five past, she came out, smiling and apologizing.

They left, eventually turning up Brook Street and walking past the little string of streets that ran parallel to their own, talking.

"Why are you checking your watch every ten seconds?" she asked after they had gone about halfway.

"Oh! I'm sorry," said Lenox. "I've an appointment at noon."

"I hope it's with someone you've hired to teach you better manners."

"The joke's on you, because it's with a duke."

"The worst-mannered wretch I ever met was a duke," Lady Jane said. As they crossed Binney Street, Lenox's eyes stayed for an extra moment on a man painting an iron fence with a fresh coat of black paint, whistling happily to himself. "Which one is it?" she asked.

"Out of discretion I cannot say."

"I call that disagreeable."

Lenox smiled. "It's a case."

She turned her gaze on him. It had been a long drought since his last case—more than a month. "Is it? I see."

Though both considered themselves tenured veterans of London now, anyone observing them would have seen two very young people, as young and resilient as the summer day. Lenox was a tall, slender, straight-backed young bachelor of twenty-six, bearing a gentlemanly appearance, and with, whatever Lady Jane said, a courteous manner. He was dressed in a dark suit, hands often behind his back, with hazel eyes and a short hazel beard. There was something measuring and curious in his face. As for Lady Jane, she was five years his junior, a plain, pretty woman of twenty-one, though she had been married for fully a tenth of those living days, which gave her some obscure right to self-regard for her own maturity. This told in her posture, perhaps. She had soft, dark curling hair; today she wore a light blue dress, with boots of a tan color just visible beneath its hem.

They had grown up in the same part of the countryside, though until he had moved to London, Lenox had never considered her part of his generation. By the time he'd noticed she was, Lady Jane had been engaged.

They neared New Bond Street, where the shops began, as the church clocks chimed the quarter hour.

In truth it was not altogether customary that *she* went shopping quite so often as she did— in most households like Lady Jane's, the task would have fallen to a maid—but it was one of the things that she liked, and Lenox liked it for that reason.

The meeting at noon was continually on his mind, even as they walked and spoke. Lenox was a private . . . well, what word had he settled on! Investigator? Detective? It was a new endeavor yet. Three years could count as new, when the field was one of your own rough-and-ready invention, and when success had been tantalizingly close at moments but remained mostly elusive.

A duke might well bring it close enough to hold with two hands.

This intersection was vastly busier than their peaceful street. She stopped at the corner and looked at a list. After she had been studying for a moment, he said, "What do you need today?"

"Are you going to bother me with questions the whole time?" she said, trying to decipher, he could tell from many years of knowing her, her own handwriting.

"Yes."

She looked up and smiled. She pointed to the window next to which they were standing. It was a barber's. "Shall we buy you some mustache grease?"

"Oh, no," he said, looking at the sign that had inspired the question. "I make my own."

"How economical."

"Yes. Though it puts you in the way of quite a lot of bear hunting."

"You are in a very amusing mood, I suppose, Charles. There—I've made it out. Let's go to the greengrocer's first."

He bowed. "Just as you please, my lady."

They made their way carefully down New Bond Street, stopping in at every third or fourth shop. Jane was very canny, while Lenox shopped almost at random; at the confectioner, as she was remonstrating with Mr. Pearson over the price of an order of six dozen marzipan cakes she wanted for a garden party she was having, Lenox decided with little prompting to order a cake to be sent to Lady Berryman, who had invited him to the country for August.

"That reminds me," Jane said to the baker. "I have an odd request. Could I order an eggless cake from you? Vanilla. It's for my husband's aunt. I wrote down the recipe she gave me. She's lord-terrified of eggs, I'm afraid."

"Why on earth?" said the baker, so moved by

this horrible information that he forgot himself.

"Can you think I have asked her, Mr. Pearson?"

"Blimey," he said. Then amended himself. "Blimey, my lady."

She raised her eyebrows. "I know. Imagine being married to her."

"I couldn't," said Pearson fervently, which was true for several different reasons.

Lenox was just about to interject that he knew the lady in question, a larger person, and that he would stand on his head if she had ever refused a dessert in her life. But as he was about to speak, Jane threw him a look, and he knew to keep mum.

In the street again, after they'd gone, she explained that she had read a recipe for an eggless cake from Germany and wanted to try it, but didn't dare insult the baker.

"You could have made it at home."

"No—no. He has the lightest hand in London, Mr. Pearson," she said. "Speaking of which, how is Lancelot?"

He made an irritated face at her, and she laughed. Lancelot was a young cousin of Lenox's on half-term from Eton and therefore in the city for two weeks of what his family had optimistically called *seasoning*. "I would prefer not to discuss it."

"Does he still want to come with you on a case?"

15

"Ha! Desperately."

"Has he gotten you with the peashooter again?"

"Please leave me in peace."

They proceeded past the cobblers, then the book stall—BACK IN STOCK, EXCLUSIVELY IN ALL OF LONDON, *Uncle Tom's Cabin*! a sign declared excitedly—before arriving at the dressmaker. Here Lady Jane went inside alone to have a word, as Lenox skulked outside, feeling like a schoolboy. Soon, though, he was meditating on the upcoming meeting.

The Duke of Dorset!

He thought of the title with a tightening in his stomach, and then of the letter that contained the entirety of his knowledge of the case thus far: *His Grace has discovered that a possession upon which he places high value is missing. He would appreciate your advice regarding its potential recovery.*

He checked his watch and saw that it was ten past eleven. They were near the end of their ramble, and he felt a quick flicker of melancholy. When he was with Lady Jane, he generally forgot himself; just at the moment, a welcome oblivion.

If Lenox's first year in London after moving down from Oxford had been characterized by his tenacious, mostly fruitless search for work as a detective, the subsequent eighteen months had been more complex and difficult. In part it was still to do with the scorn his profession drew from his peers, as they advanced steadily onward in their fields—and in part it was to do with the lonely feeling that all around him his friends were marrying, having children even, while he was still by himself.

But most of all, of course, it had to do with the death of his father. At first he had borne up under this misfortune well, he thought. Fathers were supposed to die before their children, he supposed, and he knew any number of friends who had been orphaned long ago. But recently, especially in the last six months, his grief had shown itself in odd, unexpected ways. He found himself losing minutes at a time on train platforms and in gardens, thinking; he found himself dreaming of his childhood.

Perhaps it had to do with the fact that they had never been especially close. He had loved and revered his father, but the easier friendship had been with his mother. Had he assumed there would be time, later on in life, for their relationship to grow? His father had been only sixty-one when he died; for his second son, it had been, surprisingly, not as if some venerable building in London disappeared, which was what he had always imagined—Parliament, for instance—but as if London itself had.

This past year he felt the loss more keenly with each month, not less, and he was sure

17

that was unnatural. For the first time in his life, he woke each morning with a sense of dejection—a sense that, well, here was another day to be gotten through—rather than happiness.

CHAPTER TWO

Of all people, Lady Jane perhaps sensed her friend's state of mind most delicately. When she came out of the dressmaker's, a look that was difficult to read passed across her face, as if she knew where his thoughts had turned.

"Everything acceptable?" he asked cheerfully.

"Yes, they're still making dresses."

They resumed their stroll. A few shops down the long boulevard, they passed the optician. "I really would like a barometer above anything," Lenox said longingly, pausing before a beautiful brass one in the optician's window. "Ah, well."

"What a waste of money it would be," she said.

"They say it is good to have friends who support one's interests," Lenox replied, studying the barometer.

"You are dead in the center of the largest city on earth. When was the last time you even saw a ship?"

"Ha! There you're going to feel foolish, because I see them nearly every day on the Thames."

"From a cab." She pulled his arm. "Let's go, you can't be late to your duke."

They proceeded down New Bond, talking of this and that. It seemed Lady Jane had a kind word for every person they passed, and it occurred to Lenox that just as he had been struggling to find his feet in his profession, she had perhaps felt something like an impostor in her first years in London—in the very earliest days of her grand marriage, to an earl's first son. Perhaps this was why she shopped for herself; perhaps it gave her a sense of intimacy with their leafy, occasionally intimidating London neighborhood, making a community of it. Like him, she belonged, from the first, to a small place, a village. Now she had made a small place here, in the biggest place. A village of its own.

They spent some time discussing the duke. A duke, after all! The whole of the United Kingdom, in its population of thirty million, possessed just twenty-eight such creatures. The least of them was a figure of overpowering consequence. Yet even among their rank were finer gradients, and the man Lenox was shortly to see held one of the three or four greatest dukedoms.

Theirs was the highest tier of the nobility, the dukes, first in the land beneath the royal family. Not only that, but in their innermost souls not a few dukes and duchesses would have pointed to their lineage (the title of "duke" had come into existence in 1337) and claimed a greater stake in the leadership of Britain than the come-lately family currently chattering around the throne in German accents.

After them, it went so: first the marquesses,

20

thirty-five of these, and their wives, the marchionesses. Then earls—and there it became complicated, because the title of "earl" was nearly oldest of all, originating as long ago as the year 600, historians said, when each shire of England had a *jarl* (Norse for "noble warrior"), which was the reason that in England each earl was still entitled to a small crown: a coronet.

Many earls in England (including Lady Jane's father, Lord Houghton) would not have admitted for a second to being beneath a duke. Their wives were called countesses, because nobody had ever thought to name them earlesses—which had struck many schoolboys memorizing these facts as extremely stupid indeed.

Thereafter it got greatly simpler. Viscounts were next, nearly a hundred of these, common as church mice, the poor devils. Finally came barons, last rank in the peerage.

"And there you'll be, at the very top of the heap," said Jane.

"I doubt he'll make me a duke there on the spot," Lenox said.

"Probably just a baron or something."

"I do wonder what he wants. *A possession upon which he places high value.* I only hope it's not his lucky kilt, or something like that."

Lady Jane laughed. "And the laundress has lost it, yes. I could see that being the calamity, I fear."

Lenox himself held none of these titles.

Just to confuse things, there was still one title left over, and it was here that he entered the picture: Baronets were called "sir," as Lenox's older brother, Sir Edmund, had now been in the eighteen months since their father's death.

A knight was also called "sir," but his children couldn't inherit the title. It belonged to a sole person and died with him, a great writer, say, or artist, or dear intimate of the Queen's ninth-favorite cousin.

All of these gentry taken together with their families numbered not more than ten thousand, but Lenox, as the second son even of a very old, landed, and honored baronetcy, was as far down the slopes of the mountain of aristocracy from the Duke of Dorset as the thirty-millionth Briton, drunk in a ditch, was from Lenox himself.

It was an absurd system. Almost nobody believed in it as more than a matter of chance, except for the very old aunts and uncles who kept the genealogies. Yet all of them also, somehow, believed in it implicitly.

Strange to be an Englishman, an Englishwoman.

At last they reached the turn of New Bond Street, where they saw the most dignified shop in the whole row, housed inside a handsome stone building with purple wisteria climbing its white face. This was the leecher's—the best leecher in town, people generally agreed, where they boxed the living leeches in boxes bound

22

with blue ribbon, as if they were marzipan cakes themselves.

Despite this enticement, Lenox and Lady passed by the leecher's in favor of their own favorite shop, which stood just around the corner, behind a short porch made of plain, unsanded boards. Over the door it said nothing but BERGSON in plain white stenciled lettering.

They pushed the door open and saw Bergson himself in a chair behind a broad counter, looking infernally grumpy and making absolutely no movement to rise and greet them. A duke or an earl or a murderer or anyone on God's green earth could have walked in and his reaction would have been the same.

He was a silent old Swede, Bergson, who had spent most of his life in America and then, for reasons known only to himself, come to London and set up an exact replica of the shop he had once owned in the Wisconsin territory.

An exact replica, truly exact, which meant that there were items of no conceivable use to a Londoner, like two-hundred-pound bags of cornmeal (enough to last a long cabin winter, in lesser demand here), mixed with those of delightful novelty and tireless fascination.

"Look!" said Jane, handling a necklace with a large polished turquoise at the end of two rubbed-leather ropes. "These are the fashion right now, Duch says."

Lenox looked at it doubtfully, then at the stone-faced Bergson, who, in bib overalls of a denim that was either very dark or had never been washed, did not look even adjacent to the world of fashion. Some people said he had lost his whole family to a fever, others that that he had left America when Wisconsin had become a state five years before, because he had murdered another man over a plot of property once and could not survive a land with laws.

Lenox suspected him simply of being shrewd; this was one of the most popular shops in London, its stock replenished just often enough to be endlessly fascinating.

Bergson was not telling—he barely deigned to speak to his customers—but he did sell Charles and Jane a variety of items: bars of pine soap, bags of sifted brown sugar, rough lumps of silver, a woven fishing creel that Lenox thought he might give his brother, Edmund. Lady Jane bought a handsome leather cap for her husband, who was due back from India with his troops in August. Lenox considered a tinderbox before buying Lancelot an arrowhead, silvered with mica.

"See, you do like having Lancelot," said Lady Jane as they left.

"In fact I do not, but I love Eustacia very dearly." This was Lancelot's mother, Lenox's first cousin. "As for Lancelot, he'll slit my neck with this arrowhead tonight."

She mulled this over. "Better than the tinder-box, then, all things considered, since our houses are side by side. Look, it's eleven forty, Charles. You had better go and see about your duke."

CHAPTER THREE

He arrived at Dorset House twenty minutes later, taking off his hat in the doorway and listening very attentively to Theodore Ward, the duke's private secretary, who was leading him inside.

"Just to clarify once more, our expectation, His Grace's expectation, is that we may trust in your absolute discretion, Lenox. Really, your absolute—well, you understand. You do, don't you?"

"I'm scarcely liable to change my answer the ninth time you ask, Theo."

Ward's brow darkened, and for just an instant they were two boys on the cricket pitch at school again, arguing over whose turn it was to bowl. "I say, Charlie, it really is the most highly—"

Lenox held up a hand. "I'm sorry. You have my word. My absolute word. My rock-solid bottom-of-the-ocean heaven-swear-it word. Honestly."

Ward was mollified. "Good. It's only—I don't think I have ever even seen the duke perturbed."

"I understand."

He did. In his work, Lenox had seen people of all stations experiencing the most frantic moments of their lives. Having encountered wrongdoing or violence, none of them, from scullery maid to stiff-chinned major, could stay unchanged.

26

"Just wait here a moment, then, if you wouldn't mind."

Lenox smiled. "I could live here comfortably enough for a while if you like."

The secretary followed Lenox's gaze across the enormous entryway. They had just come in from the noisy streets of London, but the cavernous silence made it like stepping into a house recessed deep in the pine-tree countryside: the vast checkerboard marble floor, the curling staircase, the high arched ceiling, a mahogany settle with the proportions of a dinghy.

"It's something rather else, isn't it?" said Ward.

"They would have slept thirty of us on that stairwell at Harrow."

Ward laughed. "They did cram us. At any rate, stay here. Find a chair if you like." He gestured toward a row of twelve of them. "Have a gander at the paintings. I'll be back when I've made sure His Grace is prepared to see you now."

Ward left, and Lenox looked around the hall.

He had seen paintings before—most of them, in his limited experience, seemed to be of streams, cows, or fine personages, and these were no exception—so instead he turned back to the entrance through which they had just come.

On either side of the heavy front door was a large vertical window. He stood close to one and looked out at the Thames, which glimmered gold under the summer sun.

He was in what some people reckoned London's most beautiful house. It was a white marble citadel built four hundred years before, sitting not all that much more than a thousand yards or so west of the Houses of Parliament and Westminster Abbey, the only private residence _on this stretch of the city. The Thames faced its front door; Buckingham Palace was a five-minute walk from its back one.

Standing there, Lenox was perhaps just conscious of a slight feeling of fraudulence. He had dressed in too warm a gray wool suit and a somber maroon tie—serious clothes, to indicate his seriousness, though in his sober face was a betraying trace of self-doubt. He was only twenty-six, and while he was passionately interested in this work, the number of serious crimes he had investigated could still be counted on one hand.

After perhaps five minutes, Ward returned, and Lenox strode back to the center of the entrance hall. He was shorter and sturdier than Lenox, Ward—a boxer in the deepest places of his heart—and there was no levity left in his manner.

"Just this way," he said. "His Grace will see you at the place of the—in his private study. His real private study."

"Is there a made-up one?" Lenox asked in a quiet voice, because now they were proceeding up the stairwell.

"There is a *public* private study, where he takes

large meetings," Ward replied, equally quietly. "I see."

And he was a duke, after all. Even Jane, whom very little impressed, the daughter of an earl, some distant day destined to be the wife of one when her husband's father died, had given Lenox a second look when he said the name Dorset. Aside from a handful of people—the Queen, Prince Albert, the old heroic red-faced Duke of Wellington, still just alive—there weren't many more powerful inhabitants of England. The Archbishop of Canterbury? Probably not. If you took the whole power of Oxford University it might compete with the duke's.

But not with his wealth.

Theodore Ward (a well-born commoner, son of a squire, which is to say a sort of untitled baronet, and grandnephew of a marquess, bound someday for Parliament in all likelihood—hence this prestigious post) was conscious of this, it was clear. He led Lenox down a red-carpeted hallway of Dorset House as carefully as if they were bound for St. Peter's gates.

When they reached the duke's study, he tapped gently upon the door. "Your Grace?"

"Come in," a voice called after a moment.

Lenox wondered again, briefly, whether there had really been any crime at all. A duke seemed a prime candidate for a cry-wolf. In they went, however.

29

"Charles Lenox, Your Grace," said Theo, bowing slightly.

His Grace looked up from behind his desk. His face was impassive. "Good afternoon, Your Grace," said Lenox.

"Come in," Dorset said. "You may sit."

It was a spectacular little room. One wall was entirely covered in windows, which overlooked the river and the bankside. Two others were taken up with bookshelves, which held innumerable small treasures; Lenox saw a scored and battered Anglo-Saxon broadsword laid along a velvet runner.

The final of the room's four walls, directly behind Dorset's immaculate French desk, was the scene of the crime.

Lenox and Ward sat in two ebony chairs, upholstered in pale green, facing the duke.

"Ward tells me you have set up as a private sort of police officer."

"Well—after a fashion, Your Grace, yes, I suppose that's correct."

The duke studied him. "He also tells me you are trustworthy."

There was no point in modesty here. "Yes, Your Grace."

The duke paused once again. He was thin, aged about fifty-five, Lenox would have said, and wore a navy suit with a gray waistcoat, like a schoolboy. He had trim gray hair, firmly set blue-gray eyes, and a mustache. He held a gold pen in one hand.

There was something ethereal in his lined face, as if a lifetime of holding his position had somehow insubstantiated him individually, his personality absorbed partially into his station. And his expression was the expression of a man who has heard the word "yes" many, many times in his life, and expects to hear it many more still, yet who is also trained to the strictest self-discipline. It was the expression of a man with dozens and dozens of servants whose existence was dedicated to him and of whose individual existences he was only loosely aware.

"I knew your father in Parliament before his death."

Lenox was a stoic, like all of his class, and only said, "Did you, Your Grace," without a question mark in the reply.

"He was a man of principle."

"He certainly was, Your Grace."

"Yes, I liked him very much. I dislike it when the ministries are out of the House of Lords, but I would have been happy to see him in a cabinet."

"He declined several posts, I know, Your Grace."

The duke barked a laugh, as if Lenox would have to dig much deeper to surprise him. "Yes, I know."

"My apologies, Your Grace. Of course you do."

31

Dorset gave him one final, appraising look, as if he were a horse up for a prize at a county fair, then nodded. "You had better leave us, then, Theo," he said.

CHAPTER FOUR

When the private secretary had left, the Duke rose and walked to a discreet stand of variously shaped crystal decanters. "Whisky?" he said.

Lenox's father's guideline flashed through his mind: Upon a first meeting, always accept the offer of a drink from a man lower in rank than yourself, never from a man higher in rank than yourself.

"Thank you, no, Your Grace," Lenox said, still sitting.

"As you like it." The duke stoppered the bottle he had opened. He turned back to Lenox. "How do you generally proceed in this kind of matter?"

"Ward told me very little."

The duke strode back to the desk. "Good. He knows very little."

"Given that, Your Grace, perhaps it would be best if you began at the start and told me as much as you could."

Lenox expected some further cavil or hesitation, but instead, after resuming his seat, the Duke launched directly into his story. Once he had taken a decision, he moved forward without reservations, apparently. Lenox stowed that away as a potentially valuable piece of knowledge.

"It's about a painting," Dorset said.

"So I had guessed, Your Grace."

The duke looked at him sharply. "Mr. Lenox?"

"The one piece of information I had from Ward was that you were missing a possession you valued." Lenox nodded to the wall behind the duke. "There are normally eight paintings on your wall, four on each side of you. At the moment there are seven. The empty space is conspicuous."

"I see. But for all you know it's been taken away for cleaning, and what's missing is a string of diamonds."

Lenox shook his head. "No, Your Grace. One of the two nails upon which the painting was hanging is ripped halfway out, the other is gone, and there is a fresh wound in the wood where it was. You can see raw wood under the varnish."

The duke turned back to look once again. "So you can."

"Not even your most careless footman would handle a painting from your study that way. Or the wall's paneling."

The duke looked at him, neither impressed (as perhaps Lenox had hoped he would be) nor displeased.

"This is your trade, then," he said curiously. "Observation."

"It is, Your Grace." Lenox hated that word, "trade," but of course it *was* his trade. Still, he couldn't help but add, "I believe that one must

34

take money in exchange for services or goods for work to be properly considered a trade, if one wished to be technical, however."

Dorset looked surprised. He pulled a gold case, engraved with his coat of arms and clasped with a ruby, from his waistcoat pocket. He drew a small cigar from it and closed the case again. "You don't take money?"

"No, Your Grace."

"I see. You are a hobbyist."

"No, Your Grace. My practices are professional. But I am—"

He hesitated. How to explain it, quite?

But the duke understood. "No, I see." He lit the cigar from a safety match struck against his lampstand. "Be that all as it may—you are correct that it is a painting that has been stolen. You may also wish to know that I want to know who took it very badly."

"Naturally, Your Grace."

"No, not naturally."

"Excuse me?"

"*Who,* I said. I only care about the *who* of the thing. The painting itself is of little consequence to me."

Lenox nodded. That was unusual. "May I assume that the painting is"—he gestured at the seven pictures still on the wall—"also a portrait?"

"It is. A portrait of my great-grandfather, the fourteenth duke."

"I would imagine that you might value the object itself in that case."

Dorset shook his head. "There you would be wrong. He had his portrait painted oftener than most. We have a dozen more scattered here and there. One is hanging in my club, where I see it every day, and another in the Lords."

Lenox squinted at the paintings. There was something wrong about them, though he couldn't yet put his finger on what.

He returned his attention to the duke. "Perhaps you are worried about your safety, then?"

"I am not," said Dorset. "New locks have been installed on the windows and door of the study, and the staff is on alert. Listen here, however. What were you looking at? Just now, behind me?"

What had he been looking at? He stared at the paintings again.

Then he realized: One of them was wrong.

From left to right the pictures might have been numbered one through eight. With, as Lenox had said, four on either side of the duke's desk. The missing one would have been numbered six in the sequence.

The first, all the way to the left, hung closest to the large windows overlooking the Thames. Lenox's inexpert eye dated it roughly to Elizabethan times. Going left to right, the paintings grew one by one slightly more modern,

36

concluding with what he felt sure was the current duke's own father.

But one of the paintings was wrong.

"I take it that these are other of your predecessors, Your Grace," he said, pointing to the four paintings on the left.

"They are, yes. Dukes of Dorset."

Then Lenox's eyes looked past the duke and to the right side of the room, where the missing painting had hung. "And the last two are, as well—like the missing one."

"Yes."

"The farthest to the right, next to the whisky you very kindly offered me from the bookcase"— the one that Lenox had numbered eighth in his own mind—"being, I would hazard, of your own father."

"Yes," said the duke again.

"But that one." Lenox pointed to the painting just over the duke's left shoulder. Number five. Just next to the missing painting, number six. "That one is very different, Your Grace."

"Different."

"The other six, I can see, are all almost exactly the same in size. This one is half as large. It is also darker, and it is less—I suppose the sitter looks less distinguished than your other ancestors. Forgive me for saying so, Your Grace."

The duke looked a shade amused for a moment, and then more serious. He gazed at Lenox for a long time.

At last he spoke. "But that painting is not the one that's missing."

"No," said Lenox. Then he added, "My instinct with crime is always to look for anything that seems off. The painting merely seems off. We needn't discuss it if you prefer."

"No. It is quite bound up in why you are here. But it is—well, I was unwilling to call in Scotland Yard for a reason. The matter is too serious. And it has to do with exactly this painting, the fifth."

So he thought of it as the fifth, too, and the stolen one as the sixth, perhaps. "I am very curious, Your Grace."

The duke leaned back in his chair, crossing his legs with the shush of very expensive cloth. "Very well. Today is Wednesday."

"Yes."

"On Monday, that is June first, the Duchess and I had planned to depart for Ireland. I have a house on Lough Leane. My son, however, who was to travel with us, fell ill that day with a fever. Out of an excess of caution—he is my only son and my heir—we delayed the date of our proposed departure to yesterday, Tuesday. He refuses to see a doctor, the stubborn fool."

Lenox took a notebook from his pocket. "The second. Might I take notes?"

"If you wish." The duke went on, his straight, slender body standing over the chair, as if he himself were posing for a portrait. "It was then, the second, yesterday morning, that I came into my study. It was just before seven o'clock. The painting was gone."

"Did you come in for any specific reason? A noise?" asked the young detective.

"No. I generally breakfast alone here, answering letters."

"What did you do when you saw the sixth painting was missing?"

The duke smiled enigmatically. "Looked at the fifth and heaved a sigh of relief."

"And then, Your Grace?"

"Rang the bell, and quickly questioned every servant I could find. None of them had seen or heard anything. My manservant, Craig, has questioned them all at greater length, and confirmed the same."

Lenox nodded, pondering this. "When was the last time you had been in the room?"

"Late the previous evening. Everything was in order then."

"Was anyone from the household in the room after you, Your Grace?"

"Only Craig. He is a Scotsman who has been with me thirty years. Before that he was in the army. He tells me that the room was in perfect order when he left, after tidying it."

"Was there any sign of how the thief might have gained access to the room?"

"Nothing could have been clearer. The door

was locked when I came in yesterday morning, but the thief left a window open. They had very definitely been shut."

Lenox looked over at the windows, which were locked now, with thin curtains tied away from them to either side. He nodded. "I see. Did the missing painting have any value?"

"I think it probably the least valuable painting on the wall," said the duke, with an odd satisfaction. "Even if it were not stolen but freely sold by its owner, myself, its worth would not exceed fifteen or twenty pounds at auction."

"Is that all?"

"If more, only because its sitter is a Duke of Dorset, perhaps. Its painter has been forgotten. Next to it, you see, is a Joshua Reynolds of my grandfather, which would obviously be a different matter." Even Lenox knew Reynolds. "Nor was my great-grandfather—who was in the sixth portrait, the missing one—a great political leader, like his own father. Or mine. He was a quiet man."

Both of those men had served in the cabinet of Parliament with relatively little distinction, Lenox knew, though that was not an opinion he would share in this proud household, where they were evidently remembered as Ciceros of the Embankment.

His eyes returned to the much smaller, smokier painting. Number five.

It was in a wood frame, not gilt like the others, and its sitter wore a plain dark shirt, open at the neck. He had a small gold earring, in the fashion of the 1810s. But the painting looked a bit older than that to Lenox's (untrained) eye. The sitter held a delicate flower carelessly by its stem, and his gaze was directed at the viewer.

There was an intelligent watchfulness to him. In the empty space by him on the canvas were a few lines of cursive writing, as you sometimes saw in old French pictures of Christ.

"Who is this, then?" Lenox asked, nodding toward the painting.

Dorset smiled, at last. "There you ask to know something that Ward does not know—that, if I am not mistaken, three people on earth know. I suppose you think I may rely upon you to be the fourth."

"I will keep it a secret, Your Grace."

It was a half-truth. He would tell Graham—of course. But the duke needn't know that.

"Very well," Dorset said. "That is the only existing oil painting from life of the writer William Shakespeare."

CHAPTER FIVE

Some hours later, at twilight, Lenox stood in the doorway of a very different sort of room than the beautiful little study by the Thames. He paused, surveying the grizzled inhabitants along their low-slung deal benches, their pint pots of ale in hand, their amiable conversations gathering into a low indistinct rumble, until a pair of heavy sailors pushed through the door and past him, carrying him partway inside.

This was a pub in Cannon Street called the Dovecote, and he was in search of a fellow named Bonden.

The sinewy, angular old landlord walked out from behind the bar to one of the pub's tables, holding four pewter jugs in each hand, foam rocking tautly atop each of them, then placed them on the table with a thud, spilling nary a drop. He returned with the table's empty tankards and laid them in a pan of sudsy water. When he was done, he looked at Lenox, who asked whether Thaddeus Bonden was there.

"Tad Bonden? I can check."

Lenox nodded. "Thank you."

The Dovecote sat squatly near London Bridge, where, being close to two dockyards, it served primarily a naval clientele. A naval clientele, at that, drawn from before the mast, the hammock rather than the officer class, rough, rough-tongued, easy with their money, generous to those they liked, violent to those they didn't.

Presumably those characteristics were also possessed by Bonden, and Lenox was on his guard.

"How'd you hear of him?" the proprietor asked eventually.

A stool at the bar had been vacated. "Could I have a pint of bitter, please," said Lenox, taking it.

The old server briefly smiled. "Lock-jawed, then," he said. "Fair enough."

As he spoke he was already turning toward the tap with a jug in hand, as automatically as if he were only a large piece in some large mechanical contraption designed to serve beer and gin to men.

"Your bitter." The old man looked at him levelly for a moment. "Well, Bonden, he's here, or he ain't, if you catch my meaning. You'll know which in five minutes. Find a table if you like."

Lenox followed these instructions and watched the barman disappear from sight, then return without looking at him. He waited nine minutes, and when that much time had elapsed, he stood, lifted his hat to the proprietor, who nodded back without a change in countenance, and left.

He was a bit disappointed, a bit relieved. Bonden would have been a risk.

It was a long westward trek back across town

43

to Mayfair, but Lenox walked it, the six-odd miles. He had a good deal to consider.

London was a very different place at this hour. The business of the day was done, and everyone but the few lone souls upon the streets had returned home from the diligent, hectic, forgetful city. Yet the late pale violet light made the houses—whose quality improved just perceptibly from street to street over the course of his walk to his own neighborhood—look so sad, cold and alone, the world an arcing, skybound, unknowable place. Those who remained outside were thrown back, with every shop shuttered, every street hawker headed to their hearths, upon little but their own thoughts.

Lenox didn't quite mind that melancholy feeling; and he needed the thoughts. The Romans, in their phrasemaking way, had hit upon it: *Solvitur ambulando*, all problems are solved by walking. In the times when Lenox had been most puzzled during his short career, it was often a long walk that had suddenly galvanized his mind.

And the duke's problem was a significant puzzle, both in itself and because it belonged to the Duke of Dorset.

The walk took him a little more than ninety minutes. His own tall, handsome home came into view when he turned off Grosvenor Square and onto Hampden Lane.

"Graham?" he called when he had reached it and unlocked the front door. "Graham, are you there?"

Nobody answered, but he heard a footstep on the stair. Then he felt a sharp crack on his face, as sudden as a bee sting. He lurched backward.

"Ha!" cried a triumphant young voice.

"You fiend!" Lenox shouted. He had been the victim of this same peashooter four times thus far. "Lancelot! Come here! I'm going to thrash you, I swear on your life!"

But this was apparently insufficient enticement; Lenox's young cousin was already thumping up to his lair on the third floor.

It was hard to conceive of a person belonging less to his name, this Lancelot being, down to his deepest essence, an instrument of mischief. Lenox loved—truly loved—his cousin Eustacia, Lancelot's mother, who had married a fine country-souled man named Stovall and led a loving, charitable, and blameless life in the far west reaches of Cornwall, near the sea.

But Lancelot made it difficult to remember that. He was a child of twelve, with continually dirty knees, brown-blond hair that spiked in every direction regardless of the ministrations it received, and a face that looked mostly innocent, but from time to time flashed a deep cunning. It was just the week before that they had celebrated his twelfth birthday, Lancelot gorging

45

himself that day on chocolate torte in a way that would have made a French courtesan blush.

"Lancelot!" Lenox shouted up the stairs.

But the only response was silence. After these attacks the boy liked to hole up in his room, which was tactically intelligent, given that, alas, it locked from the inside. According to Graham, he had turned it—the best guest room!—into a midden of discarded clothes and lurid illustrated magazines about the bloodiest subjects imaginable, werewolves, vampires, unrepentant murderers. (Lenox had swiped a few of the last. He had research to conduct.)

Lenox shook his head and hung up his hat, rubbing the welt on his cheek and scanning the floor for the projectile.

He found it. A pebble! That was hardly sporting. Really, now. As he examined it there was a far quieter footstep on the stair, and Lenox looked up to see the house's butler, Graham, a compact, sandy-haired man of roughly his own age.

"Good evening, sir. I heard a noise."

"Did you! What hearing you must have!" said Lenox bitterly. He shook his head, removing his jacket. "What does the law say about killing your cousin?"

"It's illegal, sir."

"Still!"

"I believe so, sir."

"And they call this a civilization."

Graham held forth a patched, smoky tweed housecoat, into which Lenox deposited himself, arm by arm. "Your supper is in your study, sir," Graham said.

"Oh. Thank you. Would you care to sit with me while I dine?"

Graham tilted his head. "With pleasure, sir. The Dorset case?"

"Yes. It's a good one."

Graham would not smile, indeed would not inquire further than he already had, but Lenox had known him for eight years, and from a very minor compression of the valet's lips could tell that he was extremely glad to hear it—that they had a case—for from the starting gun they had been strange, friendly partners in this business.

Passing, in the long hallways from which his study branched to the right, the table that bore his silver card-stand, Lenox saw that several people had left their calling cards while he was away that afternoon.

One of them was Sir Richard Mayne, the head of Scotland Yard.

"Mayne didn't come here himself?" he said to Graham.

"No, sir. The card was left on his behalf by a constable."

"Did he have a message?"

"He said that Sir Richard would appreciate a call when you have spare time. There is no rush."

This was mere politeness. Lenox needed the goodwill of Scotland Yard, and he would go to Mayne in the morning. He was in a position that required him to treat his few allies respectfully.

Lenox's career as a detective had been, thus far, a mixed success. The first obstacle to overcome had been the lack of work, but he had chipped steadily away at that. There were long stretches when he had nothing to do, not a case in sight, sometimes until he was very near indeed to the brink of despair. He satisfied himself during such periods with carefully designed courses of study—on poison, firearms, fraud, every criminal subject—but they never felt a substitute for a real case.

Still, something always arrived at last, as it had now. Harder to manage, and harder to bear, was the ridicule visited upon him by members of his own class.

In truth he understood their attitude. Had he been to Harrow and Oxford for this absurd shamming police work? Had he been raised to the manners of the aristocracy, ridden horses with royalty, been invited to the balls of the great metropolis and England's immortal country houses, been flattered by the mothers of young women who knew he had money and position, had he been *Charles Lenox,* only to throw it away?

No, it was agreed, by all but his close friends. Perhaps even some of them secretly agreed.

And on his other flank there was the ridicule of the police. They considered him a mere enthusiast, an amateur; a nuisance.

This was despite the two notable successes of his three-year tenure in London. The first was the case of the Thames Ophelia; the second, the bizarre matter of the businessman in Maida Vale who had gone into a top-drawer butcher's shop, come out with a pound of mutton wrapped in wax paper for his family, and upon reaching the outdoors again immediately taken a pistol from his pocket and shot himself.

Lenox alone could claim credit for solving that one.

He wondered why Mayne wanted to see him. It might well be about the duke.

There was a knock on the front door. Lenox turned, curious, having come about twenty feet into the house. He felt a sharp hunger—he could smell the cook's fragrant leek-and-potato soup, and it had been a long six miles—and hoped the caller would make no very determined demand upon his time.

Graham answered the door, spoke a few words, then closed it gently. "It is a gentleman named Mr. Bonden, sir. He asks if you'll meet him in the street."

Lenox felt a prickle across the back of his hairline. He had been followed home.

CHAPTER SIX

"Tell him I'll be with him in a moment."

"Yes, sir."

In the instant this exchange took, Lenox and Graham came to a quick, silent understanding: Graham should follow them if he could.

Lenox looked into the ancient brass stand by the door, scrolled with lions, where a walking stick and two black umbrellas stood in loose order. He took up the scarred calabash walking stick, which had been his grandfather's. Then he looked outside.

On his steps, with one foot higher than another and his hands in his pockets, was a man of an age very near the duke's, but in all other respects completely different.

He had a weathered face and wizened, piercing eyes. Despite the warmth he wore a long seal-skin jacket. He held a pipe.

"How d'you do," he inquired in a low, powerful voice.

"Mr. Bonden?" Lenox said.

"I understand that you wanted a word with me."

Lenox noticed that Bonden had not used his name. Likely he didn't know it, then. But it would not be hard for him to learn it now that he had Lenox's address.

"I did," he said, putting out his hand. "I'm Charles Lenox."

Bonden returned his handshake, then stood back and considered this information unemotionally. The embers in his pipe glimmered faintly orange, as if they, like he, were cool on the outside but very much alive inside.

"It's not a name I know."

Lenox closed the door behind him, Graham on the other side of it.

"There's no reason it should be."

"Yet you know mine," Bonden said. "That is an uncomfortable situation in some lines of work."

"Listen—shall we take a walk?" Lenox asked, gesturing up the street toward the square.

He was thinking of Lady Jane next door, the odds of running into her and her giving away their closeness, something that would put him and, worse, her in Bonden's power. Not that he had cause to think Bonden a bad man. But he was an unknown one and, perhaps given the way he had followed Lenox here, had something menacing to him.

They started west down Hampden Lane. Lenox's walking stick was clamped tightly under his right arm. He had no idea what to do with it if the cause arose, except swing as hard as he could. That would have to do.

He wondered if it had been unwise to seek help. In the Maida Vale suicide attempt, one of

51

the two cases he could claim to have solved for Scotland Yard, he had worked alone. He'd only been invited in because the police had decided he was merely mad, the gentleman, Quentin Wilkie, who had stepped outside of the butcher's and shot himself. (He had *lived* somehow, Wilkie, but was still comatose.) But Wilkie's wife had insisted that he was quite sane. It was she who had sought out Lenox's help.

Lenox, believing her, had painstakingly reconstructed the scene in the street from eyewitness accounts. One figure had slowly emerged out of those murky overlapping memories: a fellow with a diamond ring on each thumb and a bone-deep tan. Not a typical pedestrian.

Lenox had tracked him down based on the description; he was one Everett Botham, diamond miner from Cape Town.

Thereafter the story came together quickly. During a cave-in, Quentin Wilkie had chosen to haul a fortune in diamonds out of the mines with him rather than Botham, his partner, whom he left for dead. Wilkie returned to London, a rich man. But Botham had reappeared five years later, a still-richer man, and bent on either justice or revenge.

Wilkie must have known instantly when he stepped outside of the butcher's that his life would end either at Botham's hand or on the gallows.

Something like that, at least—police were still untangling the details. Among the men on the case was Mayne, who had been openly grateful to Lenox in a way none of the Yard's inspectors had.

Bonden and Lenox walked in silence for perhaps two hundred steps or so before Lenox said, "I have been wondering about the Dovecote. Why would a naval pub call itself that?"

"Before we venture onto the terrain of etymology," Bonden replied, "perhaps you could tell me why you were looking for me there."

There was a muted authority in his voice.

Lenox stopped and looked at Bonden in the shifting gaslight. They had reached the corner of Hampden Lane and Brook Street, a busy thoroughfare.

"I have been told that you are an expert at finding things, and I need something found."

"Could you please be more clear, on both counts?"

"I have heard your name twice, once from a friend inside Scotland Yard, once from a shipping officer on a case in which I was involved."

"A case?" Bonden looked up at the alabaster houses surrounding them, a smile on his face for the first time. He had taken his pipe in his hand. "You are the highest-living police constable I have met."

"I am in private business."

"Private business," Bonden repeated. He studied Lenox. "You do not have a criminal face."

"Ha! That is convenient to me, since I am not a criminal."

"Are you not? A valuable thing to know."

Lenox laughed shortly. "Listen, Mr. Bonden, we have gotten off to a poor start. I am a practicing detective, with a client who is willing to pay you for your time. My own circumstances have been mine since birth—you may ask after my identity if you wish to verify that—and I am not living on Hampden Lane as the result of any lucrative criminal enterprise. I am interested in police work, yet I am not suited for Scotland Yard. It's as simple as that."

"I see."

"What's more, I'm not after any trouble. I am looking for a specific object and hoped to enlist your aid. That is the whole of it."

Bonden again set his unnerving gaze upon Lenox.

Charles was himself headstrong at times—he was young and bright, after all, and he could have been in Baroness Lieb's parlor at that moment, with amiable company around him, or at the theater with his friend Hugo, or dining quietly with Lady Jane. He only tolerated this inspection now because of what he had heard of Bonden.

Both men—Sir Richard Mayne at the Yard, Willoughby Clark in the navy—had described him as a fellow with a nearly magical ability to locate the mislaid, the stolen, the long forgotten.

54

Neither could account for his abilities; only swear to them. Bonden had once been a seafarer, Clark had told Lenox, but was now settled in London and possessed a reputation, at least in the strange overlapping criminal and official spheres that were conscious of his existence at all, for achieving the impossible. At last Bonden seemed to come to a decision. "Not this time, Mr. Lenox," he said. "But thank you for your interest." He glanced back down Hampden Lane. "You needn't have had your valet follow us. I intend you no harm."

Very abruptly he turned and walked away.

Lenox watched him go, then peered back down Hampden Lane himself. For his part, he couldn't see Graham anywhere.

He sighed. "Damn," he said to himself.

He walked back down the street in the direction of his house, and called out to Graham to show himself.

The valet emerged from a shadowed doorway. "Sir," he said.

"He spotted you."

"Did he?" Graham frowned. "My apologies."

"Oh, don't apologize. I don't know how he managed it. Uncommonly good hearing, perhaps? I should have talked more."

They returned to the house. "That was the Mr. Bonden you have had occasion to mention, sir?"

There was little Graham didn't know of Lenox's professional life. "Yes. I hoped he might assist us on the duke's case. He declined."

"Then the duke is missing something, sir?"

"He is. No matter, though. We'll find it on our own."

And indeed Lenox believed they would. The two of them had been through a great deal in the years since Lenox came to London from university, collaborating every day, out in cold and hot together upon false trails and real ones. Aside from his brother there was nobody in the city that Lenox trusted more.

"But not until I eat," Lenox said, opening the door to his house, peering in cautiously to be sure Lancelot wasn't waiting to spring. He slotted the walking stick back into its brass stand. "I'm starved. In fact I'm happy that Bonden has turned us down, blast him."

"What was the crime to do with, then, sir?" asked Graham, as they proceeded down the long central hall.

It was kept lit to a perfect lulling low candle-light by Lenox's redoubtable housekeeper, Mrs. Huggins, who with any luck had locked cousin Lancelot into some dark, damp, and narrow closet.

"An assault upon a very august personage, in fact."

"Who, sir?" Graham.

"It will wait one moment longer—he's been dead two hundred and fifty years."

CHAPTER SEVEN

Lenox had recently taken to drinking strong tea with his supper. In the mornings he preferred to have Pekoe, the tea of his childhood, which, because it was made of the earliest spring buds, was light and fragrant; but for whatever reason, in the evenings he found that only the very black workingman's India tea, drunk by nine of ten households in England, would suffice. Taken with two spoonfuls of sugar, it gave him a few hours of vibrant energy to work before, for whatever mysterious reason, allowing him to drop into a sweet and effortless sleep.

That evening, as he ate first his leek-and-potato soup, then a very good chop with buttered potatoes and spring peas, he sipped his tea and felt himself slowly stirring into new life after his long day.

Graham sat opposite, hands closed together on the table, listening to Lenox as he described his meeting with the duke. He only interjected once, his eyes widening.

"Shakespeare!" he said.

This counted as a positive effusion from Graham, and Lenox smiled.

"Yes," replied the young detective. "I'm told he's quite famous."

Graham would not be drawn. "But that was *not* the painting stolen, sir?"

"No," said Lenox, eating his chop. "It's the poor old twelfth duke who's gone. The current one being the fifteenth."

"Perhaps the thieves took the wrong painting? A portrait of Shakespeare would be—well, priceless, of course, sir."

"The duke had the same initial thought, and so did I."

"But then, sir?"

Lenox stood up. There were madeleines on the sideboard, the specialty of his cook, Ellie. He took two, returning to the table and dunking one into his tea.

"The first thing I asked the duke was which three people's company I had joined in this knowledge, that there was a painting of Shakespeare from life sitting in the middle of London. I did not also say: if it was indeed a picture of Shakespeare, and this was not some dull, easily disproven family legend."

The duke had given Lenox his answer very simply.

"Myself, the Queen, and Sir Charles Locke Eastlake," he had said.

"Who is Sir Charles Eastlake, Your Grace?" Lenox had asked.

"The Surveyor of the Queen's Pictures."

Lenox had never heard of him before in his life.

"May I ask you about your decision to confide in him, sir?"

"It was on the advice of Her Majesty. It is a national treasure, after all."

Almost involuntarily both had at that moment glanced at the painting.

And the truth was that Lenox had just then felt an odd sort of radiant power emanating from the shabby little portrait, though in itself it was nothing, the sort of three-quarters pose that you could find stacked by the dozen at any London marketplace on a Saturday morning. An art student might have bought it simply to paint over. It was surrounded by what even he could see was much finer art.

But Shakespeare!

There were few people in England to whom his works were not as intimately familiar as the stories of the Bible, and often, as with the Bible, through lovingly wrong retellings, plays put on at local fetes, bedside stories that missed and altered dozens of details—the sort of backhanded homages that make a piece of literature more than a piece of literature, stitching it instead into a nation's culture.

Beyond the work, there were the mysteries. Who was the dark woman of his sonnets? Had Shakespeare been a secret Catholic? Where had he been during his famous lost years? Why had he left his wife his "second best bed" in his will—

as a snub or a compliment? Each was tantalizing, each impossible to answer conclusively. For Lenox—who had always preferred novels to the theater, and never quite understood the pure elation the playwright seemed to elicit in some people—they were more interesting than the work itself. Perhaps naturally, since he was a detective.

"And Sir Charles Locke Eastlake struck you as a trustworthy person, Your Grace?"

"He certainly seemed to be. Sober as a judge, very tedious. But when can one ever be sure?"

"Indeed, Your Grace."

Dorset looked at Lenox evenly. "You may have noticed several surprising people absent from that list of three. My wife, for instance."

"I had noticed that, yes, Your Grace."

"It is the great secret of the Dukes of Dorset, passed hand over hand from one to the next. It is a responsibility each duke has taken very seriously."

"And your son, Your Grace?"

"My solicitors hold a sealed letter to be given to my son in the event that anything happens to me. I shall tell him myself when he turns twenty-five. He is nineteen at the moment."

"What is his name, Your Grace?"

"Corfe."

Lenox nodded. There was a Corfe Castle in Dorset. "How did your family acquire the painting, Your Grace?"

"That is a long story, and not relevant." The duke stubbed out his small cigar and took another from the gold case. "But I hope you can now see why it matters more to me who took the painting than where the painting is?"

"I have a guess, Your Grace."

"Well?"

"Do you believe that the thief took the wrong painting?" Lenox gestured toward the wall. "The sixth, rather than the fifth, from the windows?"

Dorset looked satisfied. He checked his watch. "Yes."

Lenox, heart beating hard, said, "And yet I wonder, Your Grace."

"Eh?"

Lenox didn't speak for a moment, staring at the portraits. "Is the missing picture similar in size to the remaining ones, excluding the portrait of Shakespeare?"

"Identical. They are all modeled on the first."

They both looked toward the first and oldest portrait, next to the windows. "What gives me pause," Lenox said, "is that the Shakespeare is so very different in size, style, framing—in every detail—from the other paintings here. All of those are large, and very majestic, and very—well, ducal, Your Grace."

Dorset frowned. "But why would someone steal a painting from this room other than the Shakespeare? Or if they did, why on earth not the Reynolds?"

Lenox shrugged. "That I do not know, Your Grace. For that matter, why would they steal a painting rather than—just to take an example—your snuffbox there? Those are diamonds, if I am not mistaken?"

Dorset touched his fingertips to the box. "You are not, though I keep pen nibs in it, not taking snuff myself." He looked up at Lenox. "If they were not after the portrait of Shakespeare, I have made an error telling you about it."

Lenox inclined his head noncommittally. "At least I can promise you that I will not compound the error by telling anyone else, Your Grace, if indeed it was an error."

"Thank you," said Dorset, though his mind was elsewhere.

"Had you contemplated Sir Charles Eastlake, Your Grace, as the possible thief?"

The duke glanced at him. "I had."

Lenox shook his head. "I believe we can safely rule him out, personally. If he were the thief, I imagine he would be absolutely and entirely sure to get the right painting. It would have been an insane risk, and he has a very great deal to lose. He would have made no mistake."

"Hm."

"Moreover, he would also know how immediately suspicion must fall upon him."

The duke wore the look of a man who had found himself in deeper waters than he thought and did not like it—though Lenox could tell there was also some relief in the possibility that the portrait of Shakespeare was not part of the robber's plan.

"Yes. True. He might have told someone still, however, though he very solemnly swore to me and to the Queen that he would not."

"He might have, Your Grace."

Dorset looked at Lenox. "The Queen, of course, was not scaling the water pipe of my house on a Monday evening."

"No, Your Grace. It would not have been very stately."

"Besides, it is hers for the asking," the duke murmured, in such a definite way that it surprised Lenox—this glimpse of the intense loyalty of the medieval nobleman, who considered his life worth staking on his sovereign's slightest wish.

Their conversation had not continued much longer, and now, many hours later, in Hampden Lane, slowly eating his madeleines, Lenox sketched in its contours for Graham. He had asked for a detailed description of the painting, had inspected the windows (there was no evidence at all that they had been forced), then had inspected the room, without result.

After that, the 15th Duke of Dorset had rung for Ward and asked him to provide any general information that Lenox needed. As they left, Lenox thanked him, and the duke offered only a troubled nod.

It had occurred to Lenox how very alone he would be again in a moment.

Graham took all this in. "That is why you asked Bonden for his help, sir," he said at last.

Lenox nodded. "Yes. I wondered if there might be something about the missing painting itself, number six as I think of it, which is important after all. Perhaps nothing to do with William Shakespeare whatsoever."

"What will you do now, sir?"

"Go to sleep." Lenox smiled ruefully. "But in the morning, I intend to find this worthless painting, with or without Bonden's help."

Graham nodded but looked troubled. Both of them had it, Lenox could feel: the catch of irresolution, the absolute need to know what had happened, and why. The circumstances were too confused, too ambiguous.

"Very good, sir, though to remind you, you are engaged to have breakfast with Lady Jane Grey."

"Oh, I am, aren't I. Planning this garden party?"

"Yes, sir."

Lenox threw his napkin onto the table. "My life is a plague of obligations."

As if to confirm this bleak statement, upstairs there was a minor boom, which meant his cousin Lancelot was once again in motion—like a battalion marching under cover of darkness.

CHAPTER EIGHT

Lenox was up at the stroke of six o'clock the next morning. By quarter past, he was seated at the desk in his study, carefully reading through the papers, a pair of scissors at hand so that he could clip any article he thought relevant to his encompassing study of criminal activity in London.

It had taken him some time to be happy in this house; his rooms from the year he had first moved to London held a dear place in his heart, with their expansive view of Green Park. It was when he had made this large rectangular study comfortable that he had at last felt really at home. Now he couldn't imagine a better place to work. His books were arranged as he liked, history on one side of the room, fiction on the other. At the far end of the long chamber there was a fireplace surrounded by comfortable chairs; here, closer to the windows, was his desk, topped in red leather. From his chair he could turn and ponder the passersby a few feet below on Hampden Lane.

These morning hours were his most serious time of work. One of the reasons he had hoped to have Bonden's help was to add to his own education, to which he was ardently committed. He wouldn't have minded being a person who could find anything.

Mrs. Huggins came in. "Good morning, sir. Do you have enough tea?"

The housekeeper was a widow of approximately fifty-five, attractive and severe, with dark hair going gray in streaks—who kept house for him more exactingly than perhaps he would quite have preferred.

Lenox looked at the monumental teapot on the corner of his desk, which could have accommodated the needs of a party of eight, then at his own very small teacup.

"For now I think I'll be able to get on, Mrs. Huggins," he said, looking up at her earnestly. "Thank you."

"Mr. Graham is preparing your eggs, sir, and your toast is in the brazier."

"Thank you, Mrs. Huggins."

"If you had time to peruse a few matters of household—"

"Unfortunately it is a very busy morning, Mrs. Huggins. Could we put off the perusing until tomorrow?"

She knew very well what that meant—that he would try to put it off to the day of revelation, if he could. "Very well, sir."

He tried a slight smile. "Be sure to give me two or three reports before the food comes, though. I would like to be apprised of absolutely all this information as it becomes available."

Some days she was receptive to a joke; some

days not. Today: not. "I thought you would like to know, sir," she said stiffly.

"I'm sorry," he said, "I would. I'm very hungry." Then, pressing his luck, he said, "I also much need to take something along with me to Jane's for breakfast—to Lady Jane's—but it slipped my mind to buy flowers, or what have you, yesterday. Do we have anything sitting around?"

"Sitting around, sir!" said Mrs. Huggins.

"Well, I mean, a savory cake, or something of that sort."

She looked at him almost sadly. He knew in these moments that he seemed to her an irredeemable specimen representing the lost ways of a whole generation. "A cake, sir."

"Or something. I did say, 'or something,' Mrs. Huggins."

"I could make a tulip cake in a pinch, sir."

"Might you? I would be extremely grateful."

"In that case Mr. Graham will have to be the one to bring you up your eggs and toast, though, sir! And see to it if you need any more tea!"

Graham could have done this blindfolded and backward. He had been Lenox's scout at Balliol for three years—even now was the person Lenox liked to make his soft-boiled eggs, a duty Mrs. Huggins had only conceded after the bitterest protest—but Lenox just said, "Thank you, Mrs. Huggins. You are a brick."

67

"I suppose such emergencies are part of being in service, Mr. Lenox," she said.

Before long Graham brought the eggs and toast, and Lenox tucked into them with a hearty appetite. The valet sat down in the chair opposite, with his own cup of tea and his own stack of newspapers, and was soon as absorbed as Lenox. This was their daily ritual—or their friendly competition, you might say. Each was put out if the other found a significant clipping that he had missed.

"These are cracking good eggs," said Lenox after a long period of silence, looking up.

"Thank you, sir."

Lenox laughed. "Eh? *Cracking?* Did you pick up on that?"

"Yes, sir."

"Cracking."

"Almost painfully humorous, sir," said Graham, nodding.

Lenox frowned. "You need to get about more, Graham."

"It may well be so, sir."

Lenox glanced up at the clock on his mantel. It was close to eight o'clock. The rays of the sun were just beginning to fall more insistently across the room's dark carpet. "What time is the breakfast, remind me?" he said.

"Nine o'clock."

Lenox sat back. "I have just enough time to run

out and call on Mayne. But I doubt he'll be in the office before eight thirty, and then I shall have to turn around. It's a nuisance."

"Indeed, sir," said Graham, though this time his sympathy was sincere.

Instead of leaving, Lenox took out his notepad. He flipped to the page where he had written the duke's description of the missing painting.

"The painting was thirty inches high by twenty-two inches across," Lenox said, reading. "Or at least the *frame* was, because he swore it was the same size as the other seven, and he had asked Theodore Ward, my old school friend, to measure one of those."

"Do you have any suspicions of Ward, sir?" asked Graham.

Lenox didn't look up from his notes. "No, none," he murmured. On the wall there was a portrait of Lenox's mother's uncle, an earl himself, sitting grumpily in a chair. Lenox had always liked it. He looked over at it. "Would you say roughly that size, Graham?"

"To a first approximation, sir, certainly."

"Not easy to conceal." He looked up at Graham from his notepad. "Whereas the Shakespeare couldn't have been more than fifteen inches high and twelve across. Scarcely much larger than a sheet of paper."

"Interesting, sir."

"The background was Dorset House, in the

country—trees and that sort of thing, the duke said, a pillar. You know how those old portraits look."

Graham nodded. "Yes, sir."

Lenox frowned at his notes. "What is a jerkin?"

"A sort of sleeveless jacket, sir."

"Sounds asinine. Well, he's in a red jerkin and silver pants, this fellow, if you can credit that. Next to him is his favorite dog, a setter with long ears."

Graham nodded. "Anything else, sir?"

"It is signed by the artist very legibly, a person named Quincy Quinn. Oh, and the duke is smiling in it. That shall be a clue, if the jerkin doesn't give it away." Lenox flipped his notebook closed. "It sounds a picture of so little consequence. And yet someone went to the trouble of hiking up the side of that building, prying open a locked window, and stealing it. That is peculiar."

"You saw evidence the window was pried open, sir?"

Lenox shook his head. "No. But Dorset and his valet both swear that it was locked the night before. And it would have been far easier to break into the window than into the house, and then into the study, which itself has two locks."

"It only occurs to me, sir," said Graham, "that perhaps we are all overreaching. Perhaps it was merely one of the servants."

"I specifically asked about that possibility.

Nearly the entire staff had gone to Dorset Castle ahead of the duke and duchess. Those that were left—the duchess's maid, the butler, the duke's valet, the cook—are employees of long standing."

"None with a grudge, sir?"

Lenox tilted his head philosophically. "It is always possible. But the duke told me specifically that he pays well over market rates. That includes Ward. Why steal a painting worth less than that difference and risk the sack?"

"True, sir."

"That is what I keep wondering—why that painting? It's too large, too personal, not valuable enough . . ." He glanced at his watch. "But we can resume this discussion in a bit."

He stood up and straightened out. He didn't really mind at all going to Jane's, though it did well to pretend; his heart, the stubborn old animal, beat a little faster at the thought of seeing her. The irony was that she planned breakfasts like this one partly to help him find a wife. It would be best to leave the city soon, he thought. Behind him on the wall was a map tacked to corkboard and covered with ink: the places he intended to travel.

"Graham," he called, when the tie was done. The valet appeared. "Is Lancelot awake?"

"Not yet, sir."

"You'll see him into Mr. Templeton's hands at nine?"

This was the pimple-covered young curate in charge of showing three young Etonians on their break the sights of London.

"Yes, sir," said Graham.

Before he left his study, Lenox went over to one of his bookshelves on the right side of the room and scanned it for about ninety seconds before finding the small, very soft brown leather book he was looking for. He opened it wholly at random and read a line:

I can easier teach twenty what were good to be done, than be one of the twenty to follow my own teaching.
        —The Merchant of Venice

He frowned, considering this, then slipped the buttery-soft little book into his front pocket.

On the front hall table was the tulip spice cake, an object of perfect beauty, of course, still warm, wrapped in parchment paper, reposing regally upon a deep-blue plate.

"It's a capital cake, Mrs. Huggins!" he called out loudly. "Thank you! Good-bye!"

CHAPTER NINE

The garden behind Lady Jane's house was unusually wild compared to most of those on Hampden Lane, with vines that climbed the fences and a small sunlit knoll encircled by a few towering oak trees, shifting in the breeze.

There was a table on the flagstones outside with four places set, three occupied. Lady Jane waved to Lenox. "There you are! What a cake," she said, taking the plate from his hands. "How neatly it's iced."

"Well, of course," said Lenox with pride.

"Pass my compliments to Mrs. Huggins."

"I will not!" said Lenox indignantly.

She laughed. "You know the duchess, Charles." This was the Duchess of Marchmain, an older cousin of Jane's aged around forty-three or forty-four, very pretty, all that was amiable and kind. She gave Lenox her hand. "And this is my dear friend Miss Euphemia Somers, from Mrs. Clark's. She has just returned from a year in America with her parents."

"I'm charmed to meet you, Miss Somers," said Lenox, bowing.

She inclined her head. "And you, Mr. Lenox. My friends call me Effie."

If Effie Somers had been at Mrs. Clark's

with Lady Jane—a girls' school where Lenox's friend had spent a year perfecting her French and painting sailboats—she was probably around twenty-two. She gave an impression of great ease and good nature. She was not unusually beautiful, but her smile was, and so was her hair, a dark chestnut blond that she wore in plaits, so notably beautiful, in fact, that one might have fallen in love with her for this single trait.

Lenox sat, and the duchess said, "I hear you have been calling upon Dorset."

Lenox peered curiously at her, smiling. "Where on earth did you hear that?"

"Not from me," Jane said.

"A little chickadee saw you going into the house, I suppose."

It would be easier to find privacy in a jammed lifeboat in the middle of the Pacific Ocean than in London. "He was an acquaintance of my father's," Lenox said.

Her husband was a very different kind of duke than Dorset, his title only two generations old and won on the battlefield. But there was a great deal of money in it. "I like him."

"He pinches cheeks," said Effie Somers.

"Does he!" said Lenox, surprised.

She smiled. "He did when I was eighteen, at any rate."

"Come clean, Charles," said Lady Jane, "why were you with him?"

"It really was a social call," he said, and took a covering bite of teacake.

"Just don't go hunting with him," said the duchess.

Jane laughed shortly.

"Why not?" he asked.

They glanced at each other. Miss Somers looked at them inquiringly, evidently in the dark, too. "I suppose he kept it quiet," said the duchess.

"Kept what quiet?" asked Lenox.

Lady Jane, who had before her a small, neatly drawn diagram of the seating arrangements for her garden party, nominally their reason for being there, looked down at it. "Shall we discuss seating?"

"Come now!" said Lenox.

"Even dukes deserve privacy."

Lenox might have let it rest there, except that Miss Somers, to whom he became instantly indebted, said, "But there are only two of us. I'll keep the secret."

"So shall I," Lenox put in right away.

Lady Jane sighed. "Fine. It was about five years ago. It was terribly sad, really. A group were hunting grouse in Dorset, the duke, General Pendleton, and their two sons, and the duke accidentally shot Pendleton's son. Pure bad chance."

"And he died?"

"He lived for a month," said the duchess, her

75

cup of tea poised in her hand. "It was awful for Georgia Pendleton—awful. They have no other sons."

"Was there an inquest?" asked Effie Somers.

"Yes, with no fault found. Everyone present, including the groom, agreed that it was no more than an unfortunate accident."

Lenox reflected on this. "Pendleton commanded a brigade at Waterloo," he said. "He was made a knight for it."

"Your facts are out of date," the duchess said, "for the Queen made him a baron in the list last year. He doesn't come down from the country often, or you would have heard."

"He has no son to leave the title to," said Lady Jane.

"He has a nephew, at least," said the duchess, "with whom he has become closer. His younger brother's son."

Lenox took another bite of his teacake, which had a satisfying cracked-cinnamon sugar crust. He followed it with a sip of tea and looked up into the pure blue sky, thinking of his father and his brother for a passing moment.

"Was there bad blood between Pendleton and the duke?"

"They are not so close as they once were, of course," said the duchess. "But no, the general accepted the situation, ultimately. Of course the duke himself was heartbroken."

Lenox pictured the still, impassive face of the thin and finely dressed aristocrat.

"What a terribly sad story," said Jane's friend.

"Yes. I don't know why we brought up something so morbid!" replied Lady Jane, then with a businesslike tone went on, "Leave it aside—this seating plan. Here is where you are essential, Charles. I need to know everyone who has rejected everyone's proposals among your Oxford friends. It's vital. All the secrets, now, please."

"Why do you care?" he asked curiously.

Lady Jane looked at him for a moment with guilty happiness. "There is a chance the Queen may come. I'd like it to be perfect."

"You'd better cut those branches back, then," said Lenox, nodding upward. "It would be bad news if one fell on her."

"Leave the garden to me." Then, with sudden alarm, she said, "Lancelot will be gone in three weeks' time, won't he?"

"Yes, thank heavens."

"That's good news. It's one thing for him to target you with the peashooter, another Prince Albert."

"I'm offended at that," said Lenox.

"Who is Lancelot?" Effie Somers said.

"Don't ask," he and Jane replied simultaneously, and all three laughed, and the conversation turned decisively away from the Duke of Dorset.

Still, the story of the hunting accident stayed in his mind. And the name: Pendleton.

When they had finished eating breakfast, Lenox went inside to help Lady Jane fetch the cut flowers she was considering for the tables. He said to her, in the back conservatory, "You're about a quarter as clever as you think."

She stopped, surprised. "At least half, I would have said. But how so?"

"As if I knew more than you about who has proposed to whom! I can't even remember who's engaged."

"We have different friends," she said.

He shook his head and smiled. "I'm not going to marry Miss Somers."

Lady Jane paused, looking at him, then said, "But don't you like her? She was the dearest person I knew at Miss Clark's. Always the most popular—but never took sides, even against the worst of the girls. And her father, being a diplomat, has dragged her all over the world these last three years, meaning she's never been thrown in the way of a decent fellow."

"Well, she may be at your party. Say, look at this," he said, and pulled the small leather book from his study out of his breast pocket. "You'll like it."

She took it. "*Selected Quotations of William Shakespeare*. Why do you have it?"

"I just came across it. My father gave it to me when I went to Harrow. It was once his own."

She smiled, flipping through the pages. "There are stars by some of the lines."

"Those are his."

She read one and laughed, studying it. She was one of the people close to Charles who had known his father well.

Eventually she handed the little book back. "I'm very glad you have it."

"So am I."

Lady Jane looked him in the eye. "Don't you like her, Charles? Effie?"

He did, in fact; he liked her more with every passage of the conversation. She didn't have quite so sharp an edge as Lady Jane or the duchess, but there was something lovely about her—the effortlessness of her laugh, the ingenuousness of her wit, her clear intelligence.

He was about to say so, but there was a knock at the door. There were no servants immediately at hand, and he went to answer it himself. He saw, to his surprise, that outside was Theodore Ward.

"Hello, Theo," he said.

Lady Jane came up behind Lenox. "Hello, Mr. Ward."

The young secretary looked utterly changed. His hair was a dark upright shock, his collar loose and his face red. He only just managed to bow. "My Lady." Then he turned back to Lenox. "Charles. Thank goodness."

"What's the matter?" asked Lenox.

"The duke has been kidnapped."

CHAPTER TEN

Lenox opened the door wide. "Kidnapped! What?"

Ward shook his head. "I don't know much. I have a cab waiting. Will you come?"

"Of course. Instantly."

Soon Lenox and Ward were down the stairs and into the waiting hansom. Ward gave the address of a busy corner near Pall Mall, the quarter of Mayfair that housed the private clubs and wine and gun and clothing shops that the city's bluest-blooded inhabitants frequented.

Theo had only heard the barest details of the incident. He knew the duke had been stepping from his carriage outside the august Carlton Club, which was the luxurious and exclusive game preserve of the conservative party. It was apparently where Dorset went nearly every morning, meaning the kidnappers might well have lain in wait for him there.

"Two large men in cloaks, collars turned up, shoved him into a different carriage that pulled right up alongside the duke's."

"Cloaks?" said Lenox, interrupting.

"Yes, why?"

He turned away and looked at the passing street. "Out of season," he murmured. "Go on."

"This second carriage had sped up the street before the doorman of the Carlton could even get down the steps," Ward said, though he had blown his police whistle instantly. There had been a large crowd upon the steps of the Carlton who watched the commotion.

"Where were you?" Lenox asked.

"Dorset House."

"Did any of them provide a good description of either the men or the carriage?" asked Lenox.

Theo shook his head unhappily. "You have heard all I know. I came to fetch you immediately. The duchess is at the scene of the crime, accompanied by her cousin Sir Japheth Miles. His Lordship, the duke's son, Corfe, would naturally have gone, but his health has worsened today. He has not left his room—delirious with fever from what I understand."

"Bad timing."

"It never rains but it pours," said Ward, resorting, in his plain unintellectual but not unintelligent way, to the closest cliché at hand.

"Chin up," Lenox said, resorting to his, for Ward looked bereft. "The duke is too important to stay kidnapped. Nothing could be more certain than that."

And indeed, when they pulled up to the Carlton there were no fewer than half a dozen police wagons present. The street was blocked off in both directions. They stepped down from the cab and walked the last hundred yards to reach the scene.

The first people Lenox saw there were Sir Richard Mayne, head of the Yard, and one of his chief inspectors, Warren Sinex. Sinex was a tall, hard, dangerous fellow, shrewd but given to flights of temper. Mayne, by contrast, was a gentleman to his fingernails, equable and hood-eyed, careful.

"Lenox," Mayne said, surprised. "What brings you here?"

"I have been consulting with the duke in the last few days. His personal secretary, Mr. Ward, fetched me."

Mayne's eyes went to Ward. "You are Theodore Ward? Very well, you two, come through the gauntlet if you wish."

Journalists were ringed around the carriage, which had the Dorset family's intricate arms in raised gold leaf on each of its four doors. Inside it, Mayne showed them, were two plush blue velvet benches facing each other.

One of them there bore a large dark stain.

"Blood?" Lenox said to Mayne.

"We think so," said Sir Richard. He turned to find the journalists pressing behind him and barked, "Clear out! Clear out! Constables, yes, you two, do a better job of keeping these men back or you'll be looking for another line of work. I mean that sincerely."

The constables didn't need a second telling, and with rough shoves pushed the protesting members of the press backward.

Lenox took the chance to lean in and feel the cushion. His fingers came away a rusty red. There was no doubt of it: blood.

He looked at Ward. "Not a great amount. That is some comfort at least," said Lenox.

Mayne and Sinex returned their attention to the carriage, Sinex hanging about half a foot behind his superior, glowering at Lenox, whom he strongly disliked.

"What happened?" Lenox asked Sir Richard.

Mayne offered an account similar to Ward's, filigreed with a few more details. The carriage into which the duke had been forced had four horses—in other words, was unusually fast, might easily be halfway to Scotland by now—and both men had looked "English," to the doorman.

" 'No Indian or Negro buggers, begging your pardon, Sir Richard,' he told me," Mayne said. "I quote him directly, you understand."

"Did he notice anything about their clothes?"

"Not beyond the cloaks. But there's this," said Mayne. He took a notecard from his pocket and passed it over to Lenox and Ward.

Prepare ten thousand pounds in ready notes and ten thousand pounds in gold bullion. Await further instruction.

Lenox read it twice and turned to Ward. "I take it the duke can raise this kind of money?"

Ward, who had been pale throughout the encounter, at last had a use to which to put his nervous energy. He nodded. "Without even troubling his bankers, I should think," he said. "He owns—well, Dorset. You know that as well as I do."

It was scarcely an exaggeration. Hundreds of thousands of acres of that county were the duke's. Lenox had only asked to be sure there was no sudden, secret embarrassment in his finances.

What in all creation did this have to do with a stolen painting of a forgotten duke? What did it have to do with William Shakespeare?

"What are your men doing?" Lenox asked Mayne.

Mayne glanced up Pall Mall. "No tracks to follow, unfortunately. Cobblestones on this street; no recent rain regardless." He tapped the note against his knuckles distractedly. "I don't like the blood, obviously. Anyhow, why had you been consulting with the duke?"

Lenox, suddenly alert, said, "Do that again, would you?"

"What?"

"Hit your hand with the card, if you wouldn't mind."

The superintendent looked at him as if he belonged in an asylum, but bounced the thick notecard lightly against his knuckles. "Like this?"

"Yes." Lenox looked away, reaching for his tobacco in his waistcoat pocket. "Good. Thank you."

"Why?"

"Nothing. I was wrong," Lenox said. He had learned better than to tell the gentlemen of the Yard anything before he was obliged to do so. Motioning discreetly with his tobacco pouch, he said, "Is that the duchess?"

Ward followed his hand. "Yes," he said. "Her cousin is next to her."

This was a tall, older man who himself was very upright, with white hair and a clean-shaven face. "Perhaps I might have a word with her?"

"Better be a cautious word," Sinex put in, giving him a mirthless smile. "Don't want to be playing about in matters like this, Lenox. Liable to spill your own blood."

"Enough of that," said Mayne sharply. "Lenox, I'll walk you to Her Grace."

They left Ward and Sinex by the carriage doors. Their boots clicked on the cobblestones as they walked. "You received my card yesterday?" Mayne asked.

"I did. I had planned to call on you this morning, Sir Richard."

"Dorset wrote me to ask—well, commanded me, I suppose, to come to the Lords. He asked if you were reliable."

85

Ah, so that was why Mayne had sought him out.

"Did he?" said Lenox, who had lately learned, in conversations such as this one, too, the value of saying little.

"I asked him why he wanted to know. He would not tell. At last I gave him my reluctant recommendation."

"Reluctant on my behalf, or reluctant because you didn't know the reason it was requested?"

"The latter," said Mayne. "Mixed with some of the former, if I'm candid. You are, of course, not a police officer."

"No."

"I was also going to tell you this morning to be careful of him, Dorset. I have had cause to run across him in Parliament. He can ruin any man he pleases, and he has a streak of—" Mayne looked at the immaculate façade of the Carlton Club as they walked toward the duchess. "Not unkindness. But he believes that God made Victoria the Queen, then made him the Duke of Dorset."

"I see."

"If you feel you can tell me what he wanted I would be grateful."

"I need time to think, if you could permit it, Sir Richard. The duke entrusted me with a secret he held very close."

Mayne looked at him warily. "Very well. But if

he winds up dead and you have held something back, it will go badly for you. I say that with sincere regard, Charles. I was fond of your father."

"Thank you, Sir Richard."

"Here is the duchess."

CHAPTER ELEVEN

The duchess was, to an almost unsettling degree of accuracy, a duchess.

Which was to say, first, that she had the cool self-possession of her position; second, had the odd ability to look downward at a person of any height whatsoever; and third, was very elegant and unruffled, even in these circumstances. Her dress was conservative and self-evidently expensive, dark blue with a very wide, graceful bell-shaped crinoline spreading out from her waist, just the fashion at the moment. It must have been the devil of a time to get through doorways.

As well as her cousin, two attendants stood at her side.

She greeted Lenox with little more than a nod when she heard that he had been working for her husband, until Ward mentioned his name.

"Oh," she said, rather surprised. "Charles Lenox. I know your mother, Lady Emma."

"Ah, yes," said Lenox, nodding.

His hands were clasped behind him, in deference both to her title and her situation. "I would go so far as to call her a friend," the duchess added.

"I will remember you to her, with your permission, Your Grace," he said.

She put out her hand, and Lenox took it. She applied a gentle pressure. "Please do."

Ward asked the duchess if Lenox might pose her one or two questions, and she nodded. "Has your husband mentioned Shakespeare to you recently?" he said.

She looked at him with a surprise that would have been difficult to feign. "Shakespeare. No. Why?"

"I ask for no important reason—a misplaced thought, Your Grace," said Lenox quickly and apologetically. "Had he done anything out of the ordinary recently, may I ask?"

This was what Lady Jane called his Victoria question. He fell back upon it whenever he needed to buy time to think. Every morning, in the course of her usual business, Queen Victoria gave the orders that her chefs make a serving of curry for forty-eight.

This was despite the fact that she herself despised curry. She did it because she wanted to be prepared in case a visiting dignitary of Asian descent called upon the Palace at random.

Or forty-eight of them, Lenox supposed. The forty-ninth would have to eat whatever the Queen herself ate. All he remembered from when he had dined at the Palace as a boy was that she had eaten with incredible speed and that everyone had to stop the moment she set down her fork, which meant that nobody would have gotten enough if there hadn't been, blessedly, twenty courses.

His question to the duchess was a catchall, but being both intelligent and exceedingly private, she swatted it away. "He has hired you, evidently. Otherwise, no."

He had been raised not to contradict any woman, much less one who outranked him, but he could not let this pass. "Not hired, Your Grace," Lenox said.

"Excuse me?"

"I am an amateur."

Her cousin Sir Japheth Miles, whom Ward had introduced secondarily, said dryly, "How comforting."

Lenox had already pegged Miles—a clubman. His acerbic tone in those two words confirmed him as such: worldly, neatly dressed, faultlessly connected, probably a bachelor with voluminous memories of the gay '20s. No doubt working on a memoir. Inwardly, Lenox sighed.

"Just one more question, Your Grace," he said. "Is the duke left-handed or right-handed?"

She looked at him oddly. "Right-handed. Why?"

"Another failed thought," he said, bowing his head deferentially. "Thank you for your time."

He left the duchess and spoke to the porter at the Carlton, celebrity of the moment, who confirmed that the carriage into which the duke had been forced had four horses and was colored black, with no markings. He added that the men were cloaked in black, too.

Their behavior toward him had been undeniably violent, the porter said—no chance he went willingly into their carriage.

The duke's own driver, who was in disgrace for his failure to intervene, confirmed that.

"Why didn't you follow them?" Lenox asked.

"They knocked me clear off the box when I was getting down for to assist 'is Grace, didn't they!"

The young detective saw a developing lump on the driver's forehead now. "I didn't know that."

"Oh, yes! And in the scrumble to get out from under the wheels—'orses may always bolt, and a man kilt like the snap of your fingers—I've seen it, Your Lordships—sirs—they was gone. My goodness," he added, shaking his head in wonder. "An innocent chap can't find an ounce of sympathy."

Lenox looked through the carriage itself. He asked the driver whether there was anything missing—all he had found was a top hat, in a box beneath one of the benches—and the driver said no, there was never anything kept in the carriage. He himself cleaned its bits and bobs out completely twice a day.

Lenox thanked him, then took a step away. He put one foot up on the steps of the Carlton Club and looked down St. James's Street in the direction of Piccadilly Circus, the busiest thoroughfare in London. A quick left or right turn there and the kidnappers could have melted into traffic without any trouble.

As he contemplated this, he vaguely listened to Ward engage in an increasingly fractious discussion with Sinex about their next steps (neither had any intelligent plan for what to do, and each was ferociously committed to it), and Mayne ordering the slow and probably hopeless but necessary process of having his constables spread about the neighborhood to question the populace.

Sir Japheth was just asking when they could expect some *action,* the kind of question only a man without specific experience of action could ask, when a thought came to Lenox.

He interrupted authoritatively. "We need to speak to that fellow Jacob who sells apples outside of Savile's. It will be fastest to reach him on foot."

Everyone looked at him. "What?" said Sir Richard after a moment.

"He is a simpleton—"

"Well, that's ideal, then," said Sinex. "You two should be able to converse on an equal plane."

Lenox gave him a dead-eyed stare. "But, as I was going to say, he has perfect recall. We are in possession of one piece of information of any value aside from the ransom card: that the carriage had four horses."

"And?"

"He is always on Jermyn Street. He will know whether a carriage with four horses has passed him today." Lenox pointed. "That is the only street between here and Piccadilly, the largest street in London, where if they went, of course, they are lost to us. If they took Jermyn, however, we have a chance of witnesses."

"How do you know this simpleton?" asked Sir Japheth.

"It is my job to know something of crime in London," said Lenox curtly.

"Fine," said Mayne, siding with Lenox. "Let us go."

It took only a minute or so to reach Jacob, a popular, hulking man who sold hot chestnuts and apple cider in the winter, quinces in the summer. He greeted Lenox with a grin and a touch of his hat.

He had seen twenty-three carriages that morning (he reported), and only *two* had no markings and only *one* had four horses, and all four were dark, though one had a white diamond on its nose and another white socks, and he was sure two were mares, and certainly the driver had been wearing a cloak. He had also seen—

He would have gone on endlessly, but Lenox stopped him to ask where that particular carriage had gone, the unmarked one with four horses.

"It took a right on Bury Street," said Jacob promptly.

A little breath went through their small group. This was the first right off of Jermyn Street, and Bury Street was the opposite of Piccadilly—tiny.

Lenox started to feel a tingle of excitement. "Well done, Jacob, thank you," he said.

The duchess, from her seat in the carriage, handed over a pound note. "Please give this to him."

Lenox did so. Jacob took the pound note happily, then tried to give a basket of quinces to Lenox, who plucked just one for himself from the top and said good-bye. He got back into the duchess's carriage (a light conveyance with two horses and two doors, prettily designed) and asked its driver to turn down Bury Street.

There were five people here, Mayne, Lenox, Ward, Japheth Miles, and the duchess. The first three men were all squeezed along the bench with their backs to the horses, since the standard etiquette was that no man who was not a relative ought ever to sit alongside a woman in a carriage.

"What now?" Miles said.

Lenox had a small map of London in his pocket, folded so many times that it was white and illegible at the creases.

He took it out and spread it over his knees. "If they took Bury Street, it can only mean one thing—they wanted to get into St. James's Park as soon as possible. And the only reason for that must be that they wanted to go down

Birdcage Walk and cross Westminster Bridge."

"So they would have passed directly by Parliament," said the duchess grimly. "The Duke of Dorset trundled past the House of Lords itself like a sack of grain."

She seemed angrier at the impudence of this than worried.

"What is across Westminster Bridge?" asked Ward.

"A great deal. South London," said Mayne.

He and Lenox exchanged glances. The two of them knew very well what South London meant: crime.

"I would have a look in the opium dens," Lenox said.

"The opium dens!" said Sir Japheth.

"It is the easiest way of keeping a man sedated." This was something Lenox had learned in the course of his self-education. "It is not an uncommon method—stuff a wad of opium in a man's mouth, hold it shut until he blacks out, then leave him in a supervised daze."

"That really happens?" the duchess said.

"All the time," said Mayne, who was looking at Lenox, surprised perhaps to find him acquainted with this rough practice.

Lenox nodded. "If they have headed south, I believe it is our best chance."

And if the duke was still alive—he did not add.

CHAPTER TWELVE

They failed.

It was wretchedly hot in London by that night. Though it had been a warm, pleasant day, the evening papers reported that when the sun set the temperature was at a record high for London. This would have been bad enough, but the streets were also peculiarly breezeless, leaving the heat to radiate into the eerie air, unsoftened, from every city stone, every iron gate.

Lenox tossed and turned in his bed. He was uneasy. That afternoon at three, several dozen constables, assisted by thirty-five members of the Grenadiers sent by the Queen herself, had simultaneously raided the large and small opium houses of Battersea.

They had gone nine to each, cutting off front and back entrances, striking all at once so that nobody would be tipped off. But they hadn't found the Duke of Dorset.

Nor had any of the dozens of minor thieves or opium fanatics they'd turned out known anything—nothing at all, returned the reports to Mayne, at Scotland Yard, one after another after another, despite immense promises of reward and reprieve.

There was also a huge population of minor

criminals in the clumped low-slung drinking holes that clung like gray old seashells around the south side of Westminster Bridge, respectable boatmen and bargemen, too, and not one of them had seen a carriage of the description they were seeking pass at any time around nine o'clock. Nor thereafter. Despite this being quite literally the only place besides Parliament or his own house to which Bury Street could have most quickly transported the kidnapped duke.

At eleven o'clock, Lenox gave in to his wakefulness and lit a candle. He felt as if he were baking—his windows open, but the air outside utterly dead, the leaves as still as statues.

Suddenly he realized somewhere within that it was going to rain before the night was out, one of those pieces of natural insight, left over from his childhood in the country, that he never quite knew where he stored. He wondered if a dozen streets away his brother Edmund felt it, too.

He paced the bedroom by candlelight, thinking. The block of ice in the basin on his bedside table was a pool of tepid water now. He dipped a small towel in it nevertheless and wiped his brow.

Finally, at midnight, he went downstairs. There he discovered that he was not alone in his sleeplessness.

"Hullo, Graham," he said.

"Good evening, sir," the butler said. He

rose from the chair by the door, tucked into a miniature alcove, that he often used as a discreet way station. Despite the heat he was in a proper suit. He laid his book aside. "May I get you anything?"

"Oh, no, I'm just awake." Lenox's mind felt a little overheated by the weather, and by his doubts. "Awake, awake."

"Is it anything specific, sir?"

"Primarily the duke being kidnapped."

Graham, in the low light of the hallway, smiled. "Yes, sir," he said.

Lenox sat down opposite Graham, on one of the chairs that lined the hallway. "You know you can read in my study if you're up at night," Lenox said.

"Thank you very much, sir," Graham said, in a way that firmly rejected the notion.

Lenox sat for a moment, chin in his hand. "It's the matter of the carriage going down Bury Street that bothers me so much," he said. "Piccadilly was fifty yards ahead of them, and instead they *turned right*. Piccadilly would have meant certain safety. Whereas Jermyn Street, then Bury Street—either could have been blocked, and Bury Street brought them within sight, through the alley, of the Carlton Club, the very scene of the crime! Madness!"

"You believe the apple seller, sir?"

"Oh, without a doubt. I have tested his memory

pretty thoroughly." He sighed. "It's such an odd decision. The only reason they would have made it is to get to the other side of the river, Battersea. And nobody there saw them. Someone should have."

"You feel sure of that?"

"Absolutely sure. Yet the constables were relentless, according to Mayne. *Nobody* south of Westminster Bridge saw a thing. They have turned over every rock."

"Perhaps the carriage didn't cross Westminster Bridge, then, sir," said Graham.

"Perhaps." Lenox sat there, contemplating this. "But nothing this side of the river is closer by Jermyn Street. It would have to have been someone who didn't know London in the slightest."

Saying this, he thought of Pendleton.

"Yes, sir."

They sat in silence for a little while, Lenox tracing triangles of geography in his mind, going over and over what Mayne had told him about the massive police effort to find the duke.

At times like this he felt a sort of nausea of confusion, the feeling a doctor must have when a diagnosis lies just beyond his grasp, a writer when the plot won't come together.

It inclined him to a broad and undignified kind of despair. He was twenty-six—how soon hath time, that subtle thief!—and he had achieved nothing, he thought glumly. The police despised him, and any man or woman of his own class might dismiss him without a thought for this odd folly of his profession.

"Sir," said Graham, after a long silence.

"Yes?" Lenox replied, looking up after a beat out of the oceanic lethargy of his thoughts.

"I'm going to fetch a glass of water from the kitchen, if you'd like one."

"Oh. Why, all right. Thank you, Graham." He mustn't give in to melancholy. "I would eat some of that cold plum pudding if it happened to be in the larder, too."

Graham smiled. "Of course, sir."

Lenox pulled the little leather book of quotations from Shakespeare out of his pocket— he had found himself carrying it around all day—and, after stroking its soft cover with his thumb, opened it at random again.

> *Reputation is an idle and most false imposition; oft got without merit and lost without deserving.*
>
> —Othello

He read this carefully, but it did not strike him as particularly interesting. When he closed the book, rather, he thought of the duke's son, Corfe, whom he had visited earlier that afternoon.

He was a tall, fit lad, who was dressed but still

very pale and keeping well back of the crowd, coughing, reclined on a sofa. Still, he had not seemed delirious, despite Ward's statement. He had been with the duchess and with his sister, Violet.

This daughter, who completed the quartet of the family, had returned from their house in the country by private train car when she heard the news of her father. Few women could have been more eligible socially, but at thirty it seemed exceedingly unlikely now that she would marry. Lenox had heard of her—of this misfortune— before the duke had ever solicited his aid. Meeting her, Lenox observed that she was very sweet but painfully shy, with a large nose and small eyes: none of her mother's beauty and perhaps twice her kindness. Of the three it was she who had asked the most intelligent questions. It was also evident that her brother loved her dearly.

As Lenox went over the meeting in his mind, Graham returned with a tray bearing two glasses of water and two plates of cold plum pudding. "Would it be presumptuous of me to join you, sir?" he asked.

"No. Imagine asking that, Graham! How many times did we go divvy on a plate of chips from the caravan outside Balliol?" Lenox took a mouthful of the pudding, deliciously sweet and cool. "Ah, that's good."

They sat up for a while longer. At around one o'clock, Lenox at last went back upstairs and fell into an overheated rest, sheets kicked aside. At four he vaguely sensed, through sleep, that the heat had broken; it was raining.

The relief of the rain was enormous. Half still in sleep, skin cool, he knew that he could find the answer if he was just patient and didn't think too hard.

He lay there, listening to the hard rain, watching the branches lash around outside.

And then he had it.

He rang the bell for Graham's room—the hour be damned—and got dressed as quickly as he could. The valet appeared soon, dressed himself.

"Sir?" he said.

"Would you come with me somewhere?"

"Of course, sir," said Graham. "Shall I have the carriage taken out?"

Lenox looked into the rain. Rousing the groom and warming the horses at this hour would take twenty minutes. "We'll chance a cab if you have two umbrellas and a pair of decent boots."

If the duke hadn't been in South London, if nobody in the all-seeing population of Battersea had spotted him in a single one of its nooks and hideaways, then—he wasn't in South London.

That was the crucial fact.

And where else could doubling back to Bury Street have led the kidnappers? Suddenly it all seemed as clear as the water of a stream, the clues snapping into place: 1) that improbable bloodstain, 2) the ransom note tapped against Mayne's knuckles, and 3) the driver's account.

The only thing he still didn't understand was how the stolen painting fit in.

A few moments later they were walking hunched under umbrellas down Hampden Lane, looking up and down the street for a taxicab. At last a slow old rambler passed by on Brook Street, its horse in very little hurry.

They got in. "Dorset House, please," Lenox said.

"V'good, sir," said the driver.

It was an open cab. "Not tired?"

He was an old man, who had an umbrella himself, hooked into his trap. "Sleep less, a' my age, sir. Specially on a night so infernal 'ot as this one used to be."

It was a wet but uneventful cab ride—until, just as they were turning through St. James's Park, Graham said, in a low voice, "I believe we are being followed by a hansom."

CHAPTER THIRTEEN

"We'll step out here," said Lenox to the driver of the hansom.

"Here?" said the man in a doubtful way. He turned back to look at them from his seat on the box.

Lenox handed him a coin. "Thank you," he said, then added, "It's not like that."

"Please yourselves," the old man muttered, tucking the coin into his small waistcoat pocket.

St. James's was the trysting ground of the least savory characters of the upper classes—Lenox's own. Any constable could levy an immediate fine of a pound—an immense sum, as much as a working-class family's budget for the week—if he even suspected someone of "loitering" there, such was its ill reputation. At White's, his club, Lenox had often heard men say before supper that they were going to draw a few pound notes from the bank before it closed.

They took off on a rapid clip down one of the stone pathways. Under the moonlit rain, the park looked a bright beautiful startled green, wild and innocent.

"Anyone following now?" muttered Lenox.

"No," Graham said.

"What did you see?"

"A young man, sir. Just a glimpse. He must have seen us hail the cab and pegged us for easy marks, followed us in his own."

Lenox stopped and looked around. There was only the rainy night behind him, but it was hard to see far. He held his cane firmly in his hand and surveyed the park.

They emerged from the garden and turned down Abingdon Street. Here there was no mistaking it, under the combination of moonlight and brilliant streetlamps: They were alone. Lenox breathed a little easier.

The enormous silhouette of Parliament stood behind them; soon they had arrived at the duke's house. Both young men moved as quiet as the grave. They approached the southwest corner of the great marble house and stood there for a moment. One story up its sheer white face, a window of the duke's study was ajar, despite the rain. There was no light on inside.

Lenox smiled to himself.

He turned to Graham. "Let's try the stables."

The door to the stables was unlocked. Stupid. The only person there was a small boy, sleeping among the horses, whose fault it was not.

"Where is Perkins?" Lenox said.

That was the driver's name—the one who'd been present at the duke's kidnapping. "At home," said the boy, rubbing his sleepy face. He peered at the heavy rain behind them, which

Lenox and Graham were shaking off. "Blimey if it's not tipping down, isn't it?"

"At home?" Lenox said.

"He don't live in."

"We're going in to see Lord Vere," said Lenox. "The door is unlocked?"

The boy nodded obediently. He was too young, or it was too dark, for him to catch the subtle differences in attire that marked Graham as a valet. They must have all looked—men in suits—the same to him, like friends of the duke's son, Corfe, Lord Vere.

Lenox handed the boy five shillings, a princely sum. It was intended to mimic the aleatory tips of the drunken rich. He patted a flawless mare with a white diamond on her nose who was looking at them mildly. "Go back to sleep," he said to both horse and boy.

The detective and his valet slipped inside quietly.

Only when the door was closed behind them did Graham speak. "Is this wise?" he whispered.

"I'm wondering too," said Lenox.

There was nobody downstairs. They passed on the balls of their feet through the hard marble entranceway, leaving an unfortunate trail of moisture, before taking the carpeted steps upstairs.

Lenox led, turning left down the long hallway at the top.

They went into the duke's study. Empty. When his eyes had adjusted, Lenox could see, from the moonlight reflecting brilliantly off the Thames outside, old Shakespeare, undisturbed in his frame, fifth from the left, next to the empty spot where painting number six should be.

He struck a match against a brass candleholder and lit the new candle it held. That was life as a duke: new candles, continually replenished by an unseen hand, burning as cleanly as the conscience of the Christ child.

They stood there for a moment, and then Lenox said, in a voice low but distinct, "It's Charles Lenox, Your Grace."

There was a long, tense pause.

Then, from a closet at the far left end of the room, the duke emerged. He was in a tight-wrapped burgundy dressing gown, holding a pistol.

"What in seven hells are you doing here?" he asked, his face visibly furious even in the dim candlelight.

"I would be interested to know what you're doing here," Lenox responded.

"You're lucky you weren't shot. I have a pistol. My man Craig has a blunderbuss."

"Since we have survived, Your Grace, perhaps you could tell us why a man who was kidnapped earlier today is alone and quite at ease in his own private study."

What had come to Lenox in his half-sleep was something simple, prompted by Graham. If the carriage that had taken the duke had gone down Bury Street *without* crossing into South London, there was only one place other than Parliament on this side of the river that was closer by that route.

Here, Dorset's own home.

Now Lenox went to the duke's desk and pulled open the top drawer.

"What are you doing?" asked Dorset. "Who is this man?"

"This is my valet, Graham," said Lenox, looking with a frown of concentration through the drawer.

"What does he know about . . . about Shakespeare?"

Lenox paused and looked at Graham. "Graham?" he said.

Graham frowned. "Shakespeare, sir?"

"Shakespeare. What do you know about Shakespeare, His Grace would like to know."

"I recall that he wrote *Pericles, Prince of Tyre,* sir."

Lenox tilted his head. "It wouldn't be the first play I thought of."

"A company came to our town with it when I was a child, sir. A very engaging performance."

Lenox looked at the duke. He seemed mollified at least on this one subject; Graham was a persuasive actor. Lenox looked down into the second drawer he had opened.

He took out a notecard and inspected it—heavy, cream colored, unmarked.

He tapped it against his knuckles. "Very, very fine paper for a ransom note, isn't it?" he said. "Such as no thief or kidnapper could afford. A duke could, of course."

"Please leave," the duke said.

"That was the first thing that struck me as curious. The second was that there was so much blood *inside* your carriage, staining the cushion. If you were interrupted before getting in, as your driver and the porter testified, why would it have been there?"

"I asked you to leave," the duke said.

"You have cost the police force untold hours and your family untold worry with this absurd scheme," said Lenox. "You admit that you faked your own kidnapping?"

"Get out."

"What was it, pig's blood?"

The duke looked at him grimly. "I still believe that someone is after my family's most important secret—and very possibly after me," he said, glancing at Graham. "I thought my absence would embolden the thief to make a second attempt."

"So you arranged the kidnapping, and left your window open to entice him."

"Yes."

Paradoxically, this act of deceit proved one thing to Lenox, he thought: The duke himself was not guilty of the original crime, a possibility he had considered.

"Who were the two men in cloaks?"

"Loyal servants," said the duke brusquely.

"Did you not consider just going to the country? Wouldn't the thief be incredulous that a *second* criminal was after you?"

The duke, though briefly nonplussed, waved away this objection. "A man of my stature is under continual threat."

It was here that Lenox had a surprising revelation: The 15th Duke of Dorset was— though temperamentally suited to his rank— perhaps not especially intelligent.

"I see. Maybe. But who do you believe actually is after you, Your Grace?" asked Lenox. "It is not the Queen, nor Sir Charles Eastlake. Do you have enemies?"

"No."

"I would like very much to know how the Dorset family acquired this picture, Your Grace," he said.

Fury erupted in the duke's expression. Lenox had touched a nerve. "Please leave."

The duke knew no more than he did, but it must be possible that he entertained some suspicion, some inkling, based on the story of Shakespeare's portrait. Yet the question remained: Why the *wrong painting?*

Lenox looked at him for a long moment. He was still holding the notecard, and tapped it against his knuckles. He glanced outside. The rain had slackened, and the trees were swaying above the river.

He put the notecard in his pocket. "I am going to inform the Yard right now that you turned up at home safely overnight, without any idea of what happened. They will be able to stop expending their thinning resources on the search for you."

The duke smirked. "Do what you please."

"I consider it a courtesy to you, in fact, Duke. If you want any further assistance, you may let me know," said Lenox.

There was a subtle change there. "Duke" was how one addressed a social equal of that rank—and anyone might be a social equal to Dorset, by virtue of the subtle calibrations of money, fashion, and taste that dictated society's preferences. Lenox used the word with a feeling of recklessness. He was, in his young person's way, in a terrible haste to find the truth, and he hated the duke right now for slowing his way— for this sham of a path toward justice.

They left the study and then departed by the front door, the duke standing halfway down the steps, watching.

It would be up to him how to tell his family that he had arrived home safely.

Outside, the rain was reduced to a scattered drizzle, wonderfully cool. Across the way from Dorset's front door, leaning against the stone railing overlooking the Thames, was a man in a dark cloak. A little orange ember marked him out, not much more.

Lenox started across the empty street, under the gleam of the gas lamps. "You were right, Graham. We were being followed. Hello, Mr. Bonden."

"Good evening," said Bonden, the old seaman removing the pipe in his mouth. "I couldn't help my curiosity."

"I would be delighted to have your assistance," said Lenox. There were rays of dawn appearing between the buildings across the river. "We find ourselves in deep waters. It is a painting that we're searching for."

CHAPTER FOURTEEN

The next morning was a Saturday, which meant, per his custom, that Lenox was due, at eight o'clock exactly, in the most feared place in England.

At seven he sat in the little drawing room where he took his breakfast, a chamber directly opposite his study in which he occasionally entertained friends and family, if they numbered fewer than half a dozen. It had a fireplace and a cabinet piano, which, closed, showed a painting of Lenox House set in the countryside surrounding it.

Here he sat, a steady rain still whispering against the windowpanes, eating eggs, toast, and porridge and having his tea. The morning's newspapers were in front of him.

PEER ALIVE AND WELL!
Duke of Dorset Recovered
Safely; Police Mystified
No suspects taken into custody, questioned;
Duke recalls no details of captivity;
Ransom unpaid;
Reward of 500 pounds offered
for capture of criminals

That was the loud, confused, and rather confusing set of headlines stacked above a drawing of the 15th Duke of Dorset in the *Illustrated London Morning News*. This was a paper of greater vulgarity than the *Times*, and therefore often much more interesting. Not just to Lenox.

He looked away through the window and sat, eating his porridge and thinking. He and Bonden had spoken at length the night before and were going to meet again after the weekend. The young detective was determined to find the lost painting.

It was one of those mornings—the rain trickling down the windows, the gray skies—when for whatever queer reason he felt the loss of his father.

As he was meditating on this, Mrs. Huggins and Lancelot entered the room.

Lenox put down his fork. "What have I said about this room?" he said.

"That only Graham may enter it in the antemeridian, sir, but—" said Mrs. Huggins.

"And you told me that you'd use a shotgun on anyone who comes in but Graham, especially me," Lancelot added scrupulously.

"Sir!" Mrs. Huggins exclaimed. "Did you really? For shame, sir."

"I hate an informer," Lenox said darkly to Lancelot. "What is it, Mrs. Huggins?"

"Your brother is here, sir."

"Oh! Send him in."

"Yes, sir," said Mrs. Huggins.

Lancelot ran after her, no doubt to ask Edmund for money—which he would receive, since Edmund was, in the first place, a soft touch and, in the second, deeply grateful that he had not been imposed upon to house Lancelot for two weeks himself.

Sir Edmund Lenox had assumed his father's baronetcy eighteen months earlier, still a young man, birth-side of thirty. Nevertheless, he had subtly changed since inheriting Lenox House and the tangible and intangible legacies that came with it. He was still his cheerful, rather countryish self, stouter than his younger brother, and gentler, too, easier to smile, full of goodwill, never most at home in London.

But there was a new, decisive authority in him, and a note of service. He strove every day— silently, Charles knew—to be as good a squire to the land and its people as his father had been. It couldn't be easy.

"This is one of those nice surprises you hear about," said Lenox. "How are you?"

"Oh, very well," said Edmund, setting his cane and his hat on the windowsill. He poured himself a cup of tea. "This rain is a treat, isn't it? It was hot as Satan's hoof in Parliament yesterday."

"Lancelot is still here."

"Yes, he just asked me for a pound."

"Did you give it to him?"

"No. Four shillings. Had to draw a line."

"That's twice his weekly pocket money, you idiot," said Lenox. "I just wonder how they've kept him at Eton! Some of the stories he tells— they would have buried us alive when we were at school. Did you know he and his friend put a snake in the headmaster's study?"

"A snake!"

"Then gave each other alibis. He told me this with utter confidence that I wouldn't tell anyone. Which he's right about, blast him. Schoolboy code."

"Still, it's just another day or two," said Edmund sympathetically.

"You know very well it's six. I do wish he were staying with you. You're a father!"

Edmund took a piece of the stack of buttered toast between him and Charles. "I suspect that in fact Mother and Eustacia settled on you for exactly that reason."

"Please, help yourself to toast. But how's that?"

"Mother thinks you ought to be settling down."

Lenox laughed. "And that Lancelot will persuade me of it! What a scheme. If anything I'm going to spend the next several decades on a remote Greek hillside studying scripture in silence, like a monk."

"Not many murders there, unfortunately," said Edmund, who, perhaps exclusively among Charles's acquaintance, had never even once faltered in his support of his brother's idea of a career. "Coincidentally, on that subject . . ."

"Murder?"

"Well, no," said Edmund. "It's about Dorset."

Lenox frowned. "What about him?"

"He was at the Carlton this morning, apparently."

"Already! You weren't there?"

"Of course not." The Carlton was for conservatives; Edmund sat for the other side, in the family seat. "But the word reached me quickly enough that he was saying very foul things about you."

"Such as?"

"It was Capability Elliott who told me. I ran across him in Pall Mall and came straight here." Elliott was an ambitious young conservative, affable, full of the latest gossip. "Dorset didn't go quite so far as to blame the kidnapping on you, but he came close. Said he had asked you to consult upon a private matter, but that you were a pirate. That he had misplaced his trust, was thinking of firing his secretary. Is it really old Ward, from school?"

"A pirate!"

"Yes, Elliott emphasized that word."

This could only mean that the duke wanted his version of events spread early and quickly, to counter any tales he suspected Lenox might tell.

"Yes," said Edmund. "Of course, your friends will know that he's wrong."

"Not many people remain your friend if they

have to pick between you and a duke," said Charles, smiling.

"Ah, but there is every kind of gossip abroad about him, you know," said Edmund. "His credibility is low. If I had to guess, I would say you stand a decent chance of coming out ahead."

"Hm." Lenox sat back, arms crossed. "Well, thank you for telling me. I'm grateful."

"In brighter news, I was hoping I might speak to you and Jane, actually—two birds and all that—about Molly's birthday. I thought it would be nice to have a party for her. A surprise. Jane is such a dab hand at that kind of thing."

Molly was Edmund's wife. "What a thoughtful soul you are, Edmund. Nobody would believe that you used to chase me with that cricket bat."

Edmund reddened. "You called me fat."

"You *were* fat that year."

"I was growing into my build, and it was rude of you to point out."

"I'll see if she can come."

Lenox got up and went across the hall into his study. He tapped on the wall in code: twice, once, twice. *Come if you can, but no rush.* Then he returned to the breakfast table.

Not two minutes later, Lady Jane arrived. Both brothers stood up, smiling happily at their friend.

"When it's raining, for shame," she said.

"Oh! I am sorry," said Lenox, and he was. "I hadn't even—"

"No, it's fine. But what is it? Hello, Edmund, dear fellow. How are you?"

"He wants help planning a birthday party for Molly."

Jane, in an overcoat, brightened. "A party! Oh, and for Molly. Nobody could deserve it more."

"I'll have to leave you two to the planning," Lenox said, taking a last sip of tea. "I'm due for an appointment."

"Where?" asked Edmund.

"It's Saturday morning. I'm—"

His brother made a horrified face. "Oh, don't say the name. Don't say it. I'd forgotten. Well, go if you must."

CHAPTER FIFTEEN

At five to eight, the broad iron gates of Bedlam opened to admit Lenox. He still hadn't grown quite inured to the sound they made when they closed behind him.

This hospital was only just twelve or twenty years younger than Oxford itself, and in an inverted way as august. In 1270 it had been founded as a house for the mad, the first in the world: Our Lady of Bethlehem. Within a century its name had been shortened to Bethlem. By 1440 it was called, thanks to the local accents, Bedlam. In the centuries since then that word had lost its capitalization, and now people spoke of bedlam, of frenzied uproar, madness, mass confusion. But they also spoke of this dread place: Bedlam.

On a small plaque inside the hospital—and already he could hear the distant howls and cries of the inmates, guttural and horrifying—was a quote from the middle of the fifteenth century.

And in that place be found many men that be fallen out of their wit.
And full honestly they be kept in the place; and some be restored onto their wit and health again.

But some be abiding therein forever, for they be fallen so much out of themselves that it is incurable unto man.

Fallen so much out of themselves—that was the phrase Lenox always paused upon in the hours after his weekly visits to the hospital. On one of his first visits he had asked the warden, Dr. Hansel, under whose protection he was here, why the hospital had chosen that plaque.

"Because we have hope, you know—all of us who work here—but our final faith must be placed in God. Else I think we all of us would go mad ourselves."

He was a humble, quiet man with graying hair, Hansel. He greeted Lenox this week just as he did each time, with a gentle reminder that he could leave whenever he liked. Lenox thanked him, but he would be in Bedlam for the next eight hours.

This was part of his commitment to his career. It had started with clipping newspapers, then with seeking out the dangerous low places where crimes happened. Finally his investigations into crime, into what made a crime, had fetched him here. He had tried to convince one or two of the more open-minded officers at Scotland Yard to come with him, but they had laughed directly in his face.

Yet what could be more constructive to understanding the criminal mind than to spend half an hour in casual conversation with a man like Henry Fairfax?

By half past eight they were sitting opposite each other. Each had a cup of tea. Fairfax was scrutinizing his closely, apparently without a worry on earth. He was a handsome man with jet-black hair, as tidily dressed as one could be in the flannel garments that Bedlam provided. He was relaxed and polite. He was also a murderer.

Hansel—not given to hyperbole—thought him the most dangerous man in the hospital.

Though Bedlam still housed men like Fairfax, it was nowhere near as terrible a place as it had been thirty years before, though, as Edmund's reaction showed, not many people knew that.

Back then, after centuries of neglect, it had been a true house of horrors. The final straw was a diabolical director earlier this century, a doctor; he had published extensively in the medical journals on the need to treat lunacy humanely, while in his private fiefdom of Bedlam he had been a figure of almost limitless cruelty.

That lasted until Wakefield's famous report of 1814, which roused public indignation and instant parliamentary action. The patients at Bedlam were treated as "vermin," Wakefield had reported. Wholly coherent men, who suffered from little more than nervous anxiety, were beaten and hosed every morning, then left naked to shiver in isolation, eating one meal a day. Women were locked up in their cells, also naked, sleeping on filthy beds of straw.

Being in a group was worse still: Wakefield described ten women, "each chained by one arm to the wall; the chain allowing them merely to stand up by the bench or form fixed to the wall, or sit down on it. The nakedness of each patient was covered by a blanket gown only, nothing to fasten it."

The worst of all was the fate of those who had fouled themselves, even once. They were kept together, regardless of their particular mental condition, murderers and mild depressives alike. He had seen dog kennels in better keep, he wrote.

Fortunately, now, the horrors of those days were in decline. Two men of science, Tuke and Pinel, had published theories of treatment around the time of the Wakefield report, and the world was bending toward their kinder methods. Tuke, a genius from York, had founded near his home a place that took the gentlest and most respectful care of lunatics. Dr. Hansel was attempting to catch up to his example, though the older guards were resistant.

Tea with Fairfax was an example of how Hansel had changed the culture here, however. There were no chains in sight.

"Thank you for meeting me again," Lenox said to Fairfax.

"Not at all, Dr. Carson."

That was Lenox's name within these walls. "Last week we spoke at some length about the methods of your crime."

Fairfax looked immediately wary. "I don't quite remember that."

"Perhaps I should have said . . . of the time in your life when you felt so troubled, unlike now."

Lenox had learned on his very first Saturday the violent reaction anything less than this kind of periphrasis could elicit.

"Ah, well," said Fairfax, calming. "Yes."

Four years before, Fairfax had been employed as a solicitor in Birmingham. One evening, after a normal day at the office, he had returned to the house where he boarded and spent twelve uninterrupted hours methodically murdering everyone there. In all, he took six victims. The details were so gruesome that even Lenox, who tried to be dispassionate, could not dwell on them. (Fairfax had grown up in Lincolnshire, and his face lit up when he described his memories of hunting, gutting, and skinning animals there.) He had ethered and then bound and gagged each victim, letting them wake up on their own, one by one, before proceeding.

"Perhaps this morning I could ask about the ether," Lenox said. "How long in advance did you buy it?"

"Two weeks," said Fairfax cautiously. But

pride always got the best of him, and he added, "Two weeks to the day."

This conformed to a pattern that Lenox had slowly begun to discern. He thought it might prove important.

The men at the Yard defined all murders as being, because of their bloodiness, crimes of passion. Was it true? There could be no doubt that something hideous and visceral had driven Fairfax on the night of the attacks—but had that passion been in him two weeks earlier, too? Or could a murderer be methodical in a way that, for instance, a bank robber could? Sir Richard would have said it was impossible. But Lenox and Hansel, when they discussed it, agreed that the idea should be treated more scientifically.

Lenox had nine patients on his docket that day— among them a woman who'd slain her sisters, a wellborn and mannerly merchant named Jacobsen who had woken up one morning and killed every dog on his street, and a vagrant accused of no crime but who drew the most detailed, fond, and alarming pictures conceivable of humans butchering horses—and in all their cases he and Hansel agreed that fantasy preceded action.

If it was true, it was a compelling piece of knowledge. Could a murder be *prevented?* Just imagine.

"Two weeks," said Lenox. "Can you recall your thoughts on that day?"

"I just thought the ether might be useful," said Fairfax, mildly sipping his tea.

"Were you excited when you bought it?" Lenox asked in a quiet, distracted voice, eyes on his writing, as if he didn't especially care about the answer.

"Yes," said Fairfax.

"You were excited by the . . . sorry, just taking care of paperwork . . . the ether?"

Fairfax leaned forward. "I slept with the bottles every night. Once I used it to sleep. I bound my feet. I wanted to wake into the stupor that—"

"Yes?" said Lenox.

"That they would wake into," Fairfax said casually, looking away.

But that approached too closely to the crime itself, and Lenox steered the ship away, back to Fairfax's daily life in the solicitor's office, talk about his childhood (idyllic, in every respect, as he described it—but Lenox suspected the deepest of lies lay there), the weather on the day of the murders.

They spoke for perhaps forty-five minutes. After that, first nerves gone, Lenox went to work, a steady eight hours without more than a five-minute break to wolf down a sandwich.

By the end of these days, he was always shaken and exhausted—more than ready to leave. Today was no exception. He was due at a dinner party at nine, but thought he might send late regrets if he could not rally from this horrible sunken feeling.

Just before he departed, as he was packing away his notes, hoping they were worth what they cost him emotionally, a man approached the window. He had a tidy mustache and light, curious eyes.

"Dr. Carson?" he said.

"Yes."

"They never let me out on Saturdays." The man smiled grimly. "Because of you, I suspect."

"Me?" said Lenox.

"The name is Irvington. Captain Tankin Irvington. I am a post captain in Her Majesty's Navy. I am asylumed here under false pretenses."

They all were. "Oh?"

"If you could request to see me next week— I will tell you why it is wise never to let a member of the royal family fall in love with your wife."

Lenox looked at him curiously. "What?"

Just then a guard approached them and rapped Irvington sharply over the ear. The old methods lingered. "Back to your quarters, Belmont," the guard said, and very pointedly didn't look at Lenox as he chivvied the man away.

CHAPTER SIXTEEN

Lenox departed Bedlam's solemn gates at five minutes past five o'clock. He had politely declined his customary glass of whisky with Hansel, citing with half-accuracy his social commitment. It was at least an hour's carriage ride back to the center of London—that much was true.

He looked behind him, exhaling. Just inside the grounds of Bethlem was an unexpectedly beautiful expanse of green, washed gold now by the serene falling sun. Several inmates were playing a spirited game of bowls. One was Hellerby, among the most malicious men Lenox had ever met. His face was tight with happy concentration as he tossed his boule. He might have been on a quadrangle at Cambridge.

Lenox found his carriage a quarter mile down the road, greeted the driver, and after getting in flung himself back upon the seat, dog-tired. He spent the ride—south to north through Bromley, then on to Camberwell, before the Thames came into sight—recopying his notes from that day.

"Here will do, Robertson," he said, tapping the roof of his carriage when they were near Hungerford Bridge. He was a bit bilious from the heavy lunch Mrs. Huggins had packed. A walk would suit him. "You can take the horses home. Please tell Mrs. Huggins I'll be along in about thirty minutes."

"Very good, sir."

"My satchel is in the back here, if you wouldn't mind having someone put it in my study."

"Of course not, sir."

"Thank you, Robertson."

Lenox got out, and soon he was walking, unencumbered and alone.

There was a feeling unique to Saturday evenings in London, when it seemed both emptier than usual yet also somehow fuller—full, at least, of *imminence,* as the restaurants set out their tables and the houses prepared themselves to entertain and people walked along, looking up at addresses, unused to whatever particular street they happened to be calling upon.

Lenox strolled, unnoticed, across the river. He stopped at a park along the northern embankment. There was a small bar here, where two men played Spanish guitars with rosewood fretboards whose inlays were of intricate and lovely ivory. The notes of each instrument stood out, yet they blended effortlessly. What did it remind him of? Perhaps of love, this beautiful sound, where you could at once pick out what you saw and heard, the tone of a voice, the fall of a lock of hair, but each individual beauty was nothing without the greater whole that contained it.

He was thinking of Lady Jane, he supposed.

"Drink, sir?"

Lenox turned, brought out of his reverie by a small Frenchman in a dark tie and waistcoat, sleeves rolled up, bearing a tray. "Oh, yes. What's coldest?"

"We have an excellent white wine from Vigny on ice, sir."

"Perfect."

On the wrought-iron fence where Lenox had been standing there was a wooden box bolted to the rails, which said in gold stencil TO INSURE PROMPT SERVICE. The waiter pointedly did not look at it, and Lenox just as pointedly did not look at the waiter but found a half-shilling in his breast pocket and dropped it clattering into the box.

"Thank you, sir," the waiter said.

These boxes had shown up in all the tea gardens a few years before. The faddish thing to do was make an acronym of what the box said—*to insure prompt service,* "tips."

The wine was nicely sharp. The beautiful music continued. And the garden's flowers were in splendid form, huge purple irises bedded among the tiny speckled white flowers that they called London Pride, though Lenox's mother had always called them Whimsy, and the maids at Lenox House—Sussex girls—said everyone knew they were called Look Up and Kiss Me.

After fifteen minutes or so of quiet meditation, Lenox drained his glass, stood up, and started back through the waning daylight to Hampden Lane.

He arrived at his door and unlocked it, calling as he entered, "Lancelot, hold your blasted fire!"

His cousin—who had the unsettling gift of pretending that nothing had occurred prior to the very instant in which you happened to be conversing—said, "Fire?"

"You know quite well what I mean." Lenox paused, staring warily at the boy. "How is Mr. Templeton?"

"On Saturdays we have dancing lessons from Mr. and Mrs. Treway."

"Oh, right. Well, I jolly well hope you behaved yourself."

"We did, because Mrs. Treway had a cane."

Lenox frowned. That didn't sound quite right, even for Lancelot. "Did she cane you?"

"Oh, no. But you have to carry it if you misbehave. You look a fearful fool, and there are people everywhere, you know. Everyone being on hols. There must have been fifty people at the dance hall."

Lancelot was already turning away—his lair was the back garden—but he stopped. "I'll bet you five pence you don't know the Queen's name," he said.

"Show me the five pence."

Lancelot pulled it out. "Now you show me."

"I don't need to. Alexandrina."

Lancelot's face fell. He handed over the coin. "That's ten pence I've lost today on that. I was sure it was Victoria, but a boy from Marlborough had a little card about her coronation."

"I know for a fact that Edmund gave you four shillings, so I don't feel badly for you in the slightest."

Lancelot grinned. "See you soon," he said.

"That always sounds like a threat when you say it, you know," Lenox shouted after him.

He checked his watch. It was just past seven. He decided that he would dine out as he had planned after all. Many of his friends would be at the party, including Lady Jane, their friend Hugh, perennially lovelorn, and possibly even Edmund.

He changed and left by cab, stopping in at his club beforehand for a drink and a game of billiards. In the bar he ran into an old acquaintance from Oxford, a happy fellow named Crisp, who would lift anyone's spirits, and they split a cheerfully banter-filled pair of games before Lenox had to beg off at about five till the hour.

On his way out, though, Lenox saw someone he hadn't expected at all: the Duke of Dorset, walking straight toward him at a rapid clip.

White's was the most exclusive club in London; in the front hall at the moment Lenox could see several people he knew, including the 2nd Earl of Munster, whose grandfather had been King William the Fourth; George Byng, one of the Prime Minister's closest advisors; and half a dozen other illustrious gentlemen who were preparing, themselves, to scatter into the fashionable dining rooms and salons of the West End that evening.

"Good evening, Your Grace," Lenox said, when there could no longer be any question that the peer was approaching him specifically.

The rigid set of the duke's thin, aristocratic face now, his hands holding his cane behind his back, all bespoke his distress.

"I was dining privately but heard you were here," the duke said loudly. "I came to find you. I wanted to let you know that you are released from your position."

There was a gasp and a murmur. No business was to be conducted at White's. All eyes were fixed on the duke. "Excuse me, Your Grace?" said Lenox.

"You are sacked. You have led me into disaster."

Lenox was trembling. He had to act forcefully, which was not his strength.

But when he spoke it was in a loud, strong voice. "In the first place, if you insist upon discussing such matters here, I never worked for you. In the second, if you are in any way

133

implying that I was at fault for or complicit in your disappearance, I reject the claim outright, and suggest we go jointly to Scotland Yard right now to take it up with them." He gestured around the room. "All of these men are my witnesses that that offer stands, and will not be withdrawn."

The duke's face did not change—he was too well conditioned for that—but in his eyes was a flare of panic.

"I am implying none of that nonsense," he said stiffly. "I am merely letting you know that you are superfluous to my needs. It was a mistake to bring a commoner into a family matter anyhow."

Lenox stared him in the eye. "I was taught by my late father never to let a man feel his inferiority of rank to my own," he said at last.

There were more murmurs around the front hall. Lenox's father was remembered at White's. "I cannot pretend to care what you were taught," Dorset replied.

"No, I suppose that good manners are not incumbent upon one so exalted as a duke. Good evening, Your Grace."

CHAPTER SEVENTEEN

Lenox left, hot-cheeked, striding fast and unthinking across the genteel streets around White's in his top hat and Saturday tails, furious, sick with the feeling that he had just had an experience of great consequence but couldn't yet tell how it had gone.

His feet took him automatically to the house where he was to dine, a trek of thirty minutes or so—and indeed word of the encounter had beaten him there. By tremendous good fortune it was Lady Jane he happened to see first, standing in the hallway and handing her light shawl to a footman.

"Charles!" she said. "Have you been antagonizing dukes?"

Lenox could feel his own rapid pulse, but he answered as lightly as he was able. "Just the one. Why, did you hear something?"

"Indeed, I heard of what happened at White's word for word."

"That was quick."

Just then, their hostess, Lady Helton, sailed into the room. She was a much-courted widow who owned this small blue gem of a house on Berkeley Square. She was a year younger than Lenox, but she had two children, a husband in the ground, and a grouse farm in Scotland to manage, and thus felt herself to be, comparatively, as old as the Ganges.

"Mr. Lenox!" she said brightly. "I am so very glad you have come. I hope you can give us at least ten or fifteen minutes—at least—you young men being so much in demand on these nights, with the whole round to make. If only you could stay for dinner!"

Lenox bowed, knowing that he had been as good as slapped across the face. "You are exceedingly gracious, Lady Helton. In fact I only called to offer my apologies in person, for it emerges that I must dine elsewhere. My cousin Lancelot is in London and needs entertaining. I am most deeply sorry."

He had been explicitly invited to dine here—and while, social plans being very flexible, it was within his right to cancel his attendance even while in her house, it was a drastic demotion to be asked to stay for an aperitif when he had been invited to supper.

It could only mean that she, too, had heard of his words with Dorset.

"Oh! It is quite—quite all right," said Lady Helton, palpably relieved. "I am very, very sorry, of course, but I understand."

Lady Jane stepped forward. "And I'm afraid your footman has been too quick taking my things—I must go with him. I hope you won't be disappointed, Livia."

"Oh! What!" said Lady Helton, in a suddenly flustered voice. Lady Jane was a high prize of a guest. "Jane, no! Certainly, you—you mustn't go! Both of you must stay!"

"I have told you we will manage by ourselves," Lenox said to his friend.

But Lady Jane was already gesturing to the servant for her shawl. "Nonsense. I'm sorry, Livia," she said.

"Jane, you had—I had thought—both of you must stay," said Lady Helton desperately. "To dine."

The first thing Lenox said to Lady Jane, after the door had closed behind them, was that she of course ought to stay. She told him to shut up. They walked together through Berkeley Square, silent, contemplating, one sympathetically, the other miserably, Lenox's social disgrace.

"Where shall you go?" Lenox asked. There were a dozen parties that night. "I can take you in a hansom."

"Let's go to Chiltern's and call it a quit."

"Are you sure?"

"Of course," said Lady Jane.

This was a fallback for their crowd, a friend's open-ended Saturday salon. "I say, Jane, I am lucky to have you as a friend," he said humbly. "I know that very well."

"Tomorrow I am going to ask you for five pounds to go to the orphans of Surrey, so we shall see then if your tune has changed."

137

He smiled. "Put me down for ten."

"No, we don't want the orphans getting too comfortable," she said in a childing tone, then smiled back. "Anyway, I never once liked Lady Helton."

It was Jane's independent-mindedness exactly— her integrity—that had made her already an arbiter of London society, at this very precocious age. But Lenox could already tell that, whatever Edmund said about the duke's credibility, his own position was collapsed. A duke! There were not many of them, and their power was so encompassing, so unimpeachable, that even a few headlines had done nothing whatsoever to diminish Dorset's. Lenox thought of the famous Henry Moore, Earl of Drogheda, who had been so rich that he wrote his name through Dublin *in buildings,* each house forming part of a letter, so that a bird high above might have read it. And nothing, still, compared to a fellow like Dorset.

He stayed at Chiltern's long enough to be sure that Lady Jane was comfortably situated, then went home and to bed. He had confused nightmares about Bedlam and Shakespeare— and woke, fitfully, throughout the night, as the heat returned.

The next morning, there was a raft of correspondence on his desk. (The mail was delivered seven times daily in London, even on Sundays.) There were a few concerned letters from friends, many more "concerned" letters from assorted tattletales, and three very gracefully managed disinvitations. One of them stung. It was from an old friend of his father's, who had asked him to his box at Goodwood for the races in July.

There was a knock at the door. Mrs. Huggins answered it and returned with Jane, who often dropped round for breakfast. "I've had a letter from James," she said, referring to her husband. "The regiment is on half-rations at the moment for 'practice,' he says, in case they are ever under siege. Even he abides by it. Don't you find that appalling?"

"Toast?" Lenox said, gesturing toward the silver tray.

She laughed, took a piece, and bit it. "Yes. I might as well." She was holding a newspaper, too. "Then there's this. Someone sent it to me."

Lenox looked at the paper, which was one of the lowest rags, the *Challenger*. "Oh, botheration," he said.

She laughed. "Your oaths have stayed quite Sussex, Charles."

He didn't look up. "I am in the presence of a lady."

The article she had brought was a scurrilous and one-sided account—emphatically not Lenox's side—of the conversation he and the duke had had at White's. It called Lenox as good as a thief, connecting him, at the end, to the missing painting.

Lenox started reading it aloud in a very serious voice after he had finished, for comic effect. But when he was through he heard a kind of silence and looked at the doorway, where Lancelot was watching them, mouth agape.

"Is that true?" he said.

"Aren't you meant to be at church?" Lenox asked, frowning and not a little embarrassed.

Lady Jane shook her head. "Lancelot, come here."

He stepped forward. "Yes?" he said.

He was in short pants, a blue jacket, a gray tie, and black shoes, ready for church. For one of the few times since his arrival, he looked young to Lenox.

"Lancelot," she said, "you must know that the very *opposite* of this is true. The Duke of Dorset has behaved very badly, and your cousin Charles has behaved very *well*. Do you understand?"

He nodded. "But then why—"

"Because the duke is telling *lies* about Charles," she said. She nodded in response to his shocked expression. "Yes. Dukes can tell lies. I know there is probably a boy at your school whose father is a duke, and you all think it the grandest thing going, but dukes lie all the time."

"Cor," said Lancelot, looking at Charles.

"Go to church," said Lenox.

"Must I? It's an awful lot of rot."

Lady Jane, who was still holding Lancelot by the shoulder, patted his cheek. "On a Sunday? For shame. I will walk you out. Charles, can I have that twenty pounds you promised by the end of the day?"

"I said ten, I thought."

"For the orphans, Charles." She cradled Lancelot's shoulder. "Take pity."

"Fine," he said moodily. "I'll send Graham across with a cheque."

A long Sunday morning loomed in front of him. He was to go see Bonden the next day and begin their search for the painting but didn't quite know how to occupy himself until then. There were two small errands he could do— first, see Sir Richard Mayne, who had sent word asking him to visit, and second, check in with a friend he had at the British Library to learn more about Shakespeare, and potentially the portrait.

Neither seemed particularly promising. Still, at around eleven o'clock he put on a tie. Before he went, he looked through the new batch of letters that had arrived. There were several of interest, so it was some minutes before he saw, to his surprise, that one bore the ducal seal of the Dorsets.

As it happens I require your further assistance.
You may call upon me at three o'clock.
Dorset

Lenox felt himself flush, fury making his skin tingle. The nerve of it!

Without a second thought he took up a pen and a piece of his own writing paper, with its own proud seal, from the stand on the front hall table. Why, his family had been on the same plot of land since the Domesday Book. Longer than the duke's. There was no man he need bow in humility before for reasons of birth. He wrote his reply.

You may call upon me between five and six o'clock in the afternoon today.
If I am home I will see you. If you are willing to tell me what you actually know, I may choose to help.
Lenox

He sealed the letter and pasted a twopence-blue to it, so that it would reach the duke with all haste, then dropped it in the local letterbox outside before he could reconsider his tone.

CHAPTER EIGHTEEN

In this particular mood it was harder than ever to keep the secret of the duke's kidnapping. But Lenox did so.

"He has *no* memory of it?" Mayne asked once more.

They were sitting in the spacious, well-lit office of the Commissioner of Scotland Yard, with its view of the long avenue to Parliament. In the distance, heavy hammers worked; some tremendous bell was going to be placed in a tower right by Parliament, they said, five or six years hence.

Lenox leaned down and rubbed his shin, wincing. "He says not."

"What is it?" asked Mayne, rather rudely.

"Oh—nothing. My young cousin is staying with me for a few weeks. He hit me in the shin with a cricket ball."

"I hope you gave him a hiding."

"Ah," said Lenox, abashed. "No. I'm afraid everyone is rather soft on him. His father died when he was six."

"Oh. Shame."

Lenox nodded. He could see Lancelot's small, confused face as he held Eustacia's hand by the grave. "Battle against the French."

143

Mayne nodded. "Stout fellow. Died well."

"Indeed."

"About the duke, then—you two have had a dispute? The Palace has been in touch with me. They want no hint of a scandal, and they are worried there is a political element, given his high rank and his service in the cabinet. The ivory buttons and all that."

A cabinet minister's servants were permitted to wear ivory buttons with the Queen's seal on their uniforms. "We are meeting this afternoon," said Lenox. "I am happy to reconcile with him should he apologize."

"Do it either way."

Lenox nodded ambiguously.

They sat there speaking for half an hour or so, first discussing Dorset but then moving on to more general subjects, including a number of cases under Mayne's purview. The commissioner consulted with Lenox in this fashion more often these days, which was gratifying.

"Tell me something," said Lenox, just before he left. He was standing with his hat in his hand. "What do you know about Shakespeare?"

"I once played Ophelia in *Hamlet*."

"Did you!"

"Yes." Mayne looked dismal at the recollection. "I was nine, and I was the smallest boy at school. I wouldn't do it again for a hundredweight of coal. I've never been able to tolerate Shakespeare since."

Lenox smiled. "How were the reviews?"

Mayne brightened. "Not bad, in fact, I would have you know! We had it come happy in the wash instead of tragical—they ended up married, I think, Hamlet and Ophelia. The new king died very bloody. Gertrude, too. People liked that. I was a fair soprano then, if I say so."

Sir Richard smiled at himself, Lenox laughed, and they shook hands.

Mayne kept his grip, though, and added, "Keep me close on Dorset."

"Yes, Sir Richard."

"Good chap. Be safe."

"And yourself."

Nobody had betrayed to Lenox any reaction on his stray mentions of the name Shakespeare.

At a little after one o'clock, he stopped by the British Library. It was closed on Sundays, but Lenox's friend there, like Sir Richard, worked seven days a week. Lenox presented his card at a side door, and soon Duncan Jones came down to fetch him—a friend of long standing.

"Mr. Lenox! This is a pleasant and unexpected surprise."

"How do you do, Mr. Jones?"

"Summer could be kinder on my knees. Come in, come in—thank you, Hillhurst," he said to the library's guard, who touched his hat. Duncan Jones counted for a great deal in these noble halls.

He was a fellow of perhaps eighty-five, Jones, with short white hair and a deeply creased face. His father had been a Yorkshire farmworker. Neither of his parents had been able to read. But from an early age he had shown such brilliance in the year or two of school that was expected of him that he had simply kept advancing in his education, every year intended to be his last so that he could quit and help his family on the farm, until at last he found his way to Cambridge through the generosity of a Yorkshire squire.

Now he was perhaps the world's foremost scholar of incunabula, and the chief curator of the great library's collection of manuscripts. He still had a very heavy accent. Lenox could not quite remember whether he had been knighted; he suspected so. Nevertheless, there was no pomposity to him whatsoever. They had struck up a friendship once when Lenox requested a very old map of the Kingdom of Dalmatia, on Europe's southeastern coastline, and it had been in Jones's carrel.

"What brings you?" asked Jones, as they proceeded slowly down a long, dim hallway, striped at even intervals with shafts of sunlight from outside.

"I was hoping I could buy you a cup of tea as the price of your expertise."

"Of course. I was pottering—inexcusable, but at my age perhaps inevitable."

146

The tea was free, in a small room covered in eccentric portraits of old noblemen and women, ranging in size from a tenpence coin to twice Lenox's height.

They took cups, Jones's a proper Yorkshire cup, black with five lumps of sugar, and then retreated to a comfortable nook piled with odd cushions.

"What I was curious about was Shakespeare," Lenox said as they sat.

Jones squinted at him. "Who, now?"

"I—he was—oh, but I see now, you are having fun at my expense. Very good." Jones was laughing his wheezing laugh, which came from deep within his gentle soul. "Do you make sport of all your inferiors?"

"Do go on, Charles, do go on," said Jones, still smiling. "I apologize."

Lenox smiled, too. "What I really hoped to learn about was the portraits of him that we know to exist."

Jones brightened. "Ah. An interesting question!"

"Is it?"

"Yes, because really there is only one. That is your answer. It is the black-and-white etching that appeared in the First Folio. You would recognize it instantly. He has a very high bald forehead in it, a white ruff, and a mustache. Not a good portrait—stiff—but his friends are recorded as saying it looked very like him. The artist was Martin Droeshout, who never did a single thing of interest with the rest of his mortal hours."

"Just one picture!" Lenox said wonderingly.

"There are dozens of imitations. But only one other candidate that *could* be real. The Chandos."

Here was a name that Lenox knew well. Just at that instant, perhaps the most famous man in England was Richard Plantagenet Temple-Nugent-Brydges-Chandos-Grenville—the 2nd Duke of Buckingham and Chandos. Some decades before, he had inherited one of the world's largest fortunes. Now he was bankrupt. Indeed, they said he owed a million pounds in debt.

"The same family?"

"The very same. In the sell-off of his belongings the current duke sold it to Ellesmere last year, who to his credit immediately donated it to the nation. It is an intriguing picture. Its sitter is dressed in open collar, with a gold earring, and he has a very bright, humorous face. That makes it nice to think it is him."

"But it is not certain."

"No, it is very far from certain."

"What would a certain oil of Shakespeare be worth?"

"Worth!" Jones smiled a private smile, a librarian's smile, full of dusty secrets and happy solitudes. He thought for a moment. "I often think of Thomas De Quincey saying that the plays are not works of art—they are phenomena of nature, like the sun and the sea, the stars and the flowers. But that was not your question."

"It was still a good answer."

Jones took a sip of his tea. "There is no price that could be too high, Charles. Imagine looking into Shakespeare's eyes! The most peerie little oval of his face would be worth the moon."

"What about twenty thousand pounds?"

Jones smiled, conceding to reality. "Yes. That sounds like a decent first approximation. Twenty thousand pounds. More if there were two buyers competing for it. These Americans are getting rather rich. Gold and railroads, I'm told."

CHAPTER NINETEEN

Lenox returned home at four o'clock and went to the small sitting room across the hall from his study, to wait for the duke. He wanted the advantage of Dorset—to make him wait—and asked Mrs. Huggins to show the Duke into the study and offer him a drink if he came.

At the stroke of five the doorbell rang. The estimable housekeeper did exactly as she was asked, telling Dorset that Lenox would be there shortly. About five minutes later the detective was just preparing to go across the hall when he saw, through the cracked door of the small sitting room, something that chilled his heart: Lancelot was approaching the study.

He watched, helpless as a fly in a spider's web, as Lancelot shoved the study door open and went up to the duke.

"Hello!" he said.

"Hello," said the lean, handsome duke, looking around, a bit baffled.

The conversation halted. They stared at each other across the length of carpet that lay between them, exactly like two Parliamentary leaders negotiating a bill, except that one of them happened to have mud all over the back of his jacket; not the duke.

Lenox was just going to cross the hall to intervene when Lancelot said, in a tone that was more anthropological than anything—scientific—"You've got a perfectly enormous mouth."

The duke looked startled. "Excuse me?"

"You've got a huge mouth!" Lancelot bellowed. Then he added, with sympathy, "My great-grandfather is deaf, too."

The duke reddened to the roots of his hair. "I'm not deaf. And I'm fifty-seven."

"Oh, so it's age. Rotten luck. Well, swings and roundabouts."

"No, I—"

"Have you ever seen how many grapes you could put in there?"

"What?"

"In your mouth. Do keep up."

"Of course I haven't," he said. Dorset's hand went involuntarily to his mouth. "It's a normal-sized mouth."

"Are you that duke?"

"I am the Fifteenth Duke of—"

"I bet you could get ten grapes in there without any problem at all. After that it would be tricky."

"We could nev—"

"It's a once-in-a-lifetime opportunity. We'd simply be throwing it away not to try," said Lancelot. "Shall I ring and ask for some grapes?"

The duke, who had existed for many years

without the encumbrance of a living soul disobeying his wishes, looked truly bewildered.

"Who are you?"

"Who am I? I'm Lancelot."

"Lancelot."

"Yes, *Lancelot*."

"I am not deaf!"

"Lancelot," said Lancelot, in a soft sort of whisper. Then he said, "I go to Eton. Did you go there?"

"I was at Winchester," said the duke stiffly.

"Hadn't you the money to go to Eton?"

"The—my family has been going to Winchester for generations. Winchester and Cambridge."

Lancelot nodded encouragingly. "My father's vet went to Winchester. He had his whole arm up a cow once."

"No, he didn't."

"Well, up to his elbow."

The duke was leaning forward on his chair, irate. "No! I mean he didn't go to Winchester! Your father's veterinarian!"

Lancelot frowned. "I'm quite sure he did."

"Who *are* you? Why are you in this house?" said Dorset finally, trying to regain command of the conversation. "My God, it's like an asylum."

"They've got you in an asylum?" said Lancelot.

Lenox, in the doorway, was watching with a sort of rapt, immobilized fascination.

"No, they've not got me in an—"

152

"It's hard when they started you at Winchester, I guess."

"No, they've—"

"It's a lot to overcome."

"Winchester is—"

"The father is the child of the man, they say," interrupted Lancelot, benevolently. "That's what my headmaster tells us."

The duke, perhaps at last realizing that his role in this bewildering conversation was voluntary, stood up. "Where is your uncle?"

"In Surrey," Lancelot said instantly.

"In *Surrey*? I was told to meet him here at five o'clock! What is he doing in Surrey?"

"He collects fragments from Anglo-Saxon times."

"What are you talking about?"

"Is it hard, at your age, to keep everything straight?"

"What are you talking about?"

"My uncle Chips. In Surrey?"

"Your uncle—no, your uncle *Lenox,* you damned fool boy, *Charles Lenox.*"

"Oh, he's my cousin," said Lancelot immediately. He chuckled. "Not my uncle. Dear old duke."

"Where is *he? Charles Lenox?*"

"He said he would be back in ten minutes."

"And he left you in charge here to greet me?"

"Oh! No, I was just bored."

The duke glared at Lancelot. "Bored! When I was your age—"

153

"Long, long, long ago," said Lancelot. "Yes?"

"When I was your age, not that long ago, as it happens, I would have received a caning for the way you're speaking to me. I've half a mind to give you one myself."

"I'm so sorry," Lancelot said simply and instantly. "I hadn't meant to be disrespectful."

"But you—"

"They tell me I'm very curious. That's all."

"Hm."

Dorset looked as if he could have come up with several hundred adjectives he would have used to describe Lancelot before he reached *curious*. He sat back down in his chair, staring at the boy with distaste.

"So you really are a duke?"

"Yes."

"What duke?"

"I am the Fifteenth Duke of Dorset," said the duke with fierce assertiveness, as if he had never been more pleased to declare it. "What does your father do?"

"Have you met the Queen?"

Lenox saw the duke relax, just minutely. "Of course."

"How many times?"

"More than you could count."

"Twice?"

"No! Dozens! She is my third cousin, and my wife's third cousin once removed!"

Lancelot looked at him pityingly. "Third cousin, is that it. So she wouldn't *remember* you."

"Of course she would remember me! Her Majesty is an intimate—a close—she is of course the sovereign, and never stoops to—she—"

Lancelot took advantage of the duke's flustered tact to say, "Perhaps she would remember your face."

"Of course she knows my face!"

"Perhaps she thinks you're a footman, or something like that."

"The Queen does not think I am a footman!" thundered the duke.

"No?"

"Of course not!"

"I was always taught—by my father—that it would be the greatest honor to serve as the Queen's humblest servant. That no Englishman would hesitate to lay down his life so that she might not besmirch her gown."

"Well, of course, that is quite true!" said the duke, confused.

"Then why do you seem angry about being her footman?"

"I am not her footman!"

"Sorry, about her thinking that you were her footman?"

The duke's face was so full of anger that he stood up again, and quick as a flash Lenox realized he had to move. He crossed the hall and entered with a pointed clatter of the door.

"Your Grace," he said, bowing slightly as he came in, "I am sorry to have kept you. It was unavoidable."

The duke looked irate. "Who is this child?"

Lenox glanced at the other chair, pretending surprise. "Oh, this is my mother's young cousin, Lancelot."

"He has been speaking to me in the most—in the most—"

"I said our veterinarian went to Winchester," Lancelot told Lenox apologetically. "I'm very sorry."

"Oh." Lenox looked at Dorset. "It must have been an error, Your Grace. He is only twelve, after all."

"And he's a dashed good vet, too," said Lancelot joyfully. Lenox thought he had never seen anyone quite so intensely happy. "I'll tell you what it is, Duke, I'll write to Father. I'll bet you ten pence he went to Winchester after all! That'll please you. A distinguished alumnus for Winchester at last."

"He did not!" said Dorset angrily.

Lenox intervened. "Lancelot, excuse yourself this instant. Your Grace, I apologize."

Lancelot, who to his credit moved fast for someone who loved eating so passionately, was on his feet quickly. "Good-bye!" he said.

And as he darted cheerfully away, he winked at Lenox.

It was only then that the penny dropped: Lancelot hadn't been making random mischief. He had been exacting a specific revenge for the duke's rudeness to Lenox; he had, despite every previous piece of evidence that existed, some kind of instinctive loyalty to Charles.

Could it even be love! Just possibly. How very astonishing that would be.

"Tell Mrs. Huggins you need your tea, please."

"I will. Cheerio, Duke. We'll talk about the grapes later!"

As Lancelot left, Lenox looked at Dorset, whose face remained taut with anger. "Grapes?" he said.

CHAPTER TWENTY

A further apology ("the boy grew up quite unworldly, living in Cornwall") mollified the duke a bit, and a few moments later they were seated in the same two chairs, the duke again in some possession of himself.

"You asked to meet, Your Grace," Lenox said. The reversion to this formal address was intentional. It would be delicate work to rebalance their relationship. "I thank you for coming here. I know it must have been an inconvenience."

This gave the duke a chance to be majestic, humbly. "Ah," he said. "Well."

"May I ask why you wished to meet?"

The duke hesitated and then said, very grandly, "You may have your terms, Mr. Lenox. I will disclose to you everything I know. After that, you may help me or not as you see fit."

Lenox nodded. But his reply was noncommittal. "You can perhaps conceive why I am disinclined to do so."

The duke looked at him warily. "I can."

Indeed, Lenox was tempted to say no. The humiliation of the duke's speech to him at White's lingered—would chase him down for a long ways yet, if he knew London, like hounds to a fox.

But he also knew that he had no choice but to accept. Curiosity: a bedeviling vice, a staunch ally.

"Why have you changed your mind?" asked Lenox.

The duke, economical of motion always, tilted his head very slightly. "You caught me when Scotland Yard did not. Though that was not a happy moment, clearly you possess some skill."

"I scc."

The duke looked at him hard. At last, he said, "On my honor as a gentleman, then, I apologize to you for the harsh words I spoke at White's."

They stared at each other. A duke's apology was as rare as a winter swallow. But Lenox had been humiliated publicly, and this was an apology in private.

"Thank you," Lenox said.

He left it there and stared back at the older man. Finally, the duke said, in a voice that choked on its own concession, not out of any specific anger toward Lenox, but more for the abasement of his position, "I would be delighted if you would be my guest at luncheon at White's tomorrow."

"That is extremely kind of you, Your Grace, and I accept," said Lenox. "Let us move forward."

The duke nodded. "Yes."

There was a long pause. "Have you learned or observed anything new?" Lenox asked.

To his complete surprise, this question released

a torrential reply. Within thirty seconds the duke had stood up and was striding back and forth along the carpet, excoriating the thief of the painting, muttering dark imprecations against his own family and staff again, who he claimed were not taking the problem seriously enough, and repeatedly expressing despair at the situation.

It was clear that he had kept his emotions in check for the past day. To Lenox he suddenly seemed unwell.

"Your Grace," he said at last.

The duke, hands behind his back, stopped. "Yes."

"Tomorrow I think that with some luck I may be able to discover where the painting has gone." He was referring to his plan with Bonden. "But I cannot help but suspect that my job would be substantially easier if I knew the full story of Shakespeare's portrait."

The duke stared at Lenox as if he were not quite real—a ghost—until finally he said, "You are right that I have been concealing a few important facts from you. I will retrieve the papers that tell the story from my personal safe."

"Shall we go now?"

"Come to my house tomorrow at lunchtime— if you don't mind. The safe is in Buckingham Palace."

Lenox nodded. "I see. Very good. In the meanwhile, Your Grace, could I recommend a glass of brandy and supper with your family?"

The duke regained a measure of his composure. "Yes. Yes, of course. I shall expect you tomorrow at noon."

"I apologize again for my cousin's words," Lenox said.

He watched the duke step into his carriage and depart. Almost at the same instant, Lady Jane flew down her steps and up Charles's.

"What was that!" she said when Lenox had gone to the front door and let her in.

"He's apologized."

"Ha!" she crowed. "Everyone in Hampden Lane saw his carriage in front of your house and knew he'd come to apologize. I'm going to tell Lady Helton as quickly as can be."

"He's in a dark place, poor fellow."

Lady Jane was giddy, though. "Let him be. We've won!"

He heard that word, "we," and though he smiled, something pierced him.

It had been nearly two years since he had made the enormous error of telling Lady Jane that he was in love with her. For six months afterward they had existed in a state of tense amity, the secret always between them, and at times he had wondered if their true friendship was permanently corrupted.

Then had come something surprising. For a three-month period, Jane's oft-absent husband,

James Deere, had returned for an extended stay in London with his regiment.

Lenox had never known the man well. When Jane had married him, it had seemed quite within the cosmic order, she being the daughter of an earl, he the son of another. He was a tall, fair man, with thin nostrils, kind blue eyes, and a handsome forehead. The world thought him better-looking than Jane, and he was certainly more at home in London, having been raised primarily there.

All of this had rather predisposed Lenox to look upon him as a cavalier, one of those soldiers who marries and then never, much as they are glad it exists, off in the distance, waiting for them, thinks of their home as very real.

Yet upon Deere's return, Lenox discovered that he had been wrong. The soldier might have looked that way to the world, but as they had grown haltingly close over his three-month spell at home, at Jane's insistence really, for she would push them together—saying that Charles and Edmund Lenox were brothers to her—he had realized Deere was not at all the man he'd imagined.

His great pleasure in life was his own curiosity, Deere. He met all other human beings with a totally open interest, almost as an artist or a novelist might. When he learned Lenox—whom he had probably not spared much thought for, one of his wife's Sussex people—was a detective, he evinced no disapproval at all, but on the contrary was all delight, pressing upon him the most delicate but apposite questions, fascinated by every detail.

He was the same in all situations. He took like a duck to the culture of each place his army visited—not true, to put it mildly, of most army officers, who ate Yorkshire puddings on Sunday whether they were in New Delhi or Kabul or Yorkshire itself—and always brought home great troves of incidental objects, which he studied and collected at a high amateur level. He could name the grasses of the field, the trees of the meadow, the constellations; he had a taste for port wine and had read it up until he could describe its journey from grape to glass in the most charming, least self-serious terms; he cared deeply for dogs, knew the ancient legends about every breed, and would happily spend hours in conversation about the Clumber Spaniel with a stranger in the street.

At the end of the three months of his return to Hampden Lane, Deere hadn't merely won Lenox's affection—he had won Lenox's love, as he had once won Jane's.

This was both painful and a relief. Deere was a man of great parts, worthy of Jane's heart. One day he would make a very fine, fair, and kindhearted landowner. He loved his duty—but lightly, which was just as Lenox thought proper.

He loved his wife—and dearly, which was also just as Lenox thought proper.

After he was gone, Lenox's friendship with Lady Jane had returned to its state of initial purity. He even called her Jane again; for a while she had been Lady Elizabeth, still her name at court. For instance, they could stand here, celebrating his victory over a duke, as if they really were a shadow kind of couple.

But it was still painful to him that they were not, he realized.

"Incidentally, what do you make of my Effie Somers, upon reflection?" she said.

"What do you mean?"

"Will you marry her?"

"She hasn't asked me yet."

"I believe the custom is that you should ask her."

Lenox frowned. "That doesn't sound right."

Lady Jane laughed. "It's true that Victoria asked Prince Albert. Then again, she was queen."

"Is Miss Somers not a queen? I call that a disappointment."

"What an oldster I shall be at your wedding. Too old even for a bridesmaid."

It was an ironclad rule that the bride's bridesmaids be younger than she. "You could stand best man."

"Edmund might be put out," said Lady Jane. "Listen, I had better go. My aunt Elyssa is over for tea."

"Have you left her this whole time!"

"Don't waste your pity—she is looking through my letters right now."

Lenox spent the rest of the day reading quite an interesting book about Shakespeare that Duncan Jones had lent him—there was a theory that he had been a secret Catholic, among other things—before dining out at the Athenaeum, where several men approached him and said they were bloody glad the duke had apologized, and it was a disgrace that he had caught Lenox unawares in White's.

He slept well that night. Early the next morning he was awake, dressed, brushed, and fed by seven o'clock, waiting with the papers. He would leave soon to meet Bonden on the east side of the city, at the Dovecote.

Just as he was in the hallway preparing to leave, however, he heard the door ring.

He opened up: Bonden.

"Oh, hello," said Lenox. "I was meant to come see you, I thought."

"Hello," said Bonden. Then, after allowing himself a leisurely draw on his pipe, he said, placidly—perhaps in coming, as he did, from the watery world, where death could descend from above or below or crossways at any instant—"Your duke has shot and killed someone overnight. His manservant, Craig. You had better get there quickly, I suppose."

CHAPTER TWENTY-ONE

Lenox had begun to carry the little soft leather book of quotations from Shakespeare with him everywhere, and as his hansom cab drove toward Dorset House, he opened it.

> *Lord, what fools these mortals be.*
> —A Midsummer Night's Dream

Well, even he knew that one. He closed the tiny oracle and placed it back into his breast pocket.

Bonden had been in possession of only the most basic facts. The fatal shot had been fired at five in the morning, before first light, and though Dorset had called a doctor instantly, Craig had died after an hour's struggle. Bonden had come west to tell Lenox—he was apparently an early riser—and ask if he wanted to meet the next day or cancel altogether.

"Tomorrow will do, or sooner if I can get free," said Lenox. His feeling was that finding the missing painting might yet be very important.

"I will be at the Dovecote tomorrow morning," Bonden said. "I may be there later today, though I'm not sure."

"Very good."

Now Lenox rode in solitary silence toward

the river, contemplating this strange case. The streets on a Monday morning were crowded with carriages, and passage was slow—so slow that innumerable vendors had time to approach Lenox's open window. Whelks, spice cakes, jellied eel, lemonade, plum duff: He declined all of these as politely as he could. Such carts were the cafés of perhaps a third of London's population, who lived quite poor, and even the remaining two-thirds, up in all likelihood to the Duke of Dorset, partook of their wares at least occasionally.

At last, Lenox assented to a small boy who was selling ginger beer, and whose clothes told against his business being very successful, poor lad. He paid and tipped, then took the stone bottle and drank it—refreshing, actually, sparkly and bittersweet. The boy followed the carriage at a slow trot and took the bottle back with his thanks when Lenox was done.

They pulled clear of a traffic mixup (a "jam," as the younger constables sometimes called it, because it was so sticky) involving two hansom cabs that had locked axles, and soon enough they were at the great palatial house of Dorset, overlooking the Thames, whose austerely beautiful alabaster front now seemed a marmoreal sepulcher, ghostly and hant.

What could Lenox recall of Craig? He was of middling height; very strong; a faded Scottish accent; curt, never even marginally ingratiating. Shot! He recalled the duke's tense, nervy state the day before.

There were two unmarked police carts in front of the house, a far cry from most crime scenes, no doubt out of deference to the augustness of this one. Near one of them was Sir Richard Mayne, who had the grim and forbidding look of a powerful man in the last place he wishes to be.

He saw Lenox first and came to the hansom as Lenox was paying the driver. "Exeter would call you a bad penny."

"What would he call Dorset?"

Mayne jerked his head. "The duke is expecting you. I've never seen anything less like an arrest, I must tell you."

In the entranceway they met Ward, who was ashen. "Hullo, Ward," Lenox said sympathetically.

"I don't know what to make of it," said Ward, shaking his head. "Truly I don't. They were as thick as could be, Craig and the duke. One soul in two bodies, I sometimes thought."

"I wondered if it was an accident?" Lenox said. "The duke seemed wound tight."

Ward shook his head. "We don't know. Last night the duke had had all the portraits in his study screwed into the wall by one of the footmen. Then he hid in his closet, sleeping on a chair. Craig was in the process of unscrewing one when the duke woke up."

"Craig!" Lenox said.

In a way this attempted theft was a bigger surprise than the valet being dead. But Mayne nodded, the three of them in a tight circle just inside the front door. "The duke says he took Craig for a thief. Shot him right away."

This changed the complexion of the case completely. "Good heavens."

Just before he had come here, Lenox had quickly charged Graham with the task of finding out whatever he could about Craig—Alexander Arnold Craig, as Lenox had made note of his name when he had asked for details about all of the duke's staff.

Now he was doubly curious what Graham would uncover.

"The duke is distraught," Ward said, "though I cannot tell whether he is more upset about the betrayal or the death."

Lenox kept a dark thought to himself; it was the second time the Duke of Dorset had shot some-one accidentally—or "accidentally." Pendleton's son had been first.

"Where is the duke now?" Lenox asked.

Sir Richard, leading them through a vast and beautiful drawing room, answered. "In the family's private drawing room, with his wife and his children. We are taking him into custody shortly, but we permitted him time to shave and dress."

"Good of you," said Lenox.

"Nice to be a duke," said Mayne. "He has also asked for a private word with you should you come. Which you have."

Lenox glanced around the room, filled with delicate porcelain, medieval tapestries, satinwood side tables, and example after example of fine old Louis XIV furniture—a thin-boned Mazarin desk, just for example, of ebony and copper, inlaid with the most beautiful pattern Lenox could remember seeing in such a desk, and he had been in no few houses with pretensions to attractiveness of interior design.

Not a house for a murder.

The Dorset family was congregated in the smaller drawing room Mayne had mentioned, and they proceeded there.

"His Grace's son, Lord Vere, is still fragile, but he has risen for this occasion," Ward said just before they entered, as if they were discussing a lunch party.

Lenox nodded. This was Corfe, whose fever had kept the family in London, in a way beginning this chain of tragic events. "Understood."

The family was arranged along two sofas. The duke rose as they entered. His son and daughter remained seated, as did his wife. "Lenox," said the duke. "I requested the courtesy

170

that they wait to arrest me until I could hand you this letter."

"Letter, Your Grace?"

From the breast pocket of his handsome black suit, he withdrew a thin sheaf of papers, tied with string. Lenox saw that the reddish string was just to the left of a rust-colored stain it must have previously made on the outside of the papers—evidently it had sat somewhere for a very long while undisturbed until recently being reopened.

"After reading this there is little you will not know. Work as quickly as you can, please. Find out what Craig knew. I have instructed the servants to give you all access to the house that you wish. Ward will help as far you both see fit."

Despite their conciliatory meeting the night before, Lenox was surprised at this act of faith. "Thank you, Your Grace."

The duke looked more serene now than he had before he killed Craig, oddly. "You are my best hope. Protect it—and find it."

"Protect what?" said the duchess.

The duke ignored her. "I will be in the Tower of London if you wish to speak to me." He smiled ruefully. "My schedule there will be clear from as early as this afternoon, I understand."

As a member of Britain's nobility, it was his right to be imprisoned in the Tower. (Certain tourists from the continent would no doubt have paid a fortune to spend a night in the Tower— so long as they were allowed to leave in the morning.) He would pass his incarceration in very great luxury, that was a given. It was also the case that no common court would try him, only, if it came to trial at all, the House of Lords.

Goodness, the papers, Lenox thought for the first time. A former cabinet member; more significantly still, for circulation numbers, a Duke of Dorset.

"Very good, Your Grace."

"My daughter has agreed to act as my go-between—she will see my solicitor, call upon my friends. The duchess has a great deal of responsibility in her own right, so please call upon Violet should you need assistance that Ward cannot provide."

Lenox bowed to Lady Violet, who was sitting with great composure next to her brother. "Lady Vere," he said.

"Mr. Lenox."

Lenox watched the constables come to stand at either side of the duke. Time to go, one of them said, and the duke nodded. He looked at Lenox and said once again, to the mystification of all there except the detective, "Protect it." The fervor in his voice was remarkable; it was easy to believe that he had shot Craig without vacillation.

"I will do my level best," Lenox said.

"Thank you," said Dorset.

The elaborate process of arresting the duke commenced. The heir, Corfe, handsomely dressed, stood unsteadily, watching. As for the duke's daughter, she was full of solicitous suggestions, in a sort of ceaseless soothing chatter, telling her father about the meals that Fortnum would be delivering, naming all the ways they would be sure he was comfortable, asking which books he needed from his study, that sort of thing. None of this prevented the constables on charge from doing their duty, and locking the fifth-highest-ranking nobleman in Great Britain in a pair of scarred steel handcuffs.

CHAPTER TWENTY-TWO

He asked Ward if he could sit in some private place for twenty minutes, and the young secretary guided him to a sitting room with heavy velvet draping over the window, in the fashion of the moment. It felt stifling; when Ward had gone, Lenox opened the curtain and the window, and then at least a little breeze came in.

Lenox opened the papers cautiously. They were foxed with age, though the paper was of such quality that they had not grown brittle. The hand was legible, indeed elegant, and belonged very obviously to an earlier age.

On top was a hastily scrawled note from the Duke, written on one of the very cream-colored notecards that had given away his farcical kidnapping scheme to Lenox.

Lenox: The poem is on the portrait of S.—Dorset.

That was all it said, and Lenox frowned, not sure he understood, then riffled through the pages of the older letter beneath the notecard. He saw that there were seven in all. There was a heading at the top of the first:

Dorset House, London
22 April 1771

And on the bottom of the last, a signature:

Your father, Thomas,
13th Duke of Dorset

So this letter had been written, eighty-two years before, by the man in the stolen portrait.

In this very room, for all Lenox knew; certainly in this house.

He sat down and read.

Dorset House, London
22 April 1771

My dear Clarence,
I was pleased at the sincere curiosity with which you treated our conversation this morning. I wish to elaborate upon it in this letter, which, I flatter myself, might also serve as a guide to your heir some day when you have a similar conversation with him. Even should that not be the case, I hope you will permit your father this one circuitous story. It is indeed half-expected of men who reach my age; and I have never been voluble with you, so it may be that I can draw on that particular line of credit.

(I do not recall my own father saying more than a word or two before I first went to school. His advice when he left me there at 8 was "Don't peach, don't gamble more than your pocket money, don't cry when you're beaten, and don't be top of your class.")

To begin the story long ago:

In a lively market town in Warwickshire around the year 1570, a leather merchant and glovemaker, once very prosperous, was edging toward financial ruin.

Previously he had been one of the town's leading citizens—afeeror (here we run into a word I have watched pass out of existence in my own lifetime—an afeeror, in your great-great-grandfather's day, was the official in charge of assessing fines for which no specifically predetermined fine existed) bailiff, burgess, chief magistrate, and eventually mayor. A prominent person, you'll agree.

But on the heels of his rise came his fall. It began when the courts prosecuted him for two separate crimes, first the illegal trade of large quantities of wool, and second, usury. (This may be the crime I most abhor, as it preys on the poor and the credulous. A murderer may at least be said to have lost his ability to calculate right and wrong. Usury is done as coolly as shearing a sheep.) By 1576, this man had to forfeit his public office. There is almost no trace of him in the town records after that until his death.

This may seem like a dreary biography, with its minor apogee and depressing sequel. Certainly it would have been forgotten wholly, and I would not be recounting it to you, were it not for one of the man's children. Not Gilbert, not Mary, not Joan. No; you will have likely guessed this child's name; William. The market town was Stratford-upon-Avon, the glovemaker was John Shakespeare, and the son, our nation's greatest artist, William Shakespeare.

Even Malone knows very little (and as you know, in my modest way I have contributed to the scholarship on this subject) of the playwright's youth. Most famously, there is no record of his so-called "lost years," between 1582, when he was married at the age of 18, and 1592, when he began to make a name for himself in London. It is traditional to say that he fled to London to escape charges of poaching. I could go further into this notion (the family of Sir Thomas Lucy cling to it). But here instead I will begin a second strand of our story.

• • •

The title that I am humbled to bear, and which will one day pass to you, originated, as you know, during the reign of Queen Elizabeth, a crucial figure in this tale. I have personally never cared all that much about the schism between England and Rome. In our ancestor's time, however, religion was a choice with consequences of life and death.

You will remember the saga of Henry VIII from your schooldays. He left Catholicism and founded the Protestant church, that he might obtain a divorce. Then his daughter Mary restored the crown to the Catholic cause, before finally Elizabeth, during her long rule, made it Protestant again, a decision that her successor, King James, who gives his name to our Bible, helped finally to consecrate.

During the reign of that awful Mary, our family remained Protestant. We were rewarded for it with the title you will inherit, an extension of our lands, and a place in history's, and, we may hope, God's, graces.

Conversely, during the reigns of Elizabeth and James many men remained, at great personal risk, members of the Catholic faith.

Their reward has been more doubtful than ours. (The everlasting fires of hell, in the first place, if you wish to believe the curate at Dorset Chapel.) Foremost among these men was the rather romantic figure of Sir Edmund Campion, who took his life in his hands by returning to England from abroad with pamphlets preaching the Roman faith, dodging in and out of inlets along the coast in order to deposit them with members of the faith. He was finally caught by priest hunters—these were a cruel band of men, even we must own—and, after turning down the chance to be Archbishop of Canterbury if he would only convert, was hanged, then drawn and quartered, at Tyburn.

When Elizabeth died, in 1603, there was hope for the Catholics that they might have more freedom, but in fact Elizabeth's successor, James, took a very hard line with non-conformists. Some lived in peace; some conformed; some were banished and reprieved; some, alas, were executed.

And it is here, with hopes that I retain your patience through these twisting lanes, that my stories merge.

John Shakespeare's household was broken up and sold upon his death, two years before his Queen's, in 1601. This father had regained some of his position with his son's success, and both were, in all outward respects, good Protestants.

What is known only to a few people, however, now including you, is a truth that has long been rumored but never confirmed: The Shakespeares remained Catholic.

One hundred and fifty years ago, five years after William Shakespeare's death, there was a raid upon the house. Anti-Catholic sentiment was high in London, and they had word from an informant.

That informant, I am at once chagrined and proud to say, was an emissary from that age's Duke of Dorset, my great-great-grandfather. He was a man of iron will. He ordered and supervised the raid, and the bailiffs who conducted it found, cleverly bricked away behind the hearth, a chest full of all the markers of the secret sacrament: vestments, a chalice, the wafers and wine that papists to this day believe constitute the body and blood of Christ. Most deadly of all, they found a bundle of Campion's pamphlets.

The owner of the house could have been executed for the possession of any of those. At a minimum, his property would have been forfeit and he might have been banished.

Your ancestor was merciful, however—because he had his own motives. The Protestant church's lower officers were rude, rough men, who would have been contented to have found evidence of secret Catholicism. It was the duke who suppressed their record-keeping, because of his alternative purpose, which is a secret to this day. He was a benefactor of the theater; and discovered, as he had thought he might, more than simply artifacts of the Catholic faith: his men found the painting that I showed you this morning.

And with it, among the dusty odds and ends stored in the small bricked-off keep, a letter. It described a single hidden play.

CHAPTER TWENTY-THREE

Lenox stopped reading.

If what the letter said was true, all this had just increased dramatically in significance. He had been involved in cases of murder, and to be sure, nothing could matter more than those. But this was an issue of public magnitude upon a different order. If a lost play by Shakespeare were discovered, England would stop; the portrait would be a footnote to it. No greater treasure, shy of King Arthur's sword, could be discovered within the isle.

Protect it—the Duke had said, with a meaningful look—*protect it and find it.*

He may have meant in these last words not the portrait, but the play.

There was a knock at the door. He didn't know how much time he had passed in contemplation, but even as he rose he saw that the duke's daughter, Lady Violet, was entering the room. He turned the letter facedown.

Even at this moment, her posture and bearing were unmistakably aristocratic. She wore a plain blue house dress, and a row of dazzling emeralds pinned back her hair—though even this lightly worn fortune could not, alas, make her beautiful.

"May I have a word, Mr. Lenox?" she asked.

"Of course, Lady Violet," he said. "I am at your service."

She sat upon a plush settee near the window, so soft that she sank into it as if into a meringue. Outside there was the brisk sound of a horse passing, and Lenox remembered that there was a world beyond these walls.

"How may I help you?" he asked.

"We have just been informed by one of the constables that in fact my father will not be allowed visitors until he is processed into the Tower by the Keeper of Her Majesty's Jewels, Charles Wyndham, who has been called from a hunt in the country. Absurd, of course. But it is tradition. I myself am not allowed to see him. He will be free to receive visitors from tomorrow morning."

"You have spared me a trip this afternoon, then—thank you."

She put her hands together and looked down at them. "You can imagine that Corfe and I are exceedingly worried."

She didn't mention her composed and icy mother, Lenox noted. "Is your brother's health improving?"

"He is still low. But steady."

"Your father mentioned that he has refused to see a doctor. I know a very discreet one."

An odd, troubled look passed over her features. "He goes on refusing. But then he has always

183

been stubborn as a rock. I thank you for the offer—I will pass it on to him."

"Of course."

"Above all, both he and I are mourning Craig, and despondent at our father's misapprehension."

Lenox nodded. "Yes."

"You know better than most that he had been acting erratically. Sleeping in the study, carryings his pistol to meals. Corfe and I have heard that he was rude to you at White's."

"That is forgotten, anyhow."

"Be that as it may, it is a behavior most unlike him."

She had a melodic voice, Lady Violet, its syllables as distinct as the facets of a crystal glass; the lone beautiful thing about her, perhaps, poor soul. Sitting here, fingers worrying at the scuffed silver ring on a gold chain around her neck, she reminded Lenox of a character from Shakespeare herself—wise older sister to a dashing younger brother (still abed somewhere nearby), devoted daughter to a capricious father.

There was a reason Dorset had left her in charge of his affairs, not Corfe, Lenox realized.

"And how may I help, Your Ladyship?"

"You are working upon the . . . mystery, I suppose you would call it?"

"Yes, I am."

"Have you made progress?"

"Incrementally, Your Ladyship."

She gave him an even look. "When my father said *Protect it*—what was he referring to, Mr. Lenox?"

"There I must refer you to him, I am sorry to say."

"It is a secret?"

"I suppose you could call it that."

She accepted this calmly, little knowing what lay in the letter on the table. "Very well."

Lenox filled the silence, sensing that she wanted to discuss all of this further, this tremendous explosion of incident, but didn't quite know how. "Is there anyone you can think of who might have stolen the painting?" he asked.

She shook her head. "No."

Lenox was quiet for a moment and then said, "Anyone who might wish harm to your father?"

She looked him directly in the eye but did not speak, returning his silence. At last, she said, "Corfe wonders about . . . someone."

"If it helps you to feel more free to speak, I will not whisper a word of it to anyone."

She hesitated. "What about Lady Jane Grey?"

"No."

He was not surprised that she asked, for they were known to be close. But he was surprised when she said, next, "Is it true she is having a garden party in two Saturdays?"

"It is, yes."

"Oh! I am sure it will be lovely." She looked down, knowing perhaps that she had given herself away. "I hope for her that the weather will hold as fair as it is now."

"Would you care to come as my guest?" Lenox asked.

She looked at him. "You are very kind. May I consider it?"

He bowed his head. "Of course."

Very suddenly she said, "Corfe thinks that it's General Pendleton. I do not know whether I agree. But that is what he thinks."

"Why?" asked Lenox, just as quickly, for admissions like this one had momentum.

"It is a long story."

"No, I know the story. Why now? Why the painting?"

"Corfe doesn't say—but he . . . he feels so sure! Perhaps he knows something I do not. I thought I would tell you. In fact—" She halted.

"Yes?"

"Corfe thinks that Pendleton shot Craig in a fit of madness—grieving madness—and that our father is covering up his crime."

"Goodness me. That is an extraordinary suspicion."

"I know. Yet he has one piece of evidence," said Lady Violet.

"What is that?"

"General Pendleton is in London. He is almost never here, but he has been here for the past week."

Lenox took this in. "That is valuable information, Lady Violet. I thank you."

She nodded unhappily. "Yes."

"Is there anything else?"

"There is one thing, though I am sure it is unrelated. A servant of ours disappeared yesterday."

His eyebrows rose. "Disappeared!"

"No—that puts it too strongly, I should not have used that word. Did not come to work, I should have said. She didn't come this morning, either."

"Who is the servant?"

"Her name is Maggie McNeal. She has been a day-maid with us here for about three months. She lives in the East End, in the large boardinghouse on Garnet Street. I only know that because she took the bed of a girl who returned to Ireland. She was homesick. The previous girl, not Maggie."

"I'm amazed your father didn't tell me."

"I doubt he knows," said Lady Violet.

"Oh, I see."

"She always struck me as very reliable and obedient, Maggie. I have no reason to think ill of her. But I thought I should tell you."

"Quite. Is there anything else?"

"Nothing." She shook her head, as if she wished there were. "If you are able to bring our father home and this matter to a conclusion, you

187

and your family will have the gratitude of our family and all its descendants. I do not say that lightly."

He nodded. "I believe you. I shall certainly try."

She rose. "Thank you, Mr. Lenox. Use the room for as long as you please. Though I suppose my father has already granted you that permission. Excuse me—I am not myself."

"I think you are far more composed than anyone would expect of you under the circumstances, Lady Violet."

She smiled. All human beings are beautiful when they smile, for however infinitesimal a passage of time, and Lenox saw the ephemeral beauty in this deeply fortunate, deeply unfortunate young woman. "Thank you for your time, Mr. Lenox," she said, and left.

CHAPTER TWENTY-FOUR

When she had closed the door, he turned the letter the duke had given him over and continued reading.

. . . . a hidden play.

The portrait is firm evidence of Shakespeare's religion, the only firm evidence we have, though of course it lets in very little light upon his actual beliefs, which may have been, for all we know, atheistic. It has been observed that his work does not read as that of a zealously pious man.

The passion of my recent years has been to find the play that accompanies the portrait. The letter was destroyed by my great-great-grandfather, but we still have the portrait. Should I fail, you know now from our extensive conversation this morning all that I know: foremost, that the answer lies in my picture, which will of course be yours. In it rests, as you know, the part of the riddle that I have yet to solve. I hope that you have committed it to memory.

I make two requests of you as I pass

on this knowledge, Clarence. The first is that you keep it as private as conceivably possible. Nobody—in short—must know of the existence of this portrait. We are its protectors. Because of the clue it contains to the whereabouts of the play, it must not become public until after the play is found. Once the play is found, obviously, it would be our honor to present the picture to the King; or to keep it, but allow it to be publicly displayed, as befits its subject.

Why does all of this matter so much to me? Because I gaze upon a portrait of William Shakespeare—a real oil portrait. Nobody can stand prouder than you in his position, after I am gone, but others may be equally proud; this, on the other hand, is ours alone, and we must treasure it, and guard it, if need be, with our lives.

Your father, Thomas,
13th Duke of Dorset

Beneath this was the stamp of a signet ring with the Dorset arms on it, and after that a lengthy postscript.

To add a word, Clarence: I would be well and truly ashamed if a son of mine, or a son or daughter of his, were to subscribe to the heresy that Shakespeare did not write his own plays. He did. Every word I have read, every ancient widow I have spoken to in Stratford-upon-Avon in my travels, every document I have traced with my fingertips, every fact I have collected, confirms as much.

As you know, the primary contender for the authorship of the plays after Shakespeare is the Earl of Oxford, whose absurd family is insistent upon their forebear having "secretly" written the plays. Their argument is that Shakespeare could not have had the range of education to have composed the plays. This is a demonstrable inaccuracy. Malone tells us very clearly that Shakespeare's elementary education in Latin and religion would have been as good as yours or mine. Consider, too, that among Shakespeare's contemporaries, Spenser was the son of a clothmaker, Middleton a bricklayer, and Kyd a scrivener. Nashe was a sizar at Cambridge—a servant to the other students—and never recovered from the ignominy of it. Class was not an obstacle to literary greatness in the Elizabethan world.

As for the Oxford case—that the earl was a secret genius—it conveniently leaves out that he died in 1604, meaning that in addition to his extensive courtly and baronial duties, he would have had to pre-write plays such as *Macbeth*, *King Lear*, and *The Tempest*. Which ran out, conveniently, just when the real William Shakespeare died.

It also relies on the idea that he would have written a great deal of mediocre poetry under his own name to further the concealment, while under his pseudonym becoming the greatest genius of his or any age. An idiotic thought. Dismiss it forever, if you respect your father's opinion.

This was the end of the letter. Lenox smoothed down the creases of the pages carefully against the table. Then he read it again, this time much more slowly.

At the end of the reading he felt strangely stirred. This wasn't simply because of the long-dead duke's pride, nor because of the present duke's fanatical faith in it, which had convinced him to do no less than feign his own kidnapping and shoot a man.

It was because he thought he had found two clues. The first was in this house itself.

He rang the bell, and Ward appeared. "Ringing for me now, are you?" said his old schoolmate.

Lenox smiled. "Sorry. I didn't want to venture out of the room and get lost."

Ward looked at a fine portrait of a woman, gazing with now immortal distaste upon all she surveyed, above a nearby sideboard. His thumbs were hooked in his waistcoat. "Wish I'd never taken this bloody job," he said.

"It'll turn out for you. Listen, Theo, could I have a moment in the duke's study?"

Ward turned back to him. "By all means. His Grace said we should accommodate you however possible. I warn you that there is still blood there—and three footmen the duke has ordered to stay in the room at all times, on rotations like a ship's. The largest footmen, blast them."

"I understand."

Lenox pocketed the letter and they went up by a back staircase he didn't know. Soon they were inside the duke's study.

Lenox approached the painting, briefly attracting the attention of the three immensely tall, cow-eyed footmen standing in the middle of the room, their numerousness apparently the duke's final idea of a defense for the portrait. But Ward waved them off, and Lenox, leaning in close to the portrait, for the first time read the poem that floated in an extremely fine serif hand next to the head of William Shakespeare. How foolish of him not to have looked at it more closely to begin with. He would add that to the notebook he kept of the errors he made— a document that gave him great joy.

Ward watched him curiously, though he betrayed no particular interest in what Lenox was doing. As for the young detective, his hazel eyes were just inches from the elegant gold scroll. He read the words:

Forty miles from Charing Cross,
then back one further apple's toss,
under fields of wheat-grown gold,
doth laze a buried story told.

Lenox read the poem twice more, committing it to memory.

Beneath it was a confused squall of black ink, like the elaborate scrolled marks that sometimes appeared at the bottom of poems in fine old books.

He stepped back, so that he was nearly leaning against the duke's desk chair, and turned his attention to Shakespeare's face. It was very difficult not to see brilliance in the little daubs of brown, specked with white, that were his eyes. The genius of his and every age.

Only now, though, did he notice that in Shakespeare's right hand, held carelessly, was a lily. In faint handwriting beside it were the words *Nomen Mariae, BV.*

He wrote these words down in his notebook.

There were brand-new braces at the corners of each portrait's frame and also on each side, six in total, bolted into the wall. Anyone who wanted to remove this painting would either have to spend a great deal of time on the task or cut the canvas out. It was no longer a matter of simply removing it from a hook, as it had been with the missing portrait.

What exactly had Alexander Arnold Craig been doing?

Lenox saw that there were indeed two screws gone from the new brace. He looked to the ground, stooped, and picked them up, next to the great roped-off stain of blood. Tiny brass things, the screws. They weighed close to nothing in his palm; had cost Craig his life.

He went into the hall and wrote several pages in his notebook at a rapid rate—he was bursting with ideas—then closed it with a satisfied snap.

"I will visit the duke in the morning, if you don't mind," he told Ward.

"Not at all. In fact I could pick you up—I have to bring some papers to him. Eight?"

"Perfect," said Lenox. They shook hands. "Chin up. You'll still be Prime Minister one day."

The fastest path to a high place in Parliament, should you be unlucky enough not to have a close relative with a seat to give away, was the kind of job Ward had now, secretary to a great gentleman.

"Ha. Chancellor of the Exchequer would be enough for me," Ward said. "I've always liked numbers."

Lenox smiled. "I shall remember that if the selection is ever in my power. Actually, I once thought I would go into politics. Impossible, of course, now that I have embarked upon all this bother."

"But you have Edmund just by," said Ward.

"True enough. I can always lean on him if I have a mind to invade France. And in the meanwhile"—he was allowing himself to feel just slightly pleased, because he was sure he was on the right trail now—"being a detective isn't all bad."

CHAPTER TWENTY-FIVE

Lenox departed into the bright heat of the June day. Even on this quiet street there were carriages trotting by, and he knew that a trip to the East End, where he wished to go, would take the better part of two hours right now. He squinted into the sunlight, wondering what to do.

Then he had an idea. Straight across the street from Dorset House was a high stone rail overlooking the Thames. He leaned over it to see what was beneath him. On the quay, he saw, there were two or three small craft floating.

He cupped his hands and called out, "Down there!"

The men, in conversation, craned their necks up. "Aye?" one replied.

"How much to drop me near Whitechapel? Tower Bridge, say?"

They conferred for a brief moment, until one looked up and said, "These are junk boats, sir."

"I don't mind."

They put their heads together again, this time for longer, until the same man said, "Half-sovereign?"

It was not much more than a hansom cab would cost, and would take a fraction of the time. "It's a bargain," Lenox said.

"How will you get down, though, sir?"

But Lenox had already begun to answer that question. There was a black ladder hammered into the sides of the wall, which was thirty-odd feet in height, and he had swung himself over, to a loud, startled buzz of protest from the men below. No matter—he was climbing down. With the sublime and silly confidence of youth he felt pleasure in the lark of it, the danger, knowing that he wouldn't lose his grip.

At the bottom there was a drop-off of about his own height, and his newly hired chauffeur came and caught him with an "oof" as he came down. The half-sovereign was already in Lenox's hand.

The boat was small. It smelled of fish, but Lenox, perched on a gunwale opposite Smiley (that was the fellow's name), only noticed for a moment, because soon they were zipping down the Thames, Smiley with the rudder and the string that controlled his one small, patched sail in a single hand, manipulating them together expertly. The wind happened to be theirs, and he moved among the larger ships with ease.

Along the way he touched his cap to perhaps two dozen people, and Lenox, who loved nothing more than being on the water, partook secondhand in the glories of these associations, touching his own hat, too. The Thames seemed its own waterborne city.

"Never done this before," Smiley commented

when they were halfway. "An easy payday, with due respect, sir."

"An easy and enjoyable conveyance for me, Mr. Smiley," said Lenox.

He tipped an extra shilling when they arrived, and in a quarter of the time it would have taken by cab, Lenox was walking up the street to the Dovecote.

He had two reasons for wanting to be in this part of town. One of them was Maggie McNeal, but Bonden must come first.

Unfortunately, none of the fifteen or so men inside the pub was he, despite his remark that he might be here. Lenox went to the bar, disappointed.

The same angular man was standing behind it. He asked Lenox if he wanted ale again. Lenox said why not and, when he received it, asked if Bonden had been into the Dovecote that morning.

"Thaddeus Bonden? Why, he's directly behind you, sir," said the barman, with a look of surprise. "If he were a tiger he'd bite."

Lenox turned around.

And there he was, too, sitting at a small table with his pipe in his mouth. Lenox had passed him twice, and both times taken him for a stranger.

"How in heaven's name do you do that?" he asked angrily, lifting his tankard and taking the stool opposite Bonden.

"Sometimes at sea it pays to be very still."

"What a delightfully informative thing to know," said Lenox. "Thank you. Truly."

Bonden almost smiled. "Are we going picture hunting?"

"I hoped you would have the time."

Bonden finished off his drink. "I do. But if we wait fifteen minutes or so, we might hear a bit of information to our advantage first."

"Then we shall wait. Do they have food here?"

"I cannot recommend it." That was a serious statement coming from someone accustomed to ship's rations. "But," Bonden added, "there is a woman around the corner who makes a very decent vinegar chicken with hot potatoes and mashed turnips. One of the navvies will run round to fetch it for you if you give him a penny."

A boy of ten or so did just that, and soon Lenox was drinking his cool ale and eating a delicious plate of food, which had come under a cloth napkin with a crust of warm bread. He ate heartily, Bonden watching, and when he was done sat back, contented.

Now he felt braced for their expedition. He had heard so much about his companion's magical sense for where things were hidden, concealed, misplaced that he was eager to see him in action. But they waited patiently, and after thirty minutes a man came in who spotted Bonden right away.

He had a broad belly and a heavy beard and clattered his way to their table with no pretense toward stealth, saying hello to everyone whether he knew them or not. He looked and sounded roaring drunk.

"Bonden," he bellowed. He asked if someone named Bosun was there. (But weren't there hundreds of Bosuns? thought Lenox.)

Bonden shook his head and said no, Bosun wasn't there.

"Good," the man said. He went to the bar and ordered two pints of bitter. "He knows I'd kill him where he stood if he came in here." He said this so plainly that Lenox felt a wave of alarm. When he came and sat, the man chucked a nod at Lenox. "Mutton shunter?"

"No," Bonden and Lenox both said.

"Join a choir and save our ears, boys," the man said mildly at this simultaneous reply.

A mutton shunter, in these parts, was a police constable—so-called since they were known for wearing long muttonchop whiskers. "What news?" said Bonden.

The man drank the first pint in one draft, set it down empty, and shook his head. "Nothing," he said.

Bonden nodded. "Fair enough."

The man stood up. "If anything changes about that you'll know it first." He glanced at Lenox. "Good day, gentlemen."

As the man retreated to the back of the pub with his second pint of bitter, Bonden stood up.

He left his sealskin coat there—it was a warm day—in, apparently, the full faith that it would be there upon his return.

"The painting is not for sale in London, according to Mr. Berendo, who you just met," said Bonden, leading Lenox out of the Dovecote. "So we may begin to look for it."

"Very well," said Lenox. "Where to go?"

Bonden looked at him warily. "You asked to stick by me today," he said. "But you must follow me and pay attention, and that's all, if you please."

"Whatever you like," said Lenox. "Lead the way."

And what followed was, in fairness, one of the most interesting mornings that Lenox had ever spent in London.

The first thing they did was board an omnibus bound straight westward, the direction from which Lenox had come. Only toward the end of the trip did he realize that they were going to the duke's house. For an alarming moment Lenox thought Bonden was going to knock on the door—but they debarked the omnibus at the end of the street, just next to Parliament. It was here that Bonden's investigation began.

Almost immediately, Lenox came to understand how Bonden had followed them so subtly, and how he had disguised himself at the Dovecote.

He had a gift for slipping his body into small

areas where a person would never look twice. The overwhelming part of it was his use of the landscape, which he treated in a way that Lenox had never seen anyone do, not even pickpockets. (He had once paid three shillings to follow a pickpocket for the day. A highly illuminating experience.) He had an uncanny gift for standing just athwart of a tree, Bonden, or a quarter step inside a doorway.

This was harder with two of them, but the sailor often gestured to Lenox, primarily with his elbows, where he ought to stand. His hands stayed in his pockets, and soon Lenox's did, too.

Was this learned shipboard? In port? On some distant island where he had been marooned?

What was certain was that Lenox could not learn these tricks quickly. Perhaps the most remarkable gift Bonden had was for silence; not the silence that comes from not speaking, but some strange deeper silence that created a cocoon around them.

They began by staring for a good hour at the duke's house, from various angles. Bonden's eyes, alert, hawklike, mostly still, seemed to take in every stone of the building one by one. Occasionally he moved five or ten feet. On the pavement, people passed them without—though they were an unlikely pair—so much as a glance.

At long length, Bonden strode west away from the house, then switched directions, making a loop so that he could see it clearly from the rear.

In that hour, the only thing he said was, in a low voice, "I doubt very much that anybody went through that window."

"How do you know?" Lenox asked.

For he thought the same. But Bonden did not reply.

They spent the next hours in the streets around the duke's house. At first Lenox was baffled as to why. He was also glad that he was fairly tall, for Bonden could consume great yards of pavement when he wished, until he would stop suddenly but unnoticeably, light his pipe, then remain where he'd stopped for as long as he liked, unseen.

Only slowly did Lenox see the pattern that Bonden was tracing: He was examining every street near the duke's house in detail.

Was this wise? Was it foolish? Lenox had time to think it over, as they stood and stared at, seemingly, nothing, until eventually he realized Bonden's method: to start at the very center of the object's existence and then make slow circles away from it, considering each place the object might be.

In a way this was ludicrous. The painting could be halfway to Indochina by now. Yet on the other hand, Lenox almost believed that Bonden would ultimately make his way even to that outermost circle if it happened to be in

Indochina—there was something so dogged, so unrelenting, in his method.

He wondered, in one of the many silent moments they had, if you could do the same thing with a dead body: retreat from it in the most careful concentric circles, gathering impressions. He was making a note of the idea in the notebook he kept in his breast pocket when a low motion from Bonden, barely visible, asked him not to do it.

At five o'clock, he said they had done enough for the day. They had done scarcely anything that Lenox could discern.

Yet Lenox's faith was intact, and just before they parted Bonden seemed to confirm it. "I think I know where it might be," he said.

"Do you!"

"I think—I do not know. I may well be wrong. There are two things to check. Could we meet tomorrow?"

"Of course, though I am not free until the afternoon."

Bonden nodded. "I will call on you then."

CHAPTER TWENTY-SIX

They parted not far from the duke's house. Outside, the summer sun was just beginning to dip, filling the old streets with dusty golden light. He checked his watch. It was half past six. At this hour the city would be overcrowded in every direction between here and the east side, yet he very much wished to go there again— this time to inquire about Miss Maggie McNeal, the maid who had disappeared the day before from the Dorset household, with either suspicious or grievously unfortunate timing.

He took a chance and looked over the stone rail again. His man Smiley was there, and he called down.

"Ahoy," the riverman cried up, grinning, when he saw Lenox's face.

"Any chance of another ride? I need to go to Whitechapel, so somewhere near Katharine Pier. Same rate."

Smiley looked at the clock on the shipping tower across the Thames. "At this hour?"

Lenox was, for better or worse, unafraid of Whitechapel at night, possessing as he did a sturdy pair of fists and a quick sprint. "Yes."

Smiley shouted, "All right. If you can go now."

Lenox again scaled nimbly down the wall

leading to the dock, then crossed the pebbly strand along the Thames. Smiley asked again if he was sure and, when Lenox said he was, helped him into the boat—it was mostly full of cockles now—to travel down the river, this time nearer to the city's poorest, most thickly populated environs.

There was no more beautiful way to watch the sunset than from the river, and Lenox enjoyed the ride, the wind stinging his eyes. By the time they had reached their destination, it was nearly dark. "Are you sure you're all right here, guv?" said Smiley, tying on.

"I'll manage. Cheers," said Lenox.

He hopped off the boat in the East End with thanks, flipping the coin to Smiley, who caught it in his hat, saying he was happy to make a sovereign any day Mr. Lenox chose, then turned back upriver to sell his day's haul of cockles.

Lenox strode up a gangway and was soon in the busy weave of close-crossed lanes here. Before long he had reached Garnet Street—a rough-and-tumble but brightly lit thoroughfare, doing all sorts of busy trade even at the dinner hour, full of horses, boys, men, shopkeepers, bill stickers, newspaper criers.

"Excuse me," he said to a lad who was sprinting by.

The boy stopped. " 'S'it?"

"Is there a large boardinghouse for single maids on Garnet Street?"

The boy gave him a lascivious look. "Yes."

Lenox sighed and handed him a halfpenny. "Where?"

The boy pointed up. "Not on Garnet proper, like—on Blossom, your second right, can't miss it."

"Thanks."

"Tell the misses I said hello."

"I certainly shan't," said Lenox, but the boy was gone already.

He went to the tiny Blossom Street, and there, indeed, he found a small respectable-looking brick house, which had posted on its door a severe malediction against any male visitors who might be coming in the evening. He knocked, and was answered by a broad-shouldered, ruddy woman, holding a broom, who looked as if she had probably had fifteen children, seen five husbands into the ground, and could still put away more rum than most of the punters in the Dovecote.

Evidently it was her boardinghouse. She was impressed enough by Lenox's clothing and accent to allow him a word, and he said he had come to ask whether Miss Maggie McNeal was present.

She wasn't, the woman said.

"When was she last here?" asked Lenox, curiously.

"Never."

"Never?"

"It's not a name I've ever heard. And I know all my girls."

Lenox asked her a series of questions then. Had there been any recent turnover in the rooms? Had anyone disappeared? Gone off without paying the rent? She might have gone by any name, Lenox said.

The woman shook her head authoritatively. No. Not for several months; it was the best establishment of its kind in London for day-maids—he could believe that—and if she wanted she could fill every bed again twice over. Nobody had left since at least January, and she had seen, herself, every one of the place's girls, twenty-four of them in twelve rooms, no later than that morning, for she fed them breakfast at 5:00 a.m.

She would swear it on any Bible, or *Pilgrim's Progress* if he preferred—or a jar of jam, *she* didn't care.

He thanked her and said that none of that would be necessary, then walked off, hands in pockets, eyes ahead of him—for now it was really nighttime—confused, very confused.

Walking through this neighborhood, it paid to keep one's eyes open. Lenox must have cut a strange figure—dressed in subdued, expensive clothes, with his tall hat and a gold watch chain that he tucked away as he came back onto Garnet Street—and he stayed alert as he turned up Milk Lane. He passed a yard where two men in their shirtsleeves were splitting the chunks of an immense tree into first logs and then kindling, which would be sold up toward Lenox's end of town.

No doubt they had overpaid the country laborer who shipped the tree into London. So it went— the vast, dimly visible economy of this capital, as complex and inextricable as the vascular system of a man, crisscrossing itself a thousand times.

He caught the omnibus at the corner, kept to himself in one corner until it reached the Strand, then hopped out and took a cab the rest of the way.

When he pulled up to his own house on Hampden Lane, Lady Jane's door opened and she came out. "There you are!"

"Did I do something wrong?"

"What on earth has that duke done?" she asked.

Lenox shook his head. He lived in several overlapping versions of this city; one had to do with crime, and he sometimes forgot that word of that London could be sent back, by the passenger pigeons of society, to this one, his own.

"Shot someone."

"My goodness, so it's true." She sighed. "The papers are being very cautious, libel. So he's shot someone! Will he go to prison?"

She was leaning against the railing of her own house. He paid the driver and walked toward her. The lime tree that grew between their houses was in full leaf now, casting a dancing shadow under the gaslight.

"I would be shocked," Lenox said.

"Hm." She wore a white dress with eyelets at the neckline, and looked like summer to him. "Yes, the Lords will hush it up. They always do."

"How is your reading of Marx and Engels going?"

She laughed gaily. "I am not converted yet."

Lenox noticed that she was holding a letter and said, "What news?"

"Oh!" She folded it and tucked it into the pocket of her dress. "It is sad news, in fact— well, sad, but happy. James and his company have been dispatched to India for six months. He only has time to stop home in London for a single evening before he goes."

"I'm awfully sorry to hear that," said Lenox. She had been anticipating a long visit. "It's wicked luck."

She smiled. "No, on the contrary, he says that he hopes to be home by Christmas, and what's better still, that he will have six months in London then—for he has just been promoted."

"I say, that's something."

"Yes—there's nothing I like better than Christmas, you know." She touched her stomach, not consciously, Lenox thought. "The best thing about having a child will be Christmas morning, I sometimes think."

"Your child will be lucky in its mother and father."

"We'll see, I suppose—he'll be a spoiler, James, dear one that he is, especially if it's a girl, and I think I shall have to be the harsh and exacting disciplinarian. Girls get such a bad hand in this world that they need toughening up from the start."

"Feel free to practice on Lancelot."

She laughed. "By the way, would you like to come to supper in two nights? There will be twelve of us. I have been counting on you. Effie will be there."

"Will she? Then I must accept, I suppose."

"Good. Until then, if not before, in that case. Keep the duke from shooting anyone else in the meanwhile."

He felt particularly alone walking into his study; particularly unmarried. He reached into his pocket and opened the book at random.

The barge she sat in, like a burnish'd throne, burn'd on the water.
                    —Antony and Cleopatra

What on earth was that supposed to mean? He closed the book in disgust, sick of Shakespeare. Nevertheless, he spent the rest of the evening painstakingly making notes for himself about every element of the case, from Maggie McNeal to John Shakespeare. Graham was out, which meant that he was still investigating Alexander Arnold Craig. Finally, Lenox poured himself a glass of red wine, took down his old Latin dictionary from school, and rang for dinner to be brought up to him whenever was convenient.

CHAPTER TWENTY-SEVEN

It was raining again the next morning, a thin drizzle that was still steady enough to leave the pavement darker and absolve the city of the previous day's accumulated dust, to the delight of maids everywhere. With the streets hushed, one could hear the songbirds of London very clearly, Lenox noticed as he read the papers.

At eight o'clock, Ward appeared in the duke's carriage to pick him up.

He was alone. "Hello," he said. "Ready?"

"Is anyone else visiting the duke?" Lenox asked.

"Lady Violet plans to take him lunch."

"And the duchess?"

Ward screwed his mouth to one side and raised his eyebrows. But all he said was that he didn't know Her Grace's plans. Lenox nodded—he understood the implication. She must be a cold sort, he thought.

Ward neatened a few papers he was holding as the carriage started away. "I must say, he has been very decent to me. He wrote and released me from my position. He has offered me my pick of spots in the Lords or the Commons to go to. Says his friends will of course honor their debts to him."

"That was honorable," said Lenox.

"I declined. I will stick here for now, anyway. Though the papers are getting uglier hour by hour."

Lenox nodded. He had read the articles that morning, which were still just skirting the word "murderer." "Ward—about Craig. Will you answer me something? Who was he close to?"

Ward frowned. "Close to? I'm really not quite sure. The duke. He got on well with Lord Vere, I think—Corfe, His Grace's son."

"Below stairs, though, I mean."

Ward shook his head. "I don't know."

"Fair enough," said Lenox.

They rode through the steady rainfall. They started chatting about nothing much—bygone cricket matches and housemasters, old friends— which was rather a relief, as it happened.

That lasted until they turned onto Tower Bridge.

Then both of them fell silent, staring at the hulking dark Tower of London itself, sitting heavily on its foundation across the Thames.

A strange chill ran through Lenox. They could see its two enormous concentric defensive walls, and rising above these, the White Tower, the center of the compound, a square building with the flag of the St. George's cross flying at each of its corners.

"There's the Traitors' Gate," said Ward quietly, pointing.

Lenox looked at the waterline of the Thames and saw it—a huge arched medieval gate cut into the very stonework of one wall and plunging directly into the water. This was where barges transported the worst prisoners into the Tower. Anne Boleyn had gone through the Traitors' Gate.

"The Duke of Wellington is still the constable, you know," Lenox murmured.

Wellington, the immortal hero of Waterloo, commanded every motion in the tower unless the monarch was present. To be constable was a position of huge prestige. "Yes," said Ward.

"I would bet you that he came to see Dorset in."

"Wellington? He's eighty-one!"

Lenox nodded. "Yes. But we are wading into very old customs here. The forms must never be broken—the ravens leaving and all that. A Duke of Dorset must be received as a Duke of Dorset. We might as easily be in 1550 as 1850 once we cross this bridge."

There were always at least six ravens in the Tower of London; terrifying huge black birds with strangely human eyes. If there were ever fewer—every child knew—the Crown would fall, and with it England.

Lenox and Ward, both twenty-six, were still just within fingertips' reach of that old schoolboy awe of Albion, Henry the Eighth, Sir Walter Raleigh, Oliver Cromwell. Poor Prince Edward and poor Prince Richard with their curling blond locks. Guy Fawkes had been tortured here. Such a great number of the country's most deeply etched mythologies had emerged from within these formidable walls.

They circled halfway around the castle once they had crossed the river, to a postern gate where two tall soldiers in bright red uniform stood sentry. Ward told them they were there to see the duke, and once the yeoman guards had been informed the two old Harrovians were ushered into the austere palace where much of England's long history since 1066 had, in one murderous way or another, taken place.

"Deep breath, old fellow," said Lenox.

"Deep breath yourself," said the short, solid Ward, shoving his taller friend over on the path.

Lenox laughed.

They climbed dim, circling stone stairs, each one worn down in the middle from centuries of use.

"Here you are," the guard said, and opened a wooden door.

The suite of rooms in which they found the Duke of Dorset could not have been more eligible, except that it locked from the outside. Its stone walls were damp, true, and there were bars over the window, old, strong, thin black ones crosshatching a sweeping view of the Thames and the city. But the Savoy could not have imagined finer niceties. There was a bowl of cut flowers, a handsome desk, a pen and inkstand, books, a plush settee, every comfort. Lady Violet had arranged it all very quickly, no doubt—or who knew, the Duke of Wellington himself.

Dorset rose, a pouch of tobacco in hand. "Good morning, gentlemen."

Mysteriously, he looked better to Lenox's eye than he had two days before. Perhaps it was that he had shaved, or perhaps it was that he had made some internal decision that this was an ordeal he would conquer through attitude. His soft crimson tie was knotted impeccably. A great deal could be got out of an aristocrat in a jam, Lenox knew. It was their lone teaching (Lord knew they couldn't muster much maths) from the cradle, stiffness of spine. It did lend them a certain glory at moments of embattlement.

Ward handed the duke the papers he was carrying. "Here you are, Your Grace," he said.

"Thank you, thank you." He looked around the room, papers in hand. "Not so bad, is it? They tell me Thomas Cromwell had these rooms."

"Indeed, Your Grace?" said Ward.

Dorset smiled at Lenox, bringing him into the conversation as naturally as any host could have. "I am not sure that is as reassuring as they believe it to be when they tell you. Anyway, perhaps while you are here you may solve the mystery of the Princes in the Tower, Mr. Lenox."

218

Lenox laughed politely. "It may be so, Your Grace."

"Has the press put their oar in yet?" the duke asked.

"Not that we have seen," said Ward.

"The jailers will bring me the papers. A shilling goes quite a way here."

"That reminds me—Lady Violet sends some ready money, in notes and coin, Your Grace, and also a kidney pie for your supper. That has gone straight to the kitchens."

Ward handed over a leather billfold. "Give my thanks to my daughter, if you would," said Dorset. "She is a sound one."

"With pleasure, Your Grace."

Lenox again noticed the strange absence of the duchess from these proceedings, this conversation.

"I wonder if you would leave me and Lenox for a moment, Ward?" said the duke. "They will make you comfortable. A cup of tea, perhaps."

The secretary seemed relieved. "Yes, of course."

As Ward left, the duke walked to one of the small windows and stared through it, hands clasped behind his back. There was no glass in them, only bars; Lenox could feel the cold gusting of the rainy wind.

Dorset was silent for some time, even after Ward had gone. Finally, he turned back to his visitor. "I had never imagined that I would kill a man," he said. "Much less someone I respected so highly as Mr. Craig. He was a person of the utmost character. I am grieved, I find—fiercely grieved."

"I am told that he died painlessly, Your Grace."

Dorset, hands still behind his back, said, "My emotions are complicated by the fact that he was attempting to steal from me, I fear."

"Could you describe the events of the morning to me, Your Grace?"

The duke shook his head and shrugged, as if he were wonderstruck himself. "It was so extremely quick."

"Anything you remember."

"I had fallen asleep in the armchair. The one I moved to the closet at the east end of my study. I woke because of a noise. I stepped out and saw a figure with a paraffin lamp set on the desk beside him, unscrewing the portrait of—well, you know what portrait it is. He seemed to charge at me. It was a confused moment. I fired my pistol. I hit him square in the chest, of course."

Lenox nodded. "Seemed to charge you? Was he on the other side of the desk?"

"He came around the desk. He was holding a screwdriver. I couldn't make him out—I wouldn't have shot had I seen it was Craig, that's sure."

"You thought it was merely another intruder."

"Yes. I went over and looked at his face by the light of his own paraffin lamp, and when I saw that it was Craig I was shocked to my bones."

"You sent for the police."

"For a doctor, and the police, immediately. But he was clearly dying." A muscle flickered in Dorset's jaw. "I shall never forget it."

Lenox paused. Then he said, "I have read your great-grandfather's letter, Your Grace, if you wish to discuss the portrait. And I have read the poem; and I have an idea."

CHAPTER TWENTY-EIGHT

He drew the duke's undivided attention with this comment. Indeed, there was a hunger in his look, an avidity—he had traveled many years alone with this secret.

"An idea."

"Yes, Your Grace."

"No man who has seen the clue has yet solved it. Perhaps you may be the one to do so. Nothing would relieve me more."

Lenox removed the ancient letter from his breast pocket and returned it to the duke. "Perhaps the first thing you could do is to tell me something about your great-grandfather. In particular I am confused as to the order of succession. He was the thirteenth duke, yet you are the fifteenth."

Dorset nodded. "It is a sad story. My grandfather, Clarence, to whom this letter was addressed, died of scarlet fever at the age of just thirty-one. His wife died at the same time. And in fact the author of the letter—my great-grandfather—followed them quickly to the grave. Of grief, I have sometimes fancied, for he was only sixty-three. He had no other children and was a widower."

"But he had a grandson."

"Yes, my own father. He was only three months old at the time his parents contracted the fever, but was quarantined. Needless to say, he survived."

"An orphan."

"He was raised well loved and well tended by his mother's parents at Stowe Lodge and lived to a healthy old age himself, long enough even to become close with Corfe and Violet. They often went to stay with him at Dorset Castle. We only lost him four years ago. I think that very good of God, after his own parents died so young."

Lenox did some quick math and calculated that the duke's father must have been seventy-seven or seventy-eight. This explained why there had been four sons but only three dukes within the family in the past seventy years.

"I see."

"When my father turned eighteen, our family solicitor gave him this letter, along with several important family possessions of traditional value, in a sealed box."

"But he never heard the story of the portrait firsthand."

Dorset shook his head regretfully. "No. He was scarcely a year old when he was passed into the care of his grandparents. It would have saved us an immense amount of trouble."

"So when your great-grandfather refers to himself and his son knowing the secret that he will not spell out . . ."

"A secret lost to history."

Lenox nodded. "And your father? What happened when he eventually received the letter?"

"He was eighteen. He was at Gonville and Caius then." This was one of the colleges of Cambridge. "Shakespeare became a deep interest of his, as it has of mine. You see our position: If we make the portrait public, given that it contains a clue—"

"Yes. If the riddle were public, any unscrupulous gold hunter in Christendom might find the play, and hold it hostage for whatever sum they chose."

They were standing about five feet apart, and Dorset nodded. "Exactly. I take it as a sacred trust that this should not happen."

Lenox wanted to return to the clue, momentarily. First, he said, "Your great-grandfather's papers of research—have they been preserved?"

The duke nodded. "Yes. My father spent much time organizing and examining them. I have done the same when I had respite from my public duties."

"And what do they reveal?"

"There is no clue either to the origin of the portrait or the specific play that was found. He was too canny to commit either to print, I suppose. As to the play, there are rumors, of course."

Lenox knew these from the reading Duncan Jones had given him. The legends of lost Shakespeare plays were ten-a-penny—to begin with, those that had very definitely been performed by Shakespeare's company, the King's Men, but of which no text existed. (For instance, *Love's Labors Won*—a sequel to *Love's Labors Lost*.) Others were only rumors. The tradition had it that there was a play about Queen Elizabeth herself, as well as a variety of plays with tantalizing names: *Cardenio, Double Falsehood, Fair Em, Lancelot, Lord Cromwell.* Men spent their lives in dusty bookshops and forgotten libraries hoping to unearth one of them. Thus far none had succeeded.

Lenox nodded. "And so now we come to the poem."

The duke smiled. "Yes, the poem. A trifle that I have spent many years of my life contemplating. A rhyme scheme of AABB, one of the simplest possible. Iambic tetrameter. Seven syllables, eight, seven, eight."

"Forty miles from Charing Cross," Lenox said.

"Forty miles from Charing Cross," the duke said, and nodded.

"I take it that you or your forebears have followed the instructions."

The Duke nodded again. "Yes. With a very considerable margin of error built in."

"What do you mean?"

"In 1822, my father used a compass to draw a forty-mile radius around Charing Cross. Then he spent a month traveling the terrain by horse himself, allowing two miles on either side—anything thirty-eight to forty-two miles from Charing Cross."

"He did not forget the apple's toss, then," said Lenox.

The duke shook his head. "Believe me, we have not."

"And what did he find?"

"There were around fifty fields that matched the description in the poem. He took his steward, Crawford, under his advisement, for he was a methodical man, and together they made a search, though my father never told him for what."

"What did they do?"

"First, they looked for markers. Wherever there was anything resembling a marker, they dug—my father spending very freely on local laborers and on the men to whom the land belonged, explaining that he was chasing an old Dorset cross, not especially valuable in itself but of great worth to our family."

"I wonder that they believed that."

"Perhaps they did not," said the duke.

There was a knock on the door, and then it opened, which, since the duke had not answered, was rather surprising—until Lenox remembered they were in a prison.

It was a middle-aged maid in a coarse dress, bearing a tea tray. Behind her was the bailiff, holding the keys. "Mr. Ward sent tea through, from the Port of Whitby downstairs."

"Ah, good of him, thank you," said the duke. The maid came in and set the tea tray with its small sandwiches and scones down on a table. "That reminds me that I have not asked you to sit, Mr. Lenox. Will you join me? It is not quite White's."

The young detective smiled. "It is more interesting."

By the time they were alone again, the door shut behind them, each had a cup of tea. The wind whistled through the stone turrets.

"To return to my story: They found nothing, my father and his steward. Nothing at all. My father once told me that he had not once ever felt even close."

"Was he bitter about it?"

"Oh, no. But he was certainly determined that I should continue to look."

Lenox nodded. "And the painting itself? Have you had it inspected?"

Dorset nodded. "Numerous times. Inside, outside, backside, frontside, framed, out of frame, the frame itself."

"And?"

"No clue about the play has come from it. It is obviously of the right age—various experts

227

have attested to that. They have also noted that its sitter—"

"Is Catholic," said Lenox.

Dorset smiled faintly. "Well done. Yes. That is why the picture was hidden in John Shakespeare's house."

In his Latin dictionary, Lenox had looked up the phrase *Nomen Mariae, BV*. "In the name of Mary, Blessed Virgin," he said.

"Yes. The lily in the painting is her emblem. They are Catholic references that anyone of Shakespeare's own time would have known instantly."

Lenox nodded. He put down his teacup. "Very good, Your Grace."

The duke looked alarmed. "Are you leaving?"

"I have a solid idea of what we're working from now," said Lenox. "But I still must find that picture."

"Why? You know about the play."

Lenox was tempted to elaborate—but nothing good could come of talking before he fully knew what he was saying. "Your Grace," he said, "I wonder still whether your initial call upon my services began with an error."

"How is that?"

"Does it not strike you as implausible," said Lenox, "that someone would know of the existence of this portrait and then steal the *wrong picture?*"

Dorset frowned. "I assumed they sent a thief, who bungled the job."

Lenox tilted his head. "It is possible. Anyhow, I am very eager to learn more about your valet, and I am stubbornly still hopeful that finding the portrait will help us. If you excuse me, I promise to send you word of my progress this evening."

CHAPTER TWENTY-NINE

At home Lenox found waiting for him Graham, neat as a pin as usual in his laurel-gray suit, sandy hair combed right.

"Hello," said the detective. "Have a look at this."

He handed over the copy of the poem he had jotted down, and Graham took it and read it carefully. "New clues," he said, looking up.

"Yes, indeed," said Lenox.

They took two chairs in the front hall—this was too urgent a conference for them to make it any farther into the house—and Lenox enumerated all his discoveries of the past twenty-four hours, including the second clue he believed he had found in the letter, the one that led him to the notion of why the missing portrait had been stolen instead of Shakespeare's.

Graham listened carefully, occasionally intervening with a question. At the end of the explanation, Lenox felt obscurely relieved. It was always better to have Graham in possession of the facts of a case—always.

Meanwhile, the quiet, competent valet had himself been busy. "I have amassed the information you asked me to about Craig."

"Thank you. Anything interesting?"

"I hope so. I stopped into the Junior Ganymede, sir."

"You didn't!"

"I did, sir."

The Junior Ganymede Club was a gentlemen's club located just off of Berkeley Square, exclusively for the valets and butlers of the aristocracy. (This sort of specificity in a city with hundreds of gentlemen's clubs was not unusual—next door to White's was a very comfortable club for trout anglers, the Salmo.) Graham had joined the year before.

"I thought the first rule at the Junior Ganymede was the privacy of their masters?"

"In general it is, yes, sir. But I thought this likely would not touch on the Duke of Dorset's secrets. And more significantly, in this case there may be the chance that one of the membership has been murdered."

"Craig was a member!"

Graham nodded. "I approached a steward that I trust, sir. An Oxfordshire boy." Graham's rare smile appeared. He was himself an Oxfordshire boy. "He works the last shift. Hence my late return last night. I wanted to wait until most members had departed."

"That was clever. But I say, a servant in a servants' club. No putting anything by his masters."

"He is a stalwart fellow."

"What did you learn?"

Graham pulled a piece of club stationery from his pocket. "Alexander Arnold Craig, sir," he began. "Born in Dumferline on the fifth of November, 1810, making him forty-two at the time of his death yesterday morning."

"Too young."

"Craig joined the Scots Guards at sixteen as a private, sir, and mustered out with distinction at twenty-three. He went straight into service in the duke's household; he noted, in the Members' Book, that he had a very strong recommendation from his commanding officer, Lieutenant Pinney-May, who is a cousin of the duke's."

"Do you know why he left the military?"

"He preferred a domestic situation, sir." Graham looked down at his notes. "He went into the duke's service as a footman, but soon thereafter became a valet, upon the retirement of his predecessor to the Sussex Downs."

"They spent nineteen years together," Lenox said.

"Yes, sir. Virtually Craig's entire adult life, and much of His Grace's. Before and after he ascended to the title. No criminal record in London—the Junior Ganymede does not permit it."

"For, say, stealing," said Lenox.

"Sir?"

"If that is why he was shot, I mean."

"Yes, that sounds out of character, sir."

"Does it?"

"Craig was by universal consent a model servant, sir, at least according to the Junior Ganymede's membership. Those who had worked in the Dorset household said he was precise and rigorous in his habits."

"The military."

"Exactly, sir."

"Debts? Family?"

"He paid his bill as soon as he received it each month, sir—"

"Well done, Graham."

"Thank you, sir. That includes this month, on the first. No family listed except a cousin, Walter Craig, who is a corresponding member of the club based in Essex, with the family of Mr. Peregrine Tarrant, a landowner of means there."

Lenox crossed his legs and leaned back in his chair, studying the matter from all sides, hand across the lower half of his face. He looked up. "Did you ever see him there?"

"No, sir. But I understand that he was a regular card player on Tuesday evenings—his afternoon off—and frequently lunched in the dining room, sometimes up to four or five times a week."

"I see."

"He was not a drinker, sir."

"Never?"

"Not according to my acquaintance, sir."

233

Alexander Craig. Nineteen years in service to one gentleman, then shot by him in the early hours of the morning. It was both a damnable and bizarre situation, no matter what he'd been trying to steal. And he sounded a conscientious servant, if anything perhaps even too austere in his habits, which matched Lenox's few personal impressions of him. The farthest thing from a thief imaginable.

"I wonder if I could ask you a favor, Graham. Could you try to get in amongst the servants at Dorset's house and ask about someone named Maggie McNeal?"

"Not Craig, sir?"

"If they have any information about Craig I would be curious to hear it. But Maggie McNeal is a person I am also curious about. She departed without notice from the duke's household two days ago."

Graham raised his eyebrows. "I see. Yes, sir. Of course."

Lenox glanced up at the carriage clock on the table near the door. "If you have time after you've done that, I would be grateful if you could run a General Arthur Pendleton to ground. It shouldn't be hard. He is staying in London at the moment, I would imagine at the Army and Navy. If not there, one of the usual places."

Graham—the quickest of studies—knew the world of London clubs as accurately as any man

234

in the West End. "Very good, sir. Before you leave, you have a note from Thaddeus Bonden, sir."

"Do I? Let me see it, please."

Graham passed him a rough piece of paper folded in half.

Will be there at 3:37. No need to come east. Bonden.

It was just around noon. "Where is Lancelot?" he asked.

"Out with the curate, Mr. Templeton, sir, upon an educational trip to the museum of zoology."

"Ah, he'll hate that," Lenox said with satisfaction. "And meanwhile I can sit in my study, thinking, without a single person bothering me until—well, three thirty-seven. I wonder how he decided upon that hour?"

Graham took the note and read it. "I cannot say, sir."

"One of the things Willoughby Clark told me about Bonden is that he can multiply any two numbers in his head, just like that, faster than you could do it by hand. Large numbers."

"Interesting, sir."

"Clark called him a misfit, I think. An oddball? But I wonder if it has something to do with his gift. After all, there are all sorts of mad geniuses in painting, and that kind of thing."

"Indisputably, sir."

"Yes, laugh at me, but it's true. Perhaps Bonden is only . . . different. I don't know what I mean, I'm tired. Anyway, Lord, how I hope he has found that stupid painting. We are one piece away from knowing everything now. I'm positive."

CHAPTER THIRTY

At 3:38 p.m., Lenox and Bonden had been sitting in Lenox's library for one minute. Bonden had declined the offer of coffee or tea.

"You look different," Lenox said. "What have you been doing?"

Bonden was in a suit, a proper suit. "I broke into the duke's private study."

"You what!"

"It was necessary."

"The last man who did that was shot."

"On the other hand I was not."

Lenox frowned. "If he finds out, he'll rain every police officer in London down on you. And half the Coldstream Guards."

"I have no plans to tell him," said Bonden.

He was smoking. Lenox was torn between admiration and annoyance at his phlegmatic manner.

"Why did you do that?"

Bonden drew on his pipe and exhaled a thin river of smoke. "I wanted to see if it was possible to get in through the window."

"Was it?" asked Lenox.

Bonden shook his head. "I did it in the end. But no, it is not—practically speaking. I wouldn't care to come down with a painting, either. Even with a ladder, which nobody would dare use in plain view of the street. It would be difficult to gain entry through the window. The small hedge in front of the building makes for a sharp angle upward."

"What did you do after that?"

"Stood and watched the house for four hours."

"Four hours!"

"I wanted to see it."

"I should say you had the chance." And now Lenox felt his heart quicken, for they were coming to the point. "Do you know where the painting is?"

"Yes, I do."

"You've seen it?"

"No."

"Then how can you know its location?"

"Because I know that it's not anywhere else."

Lenox had to stop himself from scoffing. It could be in Indochina, he thought once more. "Then where is it?"

"In Lord Vere's bedroom."

The young detective was so taken aback that he just stared for a moment. "Lord Vere's bedroom."

"Yes."

Lenox took out his billfold. "Here is your payment," he said.

Bonden took half of the money Lenox held out. "For my time. See if the painting is there. If it's not, you owe me nothing more."

Lenox took the bills back and said cautiously, "You are that confident?"

"I am that confident."

"But it could be in Yorkshire now, or Florence. It could be ash."

"Yet it is not." Bonden stared at him impassively. "You hired me, Mr. Lenox. Go see for yourself if you like."

Lenox thought of what he knew of Corfe. He had seen him, sickly but dressed, on the morning of the duke's arrest.

"How can you be so arrogant!"

Bonden shook his head. "No."

"What do you mean, 'No'?"

"The person who stole the painting did not climb through the window—and they are not in Yorkshire now, or Florence. Nor do I think even Lord Vere would be stupid enough to start a fire in the dead of summer when he has a fever, so it has not been burned." Bonden paused and stood up. "Once I knew it was in the house, I paid a servant to give me the full layout of the place. There are new servants there every day, more or less. There were only four places in the house it could have been. She checked three of them for me."

It was obvious that Bonden hated speaking this much. "And that's all I'm to know," Lenox said.

"That's quite enough," Bonden replied shortly. "You may send the remainder of my payment to the Dovecote. Good afternoon, Mr. Lenox."

Lenox watched him walk down the hall and let himself out.

Magical, they had all said of Bonden. But this was the most obvious trouble with magic. It always turned out to be fake.

Still, what if it wasn't?

At seven o'clock, beneath vast gray rainclouds undercoating a heartache shade of evening, Lenox went to Dorset House. He was hoping that he would arrive in time to catch the family dining, and he did.

He was led to wait in a massive drawing room—yet another that Lenox had not seen—and nearby was a flawless Holbein (even he could recognize that much), a noblewoman against a background of pure yellow. This one was nearly priceless, he supposed. It convinced him more than ever of the significance he knew he alone suspected the missing portrait from the duke's study held—otherwise why not grab this Holbein and sell it to some unscrupulous upjumped American?

Ward entered, greeting him with an admirably friendly hello given how much of his time Lenox had demanded recently.

"What brings you here?" he asked. "News?"

"Tell me," said Lenox in a low voice. "What do you make of Vere?"

Ward frowned. "That is what you want to know about? Corfe?"

"For the moment."

"You don't suspect him of—"

"No, no."

Ward glanced over his shoulder. The cavernous room was empty. "A show-off. Not much account. At school they would have bullied him."

"Where was he?"

"Eton."

"Figures," said Lenox.

Ward smiled; Eton was the great rival to their own school, Harrow, and they both knew it to be, as an article of faith, a place full of weak-kneed, small-beer, mutton-headed coxcombs.

"D'you know who he reminds me of?" said Ward.

"Who?" asked Lenox.

"Wimple."

That said a great deal. Lord Wimple had been in Ward's form at Harrow and was widely despised. He played at the sportsman but had no physical courage; often mentioned his family, though of course every Harrovian's family was of distinction in one variety or other; and boasted incessantly about the lands he would inherit one day.

Lenox had once had a darting realization that Wimple *needed* to brag, he needed those lands to his name—there was some wound inside he was protecting with his self-importance.

Thereafter Lenox had stopped quite hating him. Still, he could never abide his company.

"That bad?" asked Lenox.

"Perhaps not quite. Civil enough to me. I've run across him socially once or twice. I've no doubt you have as well."

"Who are his crowd?"

"Horse people," said Ward immediately.

"Tell me something, would Craig ever have gone into his room? Lord Vere's?"

"Oh, yes, he usually acted as go-between for His Grace and Corfe."

"What about this past week?"

"Especially then. Corfe has been ill—his health is the reason we stayed behind, which seems a bitter irony in retrospect for poor Craig— and the duke asked for regular reports as to his condition."

Lenox had been writing in his notebook before he arrived, and he tapped his pencil against the table. The sound echoed in the huge room. "And Dorset—he seemed broken up that morning, after he had shot Craig?"

Ward looked at him curiously. "Yes, half mad. He couldn't believe it was Craig. He said that over and over."

"Has Dorset been unhappy before now, in your experience?"

"Never for a day, I would have said, before that painting went missing."

Lenox leaned forward. "I need to ask you a very great favor."

Ward looked at him. "Do you think you've solved it, Charlie?"

"I'm not sure."

Ward stared at him. "All right," he said at last.

"Is Lord Vere dining with the family?"

"Yes."

"I need you to look for the painting in his room, if you could."

"In *Corfe's?*" Ward said in a tone of disbelief so pure that Lenox experienced a sense of discouragement.

"My man, Graham, can go with you. If you need an excuse you can say that I sent him to look for some papers the duke requested."

Ward checked his watch. "It's a pretty thin alibi."

"Could you try?"

"You have a good reason for it, I take?"

"I think so."

Ward nodded. "Fine then. But dinner should only be another thirty minutes. We must go now if we're to go. Where is Graham?"

"In the anteroom."

They got him, and Ward and Graham went. Lenox waited for them with a horrible sense of dread.

When he heard a footstep in the hall, he stood bolt upright. It was only Lady Violet, however, coming to see if he needed anything.

"No!" he called very brightly and loudly. "All's well!"

She looked bemused. "Can I help you?"

"No! No! Is your supper over?"

He was still shouting; she was too well bred to point it out. "Yes," she said. "Under the circumstances we have dined *en famille*."

"Of course! A short supper!" Lenox shouted.

She took her leave—no doubt thinking him insane—and his heartbeat slowed to something like normal. Not an instant later, Ward and Graham walked back into the room.

Their faces told the story. On the way home, Lenox and Graham stopped into the telegram office and sent a message to Bonden, care of the Dovecote.

Not there STOP Very bad loss of credibility STOP Lenox

CHAPTER THIRTY-ONE

How vital it would have been to find the painting—if his suspicion about the thirteenth duke's portrait, based on that old letter, was correct.

Fool's gold, Bonden had been, fool's gold.

As the carriage pulled away from the telegram office, he took out his watch, which was made of real gold, a present from his father given on his twentieth birthday.

Nearly nine o'clock. Graham sat quietly next to him. Neither spoke—the moment was tense—and Lenox coiled and uncoiled his watch chain around his finger.

This distracted habit of his with the watch chain always made him think of Theseus in the maze of the Minotaur, the story in old books from the nursery. There were different versions. In the one Lenox knew, just before Theseus entered the maze, Ariadne, the daughter of the king, had given him a ball of yarn, so that he could track where he had been as he hunted the monster.

In the oldest tellings of the story that ball was called a clew, the name for a ball of yarn in the 1300s. It was from this word Lenox and his kind had inherited perhaps the most important word in their own vocabulary: clue.

He wished desperately that he had just one more clue now, to guide him through the maze.

For what did he know? So little, really. He placed the thief in one of three categories: a) a person who wanted the painting; b) per Dorset's original theory, a person who wanted the painting of Shakespeare and had made a mistake; c) a person who wanted the lost play.

It was the third category that alarmed him.

"You ought to turn in," Lenox said when they reached Hampden Lane. "There will be more of this nonsense tomorrow."

They both seemed to feel defeated. "Are you sure, sir?"

"I'm sure. Lord, I wish I had never heard of the Duke of Dorset."

He went to his study, loosening his tie, and poured himself a brandy and soda. Lancelot, thank the angels, was out on an "evening of astronomy" with Templeton. As an inducement for good behavior, Mrs. Huggins had entrusted to the curate a bag of licorice allsorts, despite Lancelot's vehement insistence that they would be securest in his own hands.

He almost missed the boy. He smiled, reclining in his chair and putting his feet up on the coffee table. Almost. Outside it was still quietly raining. There was a low, rumbling, dark orange fire in the fireplace, on this cold summer evening.

He missed his father.

He must have fallen asleep, because it was only the dim consciousness of a distant noise within the house that brought him to his senses. His brandy and soda, he saw, had tumbled to the carpet, and clumsily he picked up the glass and set it on the table, still half asleep. He rubbed his eyes and stretched his shoulders back. The clock on his desk told the time—past midnight.

He stood up, aching a bit, and went out into the hall.

The noise was coming from the servants' quarters downstairs, and at that moment a young footman, Fitzwilliam, came upstairs. He had hastily donned his tie and jacket.

"Hello, sir," he said. "There is a Mr. Bonden who—he has insisted that he had business with you. He brought a large parcel."

Lenox was wholly awake now. "Where is he?"

"In the servants' dining room."

Poor Mrs. Huggins. Life was hard enough for his housekeeper, and now she would have to clean whale-oil stains out of the cambric on the chairs she kept so neatly in the room where the servants took their meals. "I'm coming down."

Bonden was sitting at the enormous scarred table that dominated the room. Fitzwilliam had lit a candle, but it was dark, and Lenox asked him for more. He returned with a candelabra that held six, and the room brightened.

There, leaning against the wall, next to a table with a quarter of a kidney pie left on it, was the picture—the 13th Duke of Dorset.

For a moment Lenox just stared. He was a ruddy, weighty fellow, very different from the present duke. The picture portrayed him on a marble balcony. There was a broad verdure behind him and a chapel in the distance.

He wore a jerkin.

"Where was it?"

At that moment Graham came in, dressed for all the world as if it were noon on a Sunday. "Good evening, sir," he said.

Bonden glanced at him. "It was in Lord Vere's room, sir. He is out for the night. Recovered from his fever, apparently."

"We searched that room top to bottom," said Graham, more curious than defiant.

"Not bottom. It was nailed to the underside of the bedframe."

"Nailed?" said Lenox.

"Yes. There's some writing on the back."

Lenox's heart started to thump. He turned the painting around. Its cloth backing had been roughly and recently removed. He saw what Bonden meant: four lines, written in thin white ink, one along each side of the wooden picture frame. A single splash of water could have wiped them away.

"I owe you an apology, Mr. Bonden," he said. "If you would consent to it, I would like to learn more of your craft. I could pay you for your time."

Bonden stared at him. "Maybe," he said, putting on his cap. "For now I'll take the rest of my pay."

When Bonden had gone, paid, Lenox stood there and looked at the words on the back of the painting for a long, long time.

It was what he had anticipated.

The next morning dawned sunny. Lenox's carriage was ready at six, by his orders. On the ride across town he ignored the stack of newspapers on the seat beside him, with their increasingly frenzied questions about the duke. Instead he watched the waking city through the window, occasionally checking his breast pocket for the piece of paper he had brought.

The duke was awake, shaved, and dressed, which surprised Lenox. Even since the day before, Lady Violet (presumably not the duchess) had brought over more from home to make him comfortable. He had a sterling silver coffee set—a beautiful ancient one, covered in intricate scrollwork, upon a gleaming tray—and offered the detective a blue Wedgewood cup.

"Thank you," said Lenox.

"There are jam rolls, too," said the duke.

Lenox took one and set it beside his coffee. They were in a small nook near the corner of this large sitting room, the door to the bedroom closed. "I have new information."

"You do?" said Dorset, with a hint of suspicion.

"I do. It is about the poem."

"The poem."

"Yes. The poem as you know it is obviously tantalizing. But from the moment I read your great-grandfather's letter, I have suspected something else very strongly: that it is *incomplete*. It is a phrase he uses toward the end. The answer, he says in the letter, lies *in my picture*."

The duke was leaning forward, tense, confused. "Yes? What of it?"

"*My* picture. Then he says, *'In it is the part of the riddle that I have yet to solve. I hope that you have committed it to memory.'*"

The duke looked dangerously frustrated. "What are you saying, Mr. Lenox?"

"Everywhere else he calls the picture of Shakespeare 'the portrait' or something similar. But then he says 'in *my* picture,' though it is so clear, elsewhere, that he considers himself only a steward of the portrait."

"Lenox, for pity's sake—"

"My suspicion has been that you only have the first half of the poem, written on the portrait of Shakespeare. *That* is why there is all that

250

black paint underneath the poem—to conceal its second half. Your great-grandfather scrawled out the second stanza himself, dividing the poem for safety. Then he put the second half of it somewhere in *his* picture, as he kept referring to it. That is why he hoped his son would commit it to memory."

The effect of this idea on the duke was electric. "Of course," he said, eyes shining. "Of course. That is why the thief stole the wrong painting. It was exactly the painting he wanted."

Lenox nodded. "I think so."

The duke's face had slowly assumed a look of nearly pure grief. "And now it is lost, and the thief has the complete poem to himself. I have failed."

"No, Your Grace," said Lenox. "I have recovered the painting."

The duke stood up. "You haven't."

Lenox took the piece of paper from his breast pocket. The night before, he had reached for a piece of his cook Ellie's scratch paper and a bit of charcoal, written out the first stanza from memory, then transcribed the second, sitting opposite the silent Bonden, tilting his head to read.

It was tricky—the letter *s,* for instance, looked like the letter *f*—but he managed it quickly. He had committed the lines to memory, but he had kept the paper, too.

"The lines were written on the reverse of the painting, underneath its backing. If I am not mistaken, for the first time in nearly a century we have the whole poem."

The duke took the poem and stared at it, the whole poem, complete.

Forty miles from Charing Cross,
then back one further apple's toss,
under fields of wheat-grown gold,
doth laze a buried story told.

Kent for they who wish it found,
and dig beneath the churchyard ground
behind the name my portrait gloss,
forty miles from Charing Cross.

CHAPTER THIRTY-TWO

The duke read and reread the poem for so long that Lenox almost interrupted him. It must have been a full ten minutes that he expended studying those sixty syllables.

At last he looked at Lenox. "I am in your debt," he said.

Lenox shrugged. "It is my work."

"No. I am in your debt. What do you make of the poem?"

"I'm not sure," he replied cautiously. "Obviously knowing the play is in Kent helps."

"Mm."

"And the churchyard ground. It also makes your concern that the place might have been built over seem less likely. They don't often get rid of churches."

The duke nodded. He looked around at the walls, irritated. "I must get out of here as soon as possible—as soon as possible." He studied the paper again, as if the poem would give up more on a hundredth reading. "The third line is the one that puzzles me. *Behind the name my portrait gloss.*"

"I have a theory there." Lenox was waiting for the other shoe to drop, as young folks slanged it these days—but for now he was happy to discuss the poem. "I suspect it puzzled the thief, too, for a while."

"What's your theory?"

"If I had to guess, I would hazard that it is a pun. That would be very much in the spirit of Shakespeare, whether he wrote the poem or one of his friends did. One of his siblings, even. A fellow Stratford artist, perhaps the portraitist himself."

"A pun?"

"The gloss is the topcoat of a painting, as you know. But as I'm sure you also know there is another common sense to the word, even more common in Shakespeare's day—a gloss, from *glossa*, Latin. An explanation of a word. There is only one name 'glossed' in the portrait. In its gloss, if you will," Lenox said.

"Mary," said Dorset. "*Nomen Mariae.*"

Lenox nodded. "When we find the right churchyard, I would bet anything that the play is buried at the grave of a woman named Mary."

"A Catholic's joke," said the duke, smiling faintly. There was a beatific relief in his face. Prison was a strange place to see such a thing, but it was there. "You must be correct."

"Yes, Your Grace. A Catholic's joke."

But here it came—the other shoe, the question Lenox had been dreading. The duke, still standing, paper in his hands, said, "I have forgotten to ask you how you found the picture."

Lenox hedged. "It is a long story, and I would like to amass a bit more information. To begin with, may I ask, Your Grace, whether Mr. Craig's own financial position was secure?"

There was a river breeze in the cell, carrying on it the faint damp smell—cordage, closed spaces, open waters, salt, hardtack—of seagoing.

"I do not know to any exactitude, but I paid him well. He was unmarried and without financial obligation. He could have called on me for a loan of any size. I mean that literally."

"He knew that?"

"Yes. A Dorset is a loyal friend. What's more, I made over a parcel of land in our possession— six acres—to him. He planned to retire there. But he could have sold it for a few hundred pounds at any time, as I made clear to him. He had the deed, free and clear."

Lenox nodded quietly. "As I thought, then. With the motive of money excluded, it becomes easier."

"Easier?"

"I am still lacking information myself, Your Grace," said Lenox. "Permit me to return this afternoon. I hope to have a fuller explanation then."

The duke didn't look happy, but he was still too preoccupied with the poem—the quarry of a lifetime, that much closer to being captured— to care. "Fine," he said. "In the meanwhile I'm going to tell Lord Aston that I must leave this place as quickly as possible. He will accelerate matters. There is a play to be found now."

Lenox stood and buttoned his jacket. "Thank you for the coffee, Duke."

The duke put out a hand. "Thank you for the poem, Mr. Lenox. I owe you more than a lunch now."

"As I said, it is only my job."

Soon he was outside the Tower and in his carriage, heading back to Hampden Lane.

In all of these early cases in his career, Lenox could look back and identify some vital mistake he had made. He was still learning. For instance, the Thames Ophelia had taught him to look as carefully as he could at faces; the majority of people let faces pass before them like clouds in the sky, unremarked, without separable identities.

On Dorset's case, he had made at least this one error: He had not studied the inhabitants of the household closely enough. He knew next to nothing about Corfe, Lord Vere, who if all went to plan would some day become the 16th Duke of Dorset—just as powerful as his father.

Nor did he have any grasp of the duchess. His thoughts ran to her supercilious cousin, Sir Japheth Miles, standing with her at the scene of the "kidnapping."

Back at Hampden Lane, the young detective

heard a thumping on the staircase when he opened the door and found himself waylaid by Lancelot.

"Could I have ten pounds?" the boy asked.

"Ten pounds! What? Have you lost your mind?"

"*Please* could I though?"

"What in all the fires of hell are you talking about? That is a month of Clarissa's wages!"

Clarissa was one of the chambermaids. Lancelot nodded, his thin face as sincere as Lenox had ever seen it, to indicate that he understood this. "But Mr. Templeton knows about a horse than cannot lose in the fifth race at Anglesey. Cannot possibly lose."

"Mr. Templeton the *curate?*"

"Yes."

"MRS. HUGGINS," Lenox shouted.

"You can have some of the winnings."

"Shut up, Lancelot. *Mrs. Huggins!*"

"I would need it this morning."

"You would, would you?" said Lenox. "In that case let me go find my billfold."

"Oh, lovely, really?"

"No! Not really! You could stand here until the end of time and you wouldn't have ten pounds out of me." He paused for a second. "Why did you settle on ten pounds anyway?"

"The horse is ten to one, and I want a hundred pounds."

Lancelot explained that as if it had a Euclidean

clarity of premise. Who wouldn't want a hundred pounds? "Oh, a long shot, perfect. What could go wrong. *Mrs. Huggins, would you—*"

Finally the housekeeper appeared, and Lenox told her about the curate's apparent plan to introduce his three boys to the pleasures of the turf. He asked if he could rely upon her to find Lancelot a minder who wouldn't actually take the boy to a casino, until he could find someone at the prison to take over the job.

"You don't mean that," said Lancelot.

"I can take the three boys to the zoo today, sir," said Mrs. Huggins worriedly.

"Fine. They'll fit in marvelously. You know where the other boys are?"

"Yes, sir."

"You know where I keep my ready money. Take whatever you need. Tell Templeton he is fired, unless he can prove to me that Lancelot is lying. Actually—Lancelot, are you lying?"

"No."

"You're sure?"

"Yes."

Lenox stared at him. "Well, then fire Templeton, and watch the three boys even if you have to tie them together. One of them must have a mother in London, or something similar. I am trying to solve a murder."

"Very good, sir."

"If Templeton comes to fetch Lancelot, tell

258

him that I know every police officer in this city. Is he even a curate?"

"Oh, yes, he went to Cambridge, sir."

"That explains part of it, anyway," Lenox muttered—young and highly loyal to Oxford, he held Cantabrigians in roughly the same esteem as Etonians—and stamped out of the door into the gray day.

CHAPTER THIRTY-THREE

He took his carriage to Dorset House, studying his notes on the way. When he arrived, a servant led him into the small drawing room. She informed him that Lord Vere was just departing.

"Where is he going?" Lenox asked the housekeeper.

"To dine, sir," she said very bluntly, and she was well within her rights to be abrupt—it was an impertinent question.

"Where?" he said, pushing his luck.

When she replied, the "sir" was gone. "Out."

Lord Vere agreed to see him, however, and it was the job of this churlish housekeeper to lead Lenox to a large library that he had not seen before, on the east side of the house (it was a mansion of the sort that seemed to multiply with new rooms every day, as if breeding), where all the papers had been ironed and laid out upon an enormous oak table, just as usual it would seem—as if the oak table's owner were not in their headlines.

Lord Vere was waiting in a chair. He rose, buttoning his jacket. "Good morning," he said.

Lenox had not yet had the chance to study the young heir at close range. He was a fine specimen of his kind, perhaps four or five years the detective's senior. He wore a black frock coat; a brilliant white shirt; a paisley cravat; high-waisted checked trousers; a green waistcoat with gold buttons; and a signet ring with his seal on it. To his left was a black top hat, shining silkily under the lamplight. He was consummate: all that should be in a young gentleman.

The room was lined with shelf after shelf of books, stretching twelve feet high, a rolling ladder affixed to each wall. Dominating the center of the room was a marble of Christ and Mary Magdalene that Lenox could see was of the highest quality. He would have believed it was by Donatello.

"Lord Vere," he said, and dipped his head.

"Please, now, call me Corfe. I know your name."

"You are lunching out?" Lenox asked.

"Eh? Oh, yes. Good to get on one's feet again. Her Majesty has invited me to the Palace. To commiserate."

Good Lord, the Queen. For a moment there Lenox had nearly forgotten how high the altitude of this social sphere was, having moved into it so easily as an aide. "That is kind of her."

"Yes, she sent a considerate note. I thought after that I would toddle over to the Beargarden and scrounge up a drink."

"Ah, of course. I'm a member there myself."

"Are you! Well, we shall have to dine when this business is all over."

Lenox nodded at this queer politeness. "Of course. But for now, I wanted a quick word about your father and Mr. Craig."

Vere shook his head, face filled with consternation. He gestured for Lenox to sit. "Yes, a right collieshangie that."

Lenox, sitting and thinking of what to ask, had a fast feeling of displacement, as he sometimes did. What on earth was he doing here, playing at police like a child? But he persevered: He thought that probably everyone felt like a fraud now and then. Perhaps even the Queen.

"I wonder if you know a Maggie McNeal, Lord Vere?"

"Call me Corfe, as I said. No, I don't think I do."

"Perhaps just Maggie? She has been a servant here."

"Has she? No." He waved a hand around the room, which, though empty, did a fair job of making his point—that there were dozens of servants about. "Is she mixed up in this? Do you want her called in?"

"That won't be possible—your sister told me that the young woman hadn't been to work in a few days and hadn't given any notice."

"Oh, I see. Yes, that seems bad."

"But you don't recall her."

"Very sorry. No."

"Are there still footmen in your father's study?"

"No. It's locked inside and out now. New

locks today. Only he has the keys, in the Tower. He entrusted an outside chap with the job. I hope it will make him feel better."

"So do I."

Corfe looked vaguely troubled to have said so much, as if he sensed that it was a bit unbecoming that his father had shot a man.

He leaned forward. "You don't care to tell me what's in there, do you? The Holy Grail, one would think, from the care he's taking."

"I don't have that information myself," Lenox said. He paused. Then he said, "I have something rather delicate to ask you."

"Anything."

"The missing painting—it was recovered last night by one of your father's servants."

"But that's splendid news!"

"It was recovered from your room."

Vere did an extremely credible—indeed, an almost unfakeable—show of surprise. "*My* room?" he said.

"Yes."

"But where? What on earth?"

"The underside of your bed."

"My bed? You're joking."

"No," said Lenox.

The handsome young lord sat back and studied the books. Then he turned to Lenox. "So it must have been Craig."

"The trouble there is opportunity," Lenox said.

263

"You were in bed with fever. When would he have done it?"

Corfe frowned. "I was asleep much of the time. There was one morning I ventured out onto the terrace for a few minutes in a chair, hoping the sun would do me good."

Lenox nodded. "I see. Of course. Can I ask you about Craig, then? What do you make of him?"

For the first time something like human feeling came onto Corfe's face, which till now had been like his clothing—perfectly composed, a pose available for the world's scrutiny.

"Craig, poor chap," he said. "I hate that people will think of him as a thief. He was always very stern, but very kind to us."

"Us?"

"Violet and me, when we were small. It was always he who accompanied us to see our grandparents for Christmas. Our favorite time of the year, that, while our parents traveled to the continent."

"Can you imagine any reason for Craig's betrayal of your father?"

Corfe frowned. "Money, I suppose. It's usually money, isn't it?" He checked his watch. "Unfortunately I'll be late to meet my friend, Mr. Lenox. Could we possibly continue this conversation another time?"

Lenox hid his annoyance. The friend to whom he referred was—the Queen of England. "Of course," he said, and both rose from their seats.

He left Dorset House in a welter of emotions, confused and frustrated. He didn't know where he was going; he didn't know enough to know quite what he knew. All the facts were there. None of them would hang together in his mind. He walked in a terrible kind of anger for five blocks, then stopped.

"What have you to say for yourself," he muttered, pulling the little book of quotations from his pocket and letting it fall open to a random page.

We have seen better days.
—Timon of Athens

That was the quotation his eyes settled on. He stared at it for a long time. Then he felt something that he hadn't, in the eighteen months since his father died: tears coming into the backs of his eyes.

He blinked rapidly, and looked up at the dark gray clouds, letting his hand fall to his side. He felt a constriction inside. His face softened. Suddenly it all seemed full of meaning, the vast empty sky, its sorrowful leaden color, the world's inability to *answer* for itself.

He turned back toward the street and hailed a hansom cab. Though it was not in his plans, he directed it to a small boathouse by the side of the Thames.

Its keeper, Wilkins, greeted him with a nod. In thirty seconds he had Lenox's feather-light scull in the water, rain sprinkling the dock around them. Lenox changed in the small dark room off the boathouse, shook hands with Wilkins, and boarded the scull. Then, his back to the west, he eased into the Thames. Wilkins gave him a short salute of farewell, and he started a hard pull.

He had bought the scull four years earlier—from his and Ward's old school, Harrow—and it still pulled like a dream. For forty minutes he lost himself in the rhythm of the exercise, his mind emptied of all but the exertion.

At last, breathless, he glided onto the shore of an old hunk of rock in the middle of the Thames, Peanut Isle by name. A few trees stood high upon it, alone and old, undulating patiently in the soft wind. There was a tun of water here that the boathouses took turns filling, and Lenox pulled to, pried the lid off, took the ladle off the side of the barrel, and poured some of the fresh water gratefully over his body, the chill of chipped ice a glorious sensation on his reddened skin.

He pulled back steadily but more slowly, the rain heavier; he watched the city grow higher as he came nearer to Parliament.

Wilkins greeted him at the boathouse with a cold towel to wipe himself down with, a hot one to scrub off the sweat, and his pullover.

"Thank you," said Lenox.

"It had been a time."

"Work, you know."

"Aye," said Wilkins.

As he was changing back into his clothes, he saw the draw for the doubles race next month, a bracket of sixteen duos, eight on each side seeded by strength, thousands of possible outcomes among the matches.

It was at that moment—perhaps because the exercise had freed him from this terrible business of thinking—that everything clicked into place.

CHAPTER THIRTY-FOUR

It was a matter of numbers. Lenox had never been much of a fist at maths, but it would have looked something like $3 + x + y$, the equation he had in his mind.

He had taken on faith the duke's word that only three people knew about the painting of Shakespeare: in fact it was three plus the number those three people had told, and the number those people had told. $3 + x + y$: It might equal $3 + 0 + 0$, to be sure, as the duke was confident, but it might just as easily be $3 + 2 + 9$, or $3 + 1 + 600$. Who knew?

Or perhaps—and this was what he really suspected—the original number was not three at all. Perhaps it was four.

When he arrived at the duke's rooms this time, everything had a markedly different feel. There were numerous men in the hallways outside, and several inside as well, all of them solemn, and all of them very busy. Lord Aston's work.

The duke saw Lenox and dismissed them with a quick word; they looked at Lenox resentfully but left. The bailiff closed the door behind them.

"My apologies, Mr. Lenox," said the duke. "Solicitors, and men from the House of Lords, and the Palace, and all that."

And all that. "Of course, Your Grace."

They sat near the window again. The day wouldn't give in—still dark, still intermittently wet, and gusting with wind. They could see the ships rocking on the Thames, the taut flags on Tower Bridge.

"I have been contemplating the poem," said Dorset.

"I have been contemplating the missing picture," said Lenox.

"Yes, of course. Naturally. Where is it now?"

"In my house, Your Grace, safe under lock and key. I can have it sent back to you any time you choose."

"Where was it?" the duke asked curiously, as if it were a matter of academic significance to him, not germane to his primary interests.

Lenox took a deep breath. Here was where he felt his youth; he couldn't fluff this opportunity. "It was nailed to the underside of the bed of your son, Lord Vere."

The duke looked at him, taken aback. "Corfe? His bed?"

"Yes, sir."

The part of Lenox that had wondered whether the duke himself might be concealing something more gave way. No. His face now was unmasked and raw, his bafflement real.

"How strange that Craig would place it there. What can explain it?" said the duke.

Lenox held steady. "You mentioned to me,

269

once, your gratitude that your own father lived to a good age, long enough to grow close to his grandchildren."

Corfe had said the same that morning: Christmases with the old duke. "Yes," said Dorset. "Why? Speak plain, Lenox."

"Very well, Your Grace. It is this way.

"When your great-grandfather's portrait was stolen, the windows in your study were open and it was locked. That led us to believe that it was a thief from outside who took the painting. I believe now that that was misdirection. It would have been nearly impossible to gain access from outside the house. Which means that the thief came from inside the house."

"Yes—Craig."

"The key was his, certainly. Was he loyal to Lord Vere?"

The duke put together what Lenox's questions implied. "Are you accusing my son of something?" he asked. "You had better be very sure of your facts if you are."

And so Lenox explained the facts as succinctly and linearly and impassively as he could to the duke, who sat opposite him, intimidatingly silent:

first, that he believed that Corfe had been feigning his fever; he had rejected doctor's visits more than once without any rational explanation, according to separate, equally exasperated accounts from Dorset and from Lady Violet;

second, that he believed Corfe had done so in the hope that he might be alone in the house, but had been thwarted when his parents had delayed their visit to the country to look after him;

third, that he had decided to attempt the theft of the portrait anyway;

fourth, that he was doing so because—and here was the crucial step in the chain of speculation—his grandfather, with whom he had been so close as a child, had told him the *whole truth about the Shakespeare,* old men being famously careless with their confidences, reckoners, totters-up of debt, and above all, among dukes, in love with their eldest grandsons;

fifth, that Craig had been Lord Vere's accomplice in all matters, first offering him the key to the study, then, apparently, going to fetch the second portrait, the Shakespeare, too;

and sixth, that his motive in this must be one of two things—either, Lenox said, a maniacal interest in Shakespeare, which he could not disclose to his father without betraying his grandfather's trust, or (and privately Lenox thought this much more likely) a matter of money.

The duke took each point as a blow, wincing slightly as Lenox spoke. When the detective was done, he stood and walked away across the cell.

When he turned back, something defiant remained in his face. "Corfe has all the money he could ever need—his allowance would put the full income of most households on your street to shame," he said, with, to Lenox, a remarkable lack of delicacy.

"No doubt that is true."

"Moreover, he and I are close. If it was the portrait of Shakespeare he wanted, he would have told me. You are wrong, Lenox. I don't doubt your good faith, but you are wrong. It must be Craig."

"Perhaps. There is one point I find telling."

"Well?"

"That Lord Vere was back on his feet the moment you were taken away. Fever gone."

The duke hesitated. "Fevers come and go."

"Then look at Craig, Your Grace. Is there anyone on earth for whom he would have betrayed you other than Corfe? Listen to me—I have been delirious with fever, as I imagine you have been. To me it seems implausible that even the deepest fever sleep could remain undisturbed by a painting being hammered to the underside of one's bed."

The duke looked at him for a long moment and then slumped back. "It's not possible," he muttered. He looked out through the window, thinking. "Did you know the last person executed here was a woman?"

Lenox had not. He did not especially want to know it now. "No, Your Grace."

"In 1780. Gordon Riots."

"Oh, right, yes."

"Gordon himself, of course, went free."

Another Etonian, Lenox almost muttered, thinking of Lancelot, who was probably leading a riot somewhere right now, and Corfe, too.

Lord Gordon had been a Protestant who stirred up a mob of sixty thousand or so because some very elementary rights had been restored to English Catholics. A fool. His timing could not have been worse: directly after the American revolution, and as the French one was simmering. The Gordon Riots had become a byword for brutality now; Lenox could recall his own father's anger at the stories of violence in London that year.

"I remember now," said Lenox. "The three traitors."

Dorset nodded. "They give you a ghastly kind of introduction when you come here. Or at least they did to me. Wellington was here, which I thought civilized in him. The first thing he mentioned was that there were a hundred and twenty-two executions here between 1388 and 1780. This poor woman apparently being the last."

"Mm."

The duke got up and strode around. Lenox noticed that he had the paper with the poem on it clutched tightly in one hand. "Ninety-three beheaded. Ninety-three! Twelve hanged. Three shot. Two burned at the stake. Eleven hanged, drawn, and quartered.

"And one, he told me, with a relish that I didn't quite like, who had his stomach cut open and his entrails thrown into a fire. After that they castrated him and threw *him* into the fire. Which must have been a mercy, all things told."

"Good Lord."

The duke nodded grimly. "Yes, quite."

"Well, they're not going to execute you, Your Grace."

Dorset waved an irritated hand. "I know that, of course." Still, he looked as if it weren't the worst of the options he faced at the present moment.

CHAPTER THIRTY-FIVE

Lenox measured his words. "My friend Cabot tells me that he thinks a hundred years hence all executions will have ceased. In his opinion we will be viewed as barbarians for having had them at all."

"By 1953. Lord Cabot?"

"Indeed, your Grace."

"A sound man, if a liberal." The duke wandered around his capacious cell. Outside, the hushed chattering of the black-cloaked men continued, just audible. But the duke was not concerned with them at the moment. "If we follow your theory," he said suddenly, "why was Craig unscrewing the portrait of Shakespeare?"

There was a gleam of hope in his eye—but Lenox had anticipated this question. "I think Lord Vere believed he needed it. The second stanza of the poem."

The duke read it over. "Well?"

"The third line: It would have been easy to mistake it, *behind the name my portrait gloss,* as an indication that there was another clue about the lost play behind Shakespeare's own portrait."

"Oh, I see," said the duke, pacing again. "Yes, that is possible, I suppose."

Then he muttered something to himself that

275

sounded like "Kent." Lenox wondered: Was everything Shakespearean in the end? Because he looked like Lear now, certainly, this hopelessly rich and privileged gentleman in his cell.

"Your Grace?"

"Kent, I said. Everybody knows Kent, don't they—apples, cherries, hops, and women."

Lenox smiled politely. It was a famous line of Dickens's. "Not much else."

"No. It must be a small churchyard."

"Yes," said Lenox.

The duke seemed to have accepted the detective's theory whole cloth now. He read the poem again.

But then, all at once, he shook his head violently. "It still doesn't make sense. I told you—Corfe has an allowance that a prince would find generous. He is not a gambler—nor is there a woman I know of—and in either case, there is no financial situation from which I would be unable to extract him. We could afford ten ruinations over. He is my heir."

Lenox nodded. "Perhaps he is embarrassed."

"No. He would never risk this embarrassment rather than coming to me. I told him when he was five that there was nothing I could not get him out of."

Perhaps that was the problem, Lenox reflected. "Then it must be that he is interested in Shakespeare."

276

The duke shook his head. "I know my son. He doesn't care a whit about William Shakespeare."

That was curious. "Might he have been Craig's accomplice, then?" he suggested.

The duke rejected that idea, too, though. "After all these years?"

"Perhaps he just learned of it."

"If Craig wanted money, there were a million things he could have stolen without my even noticing. He has a key to the jewel room at Dorset Castle, for pity's sake. Anyway, I trust him—trusted him—implicitly."

"And Shakespeare?"

"If there has ever been a person less interested in Shakespeare in all of Great Britain than Corfe, it was Alexander Craig. The only thing I ever knew him to read was the army gazette."

"I see."

And indeed Lenox was troubled by this assessment of the duke's household, by its head. His mind turned the facts over but could not quite make them add up. Something was missing.

Some*one,* too. The maid, Maggie McNeal.

The duke sighed. "Will you wait to dig until I am free? We may share the credit," he said. "It is just that it should be so, given that you have sleuthed out the poem."

Lenox was shocked at this offer. He admitted as much. "You surprise me, Your Grace."

The duke gave him a tired glance, but his voice was strong, unbowed. "Then we are both experiencing a day filled with surprise," he said drily.

"If you wish, Your Grace. Of course. I had planned to sit down with an atlas myself later today and begin investigating the churchyards of Kent. But I will naturally not dig without you."

Unless you are imprisoned for life, he thought to himself.

"Find out everything you can. Just keep going. As for Corfe—and Craig—all of that, leave in my hands."

"I have one request," Lenox said.

"Not money?"

"No," said Lenox coldly. "It is that if we should search for the play together, I may be allowed a friend to come along."

The 15th Duke of Dorset looked at him for a long while. This had been his own secret for many years. But he nodded. "As you please," he said.

Lenox returned to Hampden Lane not sure how to feel. What had he solved? Who had he helped? He ate lunch, a consoling cream of tomato soup, slices of cheese with hard biscuit, and a glass of ginger ale, the meal he asked for when he wanted sleep but before he knew he wanted sleep.

He napped once more before the low warm fire in the grate, this time with a novel on his chest. He dreamed that he was a child again.

When he woke this time, he could tell that it was midafternoon. There was a glimmer of yellow light in the branches of the trees, the sun at last showing itself. He heard a knock at the front door and realized it was this that had woken him.

The knock had apparently attracted Lancelot, too, because Lenox heard a noise like a large suitcase falling from a cliff on the stairs.

Lancelot and Lady Jane appeared in his study at once, her hand protectively on his head. She held a newspaper. Evidently it had been her at the door. "Hello, Charles," she said.

He stood up. "Hello. What are you reading?"

"The afternoon *Times*. I have missed the Dunmow Flitch again," she said.

"What is the Dunmow Flitch?" he asked, still blinking his way out of sleep.

She had walked over to the fire and was prodding it, paper in one hand. "Charles, really?" she said chidingly, looking up at him.

"Am I supposed to know?"

"The winners this year were a Mr. and Mrs. Herbert Cheese. Though numerous couples received the side of bacon, obviously."

"Jane, if you value my sanity, explain what you are talking about, or leave." He glanced over at his cousin, who was rooting through his desk. "Preferably with Lancelot."

She smiled and rose. "Every Whit Monday in Essex they award a handsome side of bacon to any couple that presents themselves and swears on a Bible that they have not broken their marriage vows or quarreled for at least the space of a year and a day. The *Times* has a full column on it."

"That is one of the silliest things I ever heard," said Lenox. He sat back down and suddenly realized that for the first time in days he was in a fair mood.

"Charles! Where is your sense of romance!"

"Anyhow it is not closely associated with slabs of dead pig."

"Think how easily James and I should win. We scarcely see each other three months a year, and I cannot recall quarreling with him during those. Poor Mr. and Mrs. Herbert Cheese would stand no chance against us."

"What did they do to win?"

"They wrote a poem. Would you like to hear it?"

"Less than anything."

"*Oh Mrs. Cheese,* it begins, *who brights when I awaken—*"

"Jane, I beg of you."

"*Celebrate our love with me, and with this side of bacon.*"

"What meter is that?"

"It's only fifty lines—shall I go on?"

"No."

"Almost all of it is bacon themed."

Lenox glared at her. "Leave me alone, I beg of you."

"Lancelot, come tell your cousin about the zoo. I know from my long friendship with him that he'll want to hear every last detail you can offer about the health of Obaysch the hippopotamus."

CHAPTER THIRTY-SIX

Jane had come in part to remind him that they were meant to dine that night; she had broken up her own party because there was to be a larger one at a friend's house. Would they ride over together? she asked. He said of course, promising to fetch her at quarter past eight.

Though his visit to Bedlam was some ways off, something had been nagging at him since his last trip. When Jane and Lancelot were gone he composed a wire to Dr. Hansel, his friend at the asylum.

Wondering if you have patient Belmont STOP alternatively Irvington STOP if so would like interview STOP warm regards STOP Lenox

He sent this out by a footman. He was thinking of the man who had approached him at the very end of his last visit, claiming to be falsely imprisoned—Irvington, he had called himself, before the guard called him Belmont.

It hadn't sat well with Lenox all week, and he was glad to have gotten the wire off. That done, he sat down and faithfully recorded the events of the day both for his own edification and to keep the facts straight in his mind. The Duke might be finished with the case, but he was not.

Graham returned just before six. "Hello, sir," he said.

"There you are. I was wondering."

"I have been searching for Maggie McNeal, sir, but unfortunately without luck."

Lenox frowned. It was very rare for Graham to fail. "No sign of her?"

"None, sir. Even within the household she is not remembered except perhaps hazily—that perhaps there was a Margaret employed there for a week or two some time ago. Yet it seems implausible that she should have had a more formal name below stairs than above."

"That is bizarre."

"I thought so, too, sir."

Lenox pondered this. There were often loose ends in his cases, false trails. He didn't like this one. "Thank you, Graham," he said. "I wondered if you wanted to tackle another job for me over the weekend. No rush."

"What is that, sir?"

Lenox smiled. "Don't get too excited. It is the churchyards of Kent I have in mind."

Soon the two were upstairs in their more traditional roles, Lenox shaving, Graham pressing his evening suit, a distracted chatter passing between them. By half past seven Lenox was dressed and his cheeks patted with sandalwood—a gentleman of London town.

Downstairs, he saw that a reply from Hansel had already arrived.

Odd you mention Belmont STOP transferred by family St Cs Edbrgh this week STOP no record Irv now or past STOP welcome any time STOP Hansel

Lenox was used to the doctor's economical style. He frowned as he read this over a second time. So that dark-eyed, dark-haired man, so urgent in his entreaties, had been pulled out of Bedlam after confiding in Lenox.

He would go to the asylum soon if he could.

But for now his duty was next door. On his way out he passed Lancelot and Mrs. Huggins playing checkers intently over an enormous supper. (Lancelot sat cross-legged on the floor across from the housekeeper, about eye level with the board, chin resting on his hand. He reported that she had won thirty-seven times in a row, but he had hopes of breaking through soon, and Lenox felt a quick involuntary burst of affection.) He decided to leave without even asking about Mr. Templeton, or the long shot in the fifth race.

He picked up Lady Jane, who was dressed in a lovely rose-colored gown with a blue taffeta shrug. Her hair was whipped into a high pile of curls.

"You look lovely, Your Ladyship," said Lenox, bowing.

"And you, Mr. Lenox," she said, curtsying.

Soon his carriage was on its way, headed toward the home of Mr. and Mrs. Caliban Edwards. Cal and his wife, Emily, lived in a rather shabby house near Bloomsbury. It was the envy of all their friends. Cal was the son of a very famous explorer and an equally famous beauty, she the daughter of two houses whose lineage dated to the Norman invasion.

They didn't have a penny between them. Cal rubbed along as a writer—a novel and some stories, the occasional tale of travel. Nevertheless, there was no house Lenox knew that was more full of happiness or of, because his father was always climbing some Himalaya or wading some Nile, interesting artifacts. A crocodile with its jaw wide open greeted you in the hallway. A walking stick carved with the symbols of the natives of America—it wouldn't have been out of place in Bergson's shop—was propped against it. The walls were covered with prints from Mr. Audubon's beautifully colorful book about birds. They had all 435 in frames, given them by the artist, and rotated the birds constantly; Audubon himself had been a dedicated visitor here until his death, two years before.

They dined cheaply but happily, all their friends having brought along additional viands and drinks, Lady Jane herself providing an excellent punch, sent over earlier in the day, which tasted of raspberries.

Lenox was seated next to Effie Somers—and the time flew away, as if it were on wings.

After dinner the men and women divided. Cal's father, a noble soul with a finely shaped head and a great coiffed sweep of gray hair, briefly back in London before he left for the interior of Africa, spent a great deal of time asking Lenox about his methods and his ideas.

At the end of it he offered a word of oblique praise. "They called me mad, too, you know," he said. "Perhaps they still do. I wouldn't trade a lifetime over again in the House of Lords for a single day of doing what I loved."

The two sexes rejoined in the drawing room, and Lenox moved into other conversations. But he was heartened by that one: He did love his work.

And he was improving, surely he was improving—or he was trying to improve, at least, which must matter in its own right.

He found Lady Jane and Effie Somers together on a couch as the hour neared midnight. "You look as if you've been brooding," said Lady Jane.

They were in the center of the small, comfortable drawing room, which was populated by a mix of generations, aging Explorers Club members and young society sorts.

"Only a bit."

"What about?" asked Miss Somers, accepting a glass of champagne from a footman with a graceful nod.

"Shakespeare!" said Lenox, and grinned. "How dull."

"Did you know he minded the horses for the theatergoers?" Effie said.

"I was always told he wrote the plays," Jane replied. "But then they never educate girls."

Her friend smiled, and in that instant Lenox almost loved her. "No, it was his first job in the business. When he was new in London."

"Was it!"

"I like to think of him standing there. He must have heard the laughs and groans from inside the theater and wondered what was prompting them."

"Every long silence," said Lenox.

"Exactly," she said.

Lady Jane excused herself. "Will you take care of Miss Somers for a moment?" she asked. "I have to ask Cal something."

Her motive in leaving them alone was transparent enough that when she had gone across the room, there was a slight humorous tension in the candid look Lenox and Effie Somers exchanged.

She wore a summer dress, yellow and white. Around her neck was a gold chain with a gold ring on it. She had pinned her thick golden-chestnut hair up, and Lenox could imagine, from the trace of scent he had caught when he said hello, what it would be like to stand before her as she unfurled it just for him.

A painful absence glanced through his insides. He thought, unbidden, how he wanted someone to love.

"How are you finding your return from America to England?" he asked.

"When I was last there everyone was reading *Uncle Tom's Cabin*. But I observe that it has followed me here."

"I haven't read it."

"No? It is quite wrenching. All of the people on the right side of things—the abolitionists—have high hopes for it."

"Did you not meet anyone on the wrong side of things?" Lenox asked.

She looked at him curiously. "You are not asking because you . . . you disagree with me?" she said.

"Never in life."

"Oh! Good. I did, though, to answer your question. The population is quite mixed. The pragmatists in Newport, where we passed last summer, have set a target date of 1900. The last slave shall be freed then, they say. Others are afire for it to happen tomorrow."

"What do you think?"

"I don't know—truly I don't."

288

"My second cousin went there, on my mother's side," said Lenox. "Fourth son. He is in South Carolina. He has land, and at least ten slaves. A very amiable person as I recall him—and yet I cannot imagine his life, how he justifies it in his mind! It beggars belief."

Miss Somers glanced across the room, and her hand went to her necklace nervously. "Mr. Lenox," she said quietly, touching her necklace, "may I confide in you?"

"Of course," he replied, surprised.

He did not know if it was going to be on the subject of slavery—did she need money?—but instead she said, "I am engaged to be married."

"Are you! My heartfelt congratulations. The chap is very fortunate, very."

"It is a secret. He lives in Philadelphia. My mother and father will—it is probably only half a step too far to say that they will disown me if I become an American, so we are waiting until he is on firmer footing there. He owns a printing shop for which he has high hopes."

"Like Franklin. I am sorry that you should be separated, though," said Lenox.

"I'm telling you this because Jane, in her foolish kindness—"

He put up a hand. "Miss Somers, say nothing more. I understand."

She looked at him gratefully. "Thank you, Mr. Lenox. You are a gentleman."

He smiled. "If your fellow has a printing shop, I imagine that means he is able to send you very handsome letters even from across the sea."

They talked quietly for some time, and Lenox, after the initial surprise and a pang of disappointment, found that his sadness was not attached to the particular personage of Miss Effie Somers, even with her beautiful hair. It was attached to the idea of a woman who might love him and give him children.

He had—in other words—learned something of himself that evening. That could never be all bad.

When he returned home it was to find the final edition of the late newspaper on his step. He picked it up and read its lead headline.

DUKE OF DORSET RELEASED HOME
Servant's death ruled self-inflicted
Coroner returns verdict of misadventure

CHAPTER THIRTY-SEVEN

Early the next morning—before six—his carriage was winding its way south. He was on his way to Bedlam after all. He couldn't abide seeing the duke ensconced again at Dorset House, master of all he surveyed; not yet, anyhow. There was more to be done about Alexander Craig's death, but he would not be doing it today.

He slept for some of the drive. The journey was quicker than usual because of the time, forty minutes perhaps. As it passed he read the papers by the light of the rising sun. Nobody challenged the narrative that it had been an unfortunate accident. A few made hay of the history of the Tower—the Princes, the nine-day Queen, Anne Boleyn—but that was it.

This was the power of being a duke, he supposed, folding the papers as they came to the gate of the asylum.

When he checked in at Bedlam, Dr. Hansel greeted him with mild surprise. "You are here." The old doctor smiled. They were in a small inner courtyard dominated by an ancient oak tree, putatively the preserve of the doctor since it lay just beside his office—but even here they could hear strange moans and screeches. "What brings you?"

"I wanted to ask in person about Belmont."

Hansel nodded. "Never a patient who attracted my notice. I had a look at his papers after you wired."

There were a thousand patients or more here. "What was his situation?"

"Committed for madness three years ago—delusions of grandeur, believed he was all sorts of people, the Empress of Austria, Beau Brummel, Alexander the Great."

Lenox asked if he could see the papers. "He approached me last week."

"What did he say?"

"That he was held here under false pretenses."

"I see." Hansel frowned. "You can examine his papers, yes. Strange timing. His sister wrote and asked that he be transferred to Edinburgh on the Monday after you left."

"Giving what reason?"

"She had recently married and moved there from London, wished him close."

"Is that sort of move unusual?"

"No, not in the least. In fact I didn't even hear of it—not a decision that would reach my desk. She sent the fees to have him go by post, though, which is rather luxurious."

It also meant two large bailiffs, Lenox imagined. Hansel signaled to a young assistant—brave lad, to work at Bedlam—and asked him to fetch the papers, spelling the name Belmont twice.

"Thank you," Lenox said.

"Of course. Tell me, do you have reason to believe him?"

"I don't know, in truth. But I didn't like how it felt not to come."

"I understand. But you must excuse me—I have patients to see, even early on a weekend."

"Of course," said Lenox.

He sat down in the courtyard. No matter what went on here, the birds in the trees sang their morning songs. He pulled the little fortune-telling book of Shakespeare quotations from his pocket—he felt he was getting the hang of the bard, a bit—and opened it at random.

> *The abuse of greatness is when it disjoins remorse from power.*
> —Julius Caesar

Ten minutes or so later, the boy returned. "Here you are, sir."

"Thank you very much. Say, by chance do you keep the annual naval gazette here? I can't imagine you do."

"Oh, yes. We have quite an extensive library, sir. Would you like to see it?"

"Who uses it?"

"The inmates."

Lenox felt a trickle of panic at the idea of being in a room with them—but he nodded. "If you don't mind, thank you."

The boy led him to a desk with a green banker's lamp. Lenox glanced around nervously, but everyone there seemed absorbed in scholarship. He could imagine what some of them must have done to come to arrive at this station in life, yet all were calm now.

Belmont's file was a disappointment. The fellow had been here for two years. His health was good. He had never caused trouble. There were regular additional monies allotted to him for small luxuries: tobacco, newspapers, and so forth.

Lenox flipped through the pages twice but noticed nothing else.

Then he turned to the long row of annual gazettes to which Hansel's assistant had guided him, bound in blue leather, with gold lettering on their spines. He tried the one from two years before. There was no mention of a Captain Irvington in the index—the name Belmont had said was actually his own. He tried the year before and after. Nothing.

But then he did find something. In the gazette for 1849, this short entry from November:

Captain T. Irvington, Hants, formerly HMS Bella, Livia, Aurelie, *lost in solo hunting expedition from HMS* Victoria *near Storm Bay, Van Diemen's Land, Australia.*

Search fruitless; numerous inlets along "Tasmania," as locals call it; small parties gave up after several days; funeral services held at sea; Lt. Pilon breveted to Captain for remainder of voyage by Rear Adm. Weber.

Lenox felt a rush of excitement. He looked through the previous years' gazettes methodically and found no mention of an Irvington except in the year 1842, when he had received his first captaincy aboard the *Aurelie*.

Was it possible that Irvington had been whisked away, his disappearance covered with this tale, and then pressed into his imprisonment here in England?

He turned back to Belmont's file. Something was bothering him.

Only after studying it carefully did he suddenly realize what it was: His visitor log for the past two years, despite his having this sister so eager to bring him with her to Edinburgh, was entirely empty.

He got up and went to the offices to send a few wires, one to a friend in the naval office, another to the asylum in Edinburgh, and a third to the sister there, return post paid, asking if Belmont had arrived safely.

He felt sure he was onto something. What had Belmont said? Never to let a member of the royal family fall in love with your wife. It seemed ridiculous to imagine an officer of the navy being interned here under a false name simply by royal fiat, but in the same thought he remembered the headline that had greeted him in the paper the night before, and all those clerks and solicitors in their efficient swarm around the duke in the Tower.

It was past nine o'clock by the time Lenox left, and he was hungry. They stopped at a coaching inn in Penge called the Sycamore, which his driver said was good—and though it was relatively quiet, he was right. They sat at a small knotted table together and fell ravenously upon eggs on toast, a piping hot Welsh rarebit, sausages, and strong dark tea, with a measure of whisky for the driver, to aid, he said, his concentration upon the roads.

"That works, does it?" said Lenox, ingenuously.

"Works a treat, sir—works a treat."

It was the first meal they had ever shared, but then there was something democratic about a coaching inn. It was different from a regular public house. A coaching inn was much larger, for a start, and generally located along a main road, since horses could be stabled there. All of them had private dining rooms and sleeping quarters for travelers; unlike a pub, a coaching inn never closed.

Some of the best memories of his childhood

were of a coaching inn. When they were young, his and Edmund's father had taken them up to town by himself once a year for the start of Parliament, so they could sit among the spectators.

There had been something delightful about traveling without their mother, love her though they dearly did. It was more of an adventure with their father. He didn't have any particular rules, for one thing.

They had always stopped at the same inn halfway, the Admiral Nelson. It was a wonderful, uproarious place, full of the scent of beer and coffee and horses. Class vanished. Men of every stripe—he had never seen a woman there—traded stories, those coming from London, those headed there, over tankards of ale and the latest newspapers.

Most of all Charles remembered the food: His father, generally ascetic, had let the boys have whatever they wished.

Edmund's taste tended to mutton, but for Lenox the best sight was the huge black pot, trembling when there were footsteps nearby, that always hung over the fire, full of a delicious stew. It came in a tremendous bowl—what had seemed tremendous at the time, anyway—with hunks of bread and a pitcher of freshly chilled milk.

Edmund and Charles watched how their

father handled himself, as they ate and their horses were watered and fed; he was civil to all, familiar with few, a figure, whether because of his clothes or because someone had whispered his name, of instant significance and respect.

He could so easily recall that awe.

Once he had told them—Lenox had never forgotten—about England's two most famous coaching inns, just a few hundred yards apart on the same road in Buckinghamshire.

Their father, eyes twinkling, said, "They are famous for their tall tales. Have been for centuries now. Nobody goes there expecting the truth—only for a good rattling yarn. And do you know what they're called?"

"What?" Charles and Edmund had said simultaneously.

He smiled. "The Cock and the Bull, lads," he had said. "That is why you shouldn't let anyone at school tell you a cock-and-bull story."

Lenox and his driver finished their breakfast and by ten had returned to Hampden Lane. Lenox had fallen deeply asleep again, full and tired, but apparently the driver was right—the whisky had kept him alert.

He woke up thinking of the dozens of words that he had been scrawling in his notebook before he fell asleep, trying to force his hand to generate what his mind could not: *Corfe, money, Craig, 20, Shakespeare, Vere, terrace,* a loose association. He read over them again as the carriage stood patiently in front of his house.

Something was still wrong. But what? The page wouldn't give it up to him, even after twenty minutes. At last he sighed and went inside.

CHAPTER THIRTY-EIGHT

Graham greeted him. "How was your journey, sir?"

"Puzzling. What have you been doing?"

"Housework, sir. But I have the maps of Kent laid out in the large drawing room, where with your permission I will consult them. Before that, if you have no need for me here, I thought I would find General Pendleton for you, and try one last trick to run Maggie McNeal to ground."

"Thank you, Graham," Lenox said. "If you have time, could you also do a bit of research for me? It would be on a sea captain, dead, by the name of Tankin Irvington. Only if you have time."

Graham was writing the name down. "Of course, sir."

"Thank you, Graham. Incidentally, where is Lancelot?"

"The junior curate at St. Michaels's, a Mr. Wilfrid, has agreed to superintend the three children for the next week, sir. Mr. Templeton has been reprimanded and placed on a month's involuntary leave. He is apparently somewhat susceptible as a gambler."

"Poor Mr. Wilfrid," said Lenox.

"Yes, sir," said Graham, with what amounted

to fervent feeling for him—a slight rise of his eyebrows.

The confused state of Lenox's social status in London was clear from the table in his front hall: two more invitations stylishly withdrawn, but also a dinner invitation to White's from his father's old friend Lord Salisbury, a touching marker of good faith to which Lenox immediately replied in the affirmative.

A detective—and now bound up in the mess of Dorset. Before the summer of 1853 was out he would be an untouchable.

He riffled through the rest of his letters as he walked to his study. But perhaps Salisbury's loyalty stayed in his mind, for when he sat at his desk—through the windows it was turning into a clear, warm June day—he had a thought.

Wasn't it far more likely that Craig had died out of loyalty to the duke than anything else? It was the duke who had given him employment for close to two decades. He might have felt affection for the house's heir, but nobody so serious as Craig had been, both by appearance and by all accounts, would have risked everything for a silly young fool like Corfe.

And there was still the uneasy matter of Corfe's motive.

Solvitur ambulando. It had already been a long morning, but he decided that he would go out into the sunny morning and think it all

301

through. He told Mrs. Huggins (coaxing a cat with milk, in the hallway) that he would be back shortly, then went out and headed in the direction of the river.

He kept a steady, unthinking pace, rather as he did when he rowed. For perhaps twenty minutes he didn't think of anything particular—only watched the city fold and unfold itself around him, the milkman delivering to a café, four boys playing skittles down an alley, an old woman walking with her spine very straight, and behind her a lady's maid holding a King Charles spaniel.

He stopped short at a bookshop on Bond Street and went inside and bought the first volume of *Uncle Tom's Cabin*, which was sold in separate parts.

"Flying off the shelves it is, sir," the lean young clerk told him.

"Is it any good?"

"Haven't read a word of it, sir. Here's three-pence back. Enjoy the day."

He tucked the book into his jacket pocket and went on walking, thinking of Effie Somers and her secret engagement. He liked her. The night before she had told them amusing stories of her time in America, gently caricaturing her father, a diplomat who in his spare time was working on an apparently infinitely proliferating history of the American continent. (It was at nineteen planned volumes thus far—half of a quarter of the first one written.)

When he reached Pall Mall he leaned against a wall and lit his pipe, smoking and studying the comings and goings at the Reform Club. After a moment he reached into his pocket and took out the novel, and soon found himself consumed by its quick-moving story. He read for fifteen or twenty minutes, as long as it took his pipe to run cold.

Just up the street was the Army and Navy Club, and he had the idea that he would go in. In the carpeted front hall he was greeted by a smartly dressed majordomo, clearly ex-military himself, who asked if he could help. There were portraits of various generals running along the walls, and beneath them paintings of famous battle scenes.

"I was hoping to call on General Pendleton," he said.

"The general is not in town at present."

"No? When did he leave?"

"He was last here in April, sir."

Lenox raised his eyebrows. "Perhaps he is staying somewhere else."

The steward laughed. "Impossible, sir."

"I see. Well, thank you."

Lenox went outside, book tucked under his arm. The sand kept slipping through his fingers. He walked the beautiful green stretch of the mall in a deep study, the beds embanking it abloom with tens of thousands of yellow wallflowers and red tulips, tender sprays of purple salvia. The avenue was filled with prams, children, and couples—it was Saturday, a day to be outside.

Then, in the distance, he spotted a woman he momentarily thought was Effie Somers.

He saw when she turned that it wasn't, but it was this that caused him to reverse course, walking rapidly now, toward Dorset House.

He had it. He was all but sure—he had it. That glimpse had resolved all of his doubts.

One he reached Dorset House, he didn't approach it. Instead, he slouched back against the wall facing it, using the tricks that Bonden had taught him, or trying to, anyhow. It helped to be reading something, Bonden had said, and Lenox made it through a long stretch of *Uncle Tom's Cabin*; it helped to be eating something, so he bought some chestnuts from a passing woman; it helped to be smoking.

He moved fifteen feet here or there, and at least did not think he was observed. The same constable—one that he knew to say hello to, in fact, Sam Shepperton—passed by on his beat five times over the course of the next few hours without noticing Lenox once.

He observed the house's comings and goings. The duchess left and returned four times, three of them by carriage. The duke went out just once—for lunch, Lenox presumed—and returned after about ninety minutes. Lord Vere came out twice, once very quickly to run around the corner, returning with a bouquet of flowers, and then a second time to get into his carriage. Busiest of all was Ward, constantly in and out down the road to the Lords, though naturally various servants came and went too many times to count. They took deliveries from the butcher, the upholsterer, and the postman.

Staring at the house for such a long while, Lenox begin to grow almost fond of it. There were six majestic marble archways on its face forming an arcade that reached past the second floor. Above them were large Corinthian columns with rectangular windows between them. At the very height of the house were two enormous round windows, with a statue of the 1st Duke of Dorset standing between them, and statuary representing England and the county of Dorset around him.

Who made such a thing! It was glorious and absurd in equal measure; it belonged in the deepest woodlands of Pembrokeshire, not *here,* taking up a hundred feet on the river in the most densely populated city on earth.

But then, it always helped to have built in the year 1550—plenty of space back then, 250-odd years before they even conceived of Buckingham Palace.

He stood there as the long summer hours passed, watching. By the time the sun began to glow over the river he had finished the first third of *Uncle Tom's Cabin* and was desperate to eat something other than chestnuts—and he was very tired.

At four o'clock, he left. He knew it all now. It was just a matter of braiding the strings together. He felt exhausted, but triumphant.

He hailed a cab and went to Scotland Yard. Sir Richard Mayne, fortunately, worked seven days a week, was known for it.

He greeted Lenox warily, as if expecting to be criticized for the duke's release. "Well?" he said. "What is it?"

"I know what happened," Lenox said.

"What do you mean?"

"I mean that the coroner was right. The duke is innocent. Listen—will you travel down to Dorchester with me tomorrow morning? I do not feel equipped to go alone."

Mayne looked at him inquisitively. "Dorchester? Could one of the inspectors go? You may have your pick."

Lenox shrugged. "If you prefer," he said. "But it is the Duke of Dorset we are discussing. The Queen herself intervened in his release."

Mayne nodded. "Very well. Dorchester."

CHAPTER THIRTY-NINE

They consulted the timetable in Bradshaw's. There were thirty trains to Dorchester from London each day. They picked the earliest one, agreeing to meet on Platform 19 at Waterloo at five past six o'clock the next morning.

Lenox went home and had a quick dinner, doubtfully enlivened by a long monologue from Lancelot, which might, had he been presenting it to the Royal Academy, say, have been titled "A Schoolboy's Field Guide to the Practical Uses of Laxatives." From the sound of it there was not a beak at Eton who had gone unpunished by Lancelot and his two apparently likewise Luciferian friends, Mott and Wutherington-Fassett.

"Except the Head," said Lancelot, wistfully. "We can never get near his tea. He keeps it in a flask."

"That is how you get to be Head."

"They always say there must be something 'going the rounds,' which is awfully funny, don't you think? The way they bolt from their desks in the middle of a lesson."

"I do not think it is funny," said Lenox. He made a mental note not to drink anything whose decanting he had not personally supervised for the rest of his cousin's visit. "Did Templeton's horse win, by the way?"

"Dead last," said Lancelot cheerfully, and returned to his game pie with his customary gusto.

"I suppose the lesson there is not to gamble."

"The lesson," Lancelot corrected him, mouth full, "is not to trust a scrub like Templeton."

Lenox gave up. He finished his supper and soon was upstairs. Though it was barely eight o'clock, he fell immediately and deeply asleep.

The next morning he arrived at Waterloo early.

It was only five years old, this rail station, fresh and clean—it had replaced Nine Elms, though that superannuated terminus had remained open for the convenience of one cantankerous young person: Queen Victoria, who liked the privacy of traveling from a vacated station.

Lenox bought a cup of tea and a soft chocolate crescent roll, still warm, from a stallholder, then stood on Platform 19, watching through the enormous windows as the mist rose over London's uneven buildings.

Soon enough Mayne strode up the platform hailing Lenox, accompanied by his highly efficient secretary, Wilkinson. "You're sure of this?"

"Quite sure," said Lenox.

"On we go then."

The first-class carriage was comfortable;

the trip took two hours and twenty minutes, during which time Lenox consumed much of the second volume of *Uncle Tom's Cabin*, which he had had a footman run out to buy for him. As they were pulling into Dorchester Station, he pulled his little leather book out for luck and let it fall open.

In nature there's no blemish but the mind; none can be call'd deform'd but the unkind.
—Twelfth Night

He frowned. No idea what that one meant.

At the station they hired a carriage. They were in it for around forty minutes, until roughly twenty-five past nine, before they reached an immense black gate. They had arrived at Dorset Castle.

Except that it then took a long and winding drive down a tree-lined alley, ten minutes in its own right, to reach the building itself. Only at the last instant did it come into view—beautiful, isolated, a working wreck.

It was built as an extension from the partially ruined foundations of a very ancient castle. On one side there was a high turreted tower, but more recent architects had built behind it: two long sides in similar gray stone, around an open, grassy courtyard. It looked something like a college at Oxford, except the wrong color. To the west there were miles of wild gardens and forest—the opposite of the tamed and mown beauty at Lenox House, but immensely bigger, and impressive as only nature left to itself can be.

They knocked upon the heavy oak door. There was no answer. A quick sortie from Wilkinson revealed that the real front door was around the side (the private private door), where evidently the living quarters were situated.

A dignified, silver-haired butler answered. "May I help you?" he said with a face full of perfect incuriosity, though he must have heard the carriage coming for at least the last five minutes.

Mayne produced his royal seal. "We are with Scotland Yard. May we come in?"

The butler examined the identification and then surveyed the three of them unflappably— clothes, faces—before finally saying, "Excuse me for a moment."

They stood and watched the door close in front of them. They waited for about a minute, and then it swung open.

It was Lady Violet Vere. "Mr. Lenox?" she said.

"How do you do, Lady Violet," he said, bowing.

There was a moment of confusion upon her face, and after that—she was a bright woman—

a moment of realization, then one of resignation.

That quickly! She had a rapid mind; she had outfoxed everyone more than once.

"Come in," she said with poised courtesy. "Come in."

When Lenox had stood before Dorset House in London the day before, he had watched every person who came and went—Corfe, the Duke, the Duchess—but in that time he had not seen Lady Violet once. This had been the confirmation of his suspicions that he needed.

She led them into a dark room full of heavy old furniture, its roughly coursed stone walls decorated with medieval hunting tapestries. It was cool here, by ancient design; the warmth of the day could not penetrate the walls.

She offered them tea, which they accepted. When they had sat down near the empty fireplace (there was a skeleton staff here, as she told them, but you wouldn't have guessed— Lenox never saw the same face twice as people tramped in and out of the room bearing tea, scones, cakes, and sandwiches), she gathered her skirts under her.

Why was she not beautiful? The world was treacherous hard on women, he thought. For Lenox, the whole impression was his only means of judging these things, really. He knew, or did not know, whether a person appeared attractive to his eye. If he focused he could see that Lady

Violet's eyes were too close together and too small, her chin and nose too sharp, her cheeks low, her forehead high.

He knew his own looks—he was about the average run of the gentlemen of his class, he reckoned—and had the luxury of thinking about them rarely.

For Lady Violet Vere, by contrast, born to everything, absolutely everything, *except* beauty, and in a world where even for an heiress it must matter—he could only imagine how the fact had racked her days, her weeks, her years with self-doubt and self-hatred.

At last the tea was all set before them, she having poured four cups and added sugar and cream as directed, an ideal host, and Lenox could speak.

"You shot Mr. Craig, I think, Lady Violet?" he said.

She took a careful sip of her tea and then set it down with its saucer, which had been in her left hand. "Yes, that's so," she said.

"Your father was not there?"

"He was not. Mr. Craig was sleeping in the closet, it would seem, to surprise intruders. I went to get the portrait. He surprised me."

"You know about the portrait, then."

She looked at Mayne, who was wide-eyed and silent. In much of the world he was a great man, but she was the daughter of a duke, and her glance toward him was dismissive. "Yes," she said.

"Why were you carrying a gun?" asked Lenox.

"I wasn't. Craig was. I shoved him and it went off, just like that."

Lenox nodded. It had been a detail of great uneasiness to him that the wound the duke had supposedly inflicted on Craig went *upward* through his chest, since the duke was the taller of the two men. But Craig would have had six inches or so on Lady Violet, and if the gun was between them, a stray bullet might easily have been fired upward.

For all that, he was not sure still that it was a stray bullet.

"Did he know it was you?"

"I don't think he did," said Lady Violet. "I did not know it was him. I thought it might be you, or a police officer my father had hired. I was scared."

"I'm very confused," said Mayne.

Lady Violet took a sip of tea. "I started out with a very simple plan. As it happens it has turned into a nightmare."

"You wanted to steal your father's portraits?" said Mayne.

Lenox intervened. "There is reason to believe that the two portraits, together, hold the clue to a very significant treasure."

"But you are—"

The commissioner did not finish his sentence, but his meaning was clear. She was privy to immense wealth. Hundreds of thousands of acres in any direction were rented to pay for the glories of her life, in immemorial custom. Out upon the heaths men raised crops and paid their duty out of them to the duke, and those sheaves of corn, those bushels of potatoes, transmuted magically into silver dinner plates, ruby necklaces, kid gloves, boxes at the opera. Ball gowns, taffeta, silk.

The tarnished ring on a gold chain that never left her neck.

It was in fact Miss Somers who had unwittingly forced upon Lenox the revelation that Lady Violet might be the prime mover behind the whole mystery. Lady Jane's friend had spoken of her American courtship, and her hand had gone unconsciously to the ring on a slim gold chain around her own neck—a ring not very different from Lady Violet's. When he had seen her doppelgänger the afternoon before, he had connected the two.

"I believe Lady Violet is engaged," Lenox said gently, "but that her parents will not approve the match. Thus it was that she needed money."

She looked at him. "Yes, that's the way it stands," she said, looking at him coldly, daring him to go on.

"Her grandfather had once told her of a

treasure that might be had from the paintings she stole." Mayne looked puzzled and sat silent. The word "treasure" sounded foolish even to his ears, but Lenox pushed ahead. "The question now, as I see it, is whether Sir Richard will arrest you."

CHAPTER FORTY

The staircases in medieval castles were all identical—narrow and spiraling upward to the right. This design served two practical purposes. First, they were slower to ascend; second, they blocked the right arm on ascent but freed it on descent, meaning that only someone coming down from the keep had the use of his sword.

In the sieges of the very old days, they said, some unfortunate improvised troop of left-handers always had to make the first assault upon the stairs.

Lady Violet's rooms were in the castle's keep, she said, not in the modern wing. Sir Richard Mayne insisted that they had to accompany her as she gathered her things, to prevent some act of self-harm. She was to be taken in, Mayne said, and held until they consulted the duke.

They did not enter her actual bedchamber but lurked just outside, watching her consult with her maid. Lenox felt, to use Lancelot's words, a scrub, standing in the doorway.

Nor did he like Mayne's plan. "Are we to let her walk into the streets of London?"

Sir Richard turned full upon him. He had a great deal of authority he had suppressed in front of Lady Violet, and he let the store loose upon the young detective. "I suppose we are, Lenox, yes."

"That seems wrong."

"It certainly does."

They agreed then. The Queen made no intercessory requests about the fate of the prostitute who put a knife into the ribs of a man assaulting her. And it would take longer than they had now to ponder the father who would not allow his daughter to marry to suit her happiness, yet was willing to risk a trial for murder rather than let her come to public shame.

"I think of Craig," Lenox murmured.

"He will not wake up tomorrow morning either way."

Lenox could not let it go. "Is that the point of justice?"

"That is the reality of justice," said Mayne. "You would call upon it yourself if it were your brother or your nephew in question, I reckon."

And there he had Lenox. Every aristocrat with his politics wanted greater fairness, but they went on sending their sons to Oxford. How would any of it ever change?

Lenox fell silent and set to wondering about that tarnished ring around Violet's neck. What declarations had come with it, and how sincere they were. Most of all who had given it.

But she refused to say. After having packed, she was very becoming in following their instructions, in attending to their plans—she would be confined to Dorset House in London, with a constable—but would not add a word to what she had confessed.

She did ask how Lenox had known. "Was it just the ring? Such a minor error. Though I suppose it is out of keeping with my habits that it should be tarnished and made of nickel."

He shook his head. "You overplayed your hand, my lady. When I realized that I could find neither the maid Maggie McNeal nor General Pendleton anywhere in London, I knew that you had tried to misdirect me."

She looked at him. "I see."

"Nor could I, for the life of me, make any of it stick to Corfe."

"No, he is an innocent sort, my brother."

When they reached the gravel courtyard, Mayne asked if he might retire inside before their return trip, which they would take in her ladyship's carriage. Wilkinson was a little ways off, smoking.

Quickly, Lenox said, "The poem—you have misread it."

Lady Violet looked at him expressionlessly. "Is that so?"

"The clue is not in Shakespeare's portrait."

She studied him, then turned away in the gravel courtyard and touched the nose of one of her horses, feeding him a cube of sugar from her pocket. "What is the clue, then?"

"Were you planning to leave the country while your father was in the Tower?"

She turned back to him. "What a contemptible idea. Of course not."

"Yet you would have run away from him if you had found and sold the play."

"To the Americas or India, yes."

"Who is the young man?"

She ignored the question. "I could not live upon a single strand of pearls, like some heroine in a novelette. My own possessions are pretty but minor."

"But the play . . ."

She rubbed the horse's nose. "I consulted a friend who said that the bidding between Oxford and Cambridge and the British Library would be fierce. And there are these Americans, you know, coming pretty hardy into the fray. The Astor family has unlimited wealth, they say. Unlimited. Soon enough people like you will be marrying them."

"People like me," Lenox murmured, and smiled. "How much did you think you could fetch?"

"I was told I could be guaranteed a minimum of thirty thousand pounds in a private auction. My father need never have known."

"Your grandfather told you the legend?"

"He told us a great deal, yes. He was a wonderful person."

"Corfe was in on this scheme, then?"

"My brother?" she said. "No."

She turned away, walking a few steps to the third horse in her cortege of four. So much money around her! Each of these horses was flawless, twice the price of a house. Yet she needed her very own thousand pounds a year to live happily—even in love.

"What about Craig? He helped you?"

"He and I have always been friends."

"And now he is gone."

She brushed the remaining sugar off her hands. "Excuse me," she said, and stepped into the carriage.

They spent much of the ride back to London in silence, an unreadable silence on the young woman's part, a respectful one on Mayne's and Lenox's. Wilkinson rode on the box. The horses pulled them swiftly and surely—perfect beasts.

When they had arrived within the limits of London, Lenox begged Mayne to let him off at the Wilcombe Tavern. When asked why, he said he had some business to conduct here. He would meet them at Dorset House.

Receiving no farewell from Lady Violet, Lenox watched the carriage go.

Then he sprinted inside and asked for the hostler.

A grizzled old gentleman with squinting eyes met him. "I need a horse, your fastest."

"Three shillings and a five-pound bill of debt for collateral. Standard."

"Done."

Within a few minutes Lenox was in the saddle. He rode as hard as he could, aiming for the center of London.

It was a rough ride over uneven ground, and before long both man and horse were sweating. But they made excellent time—slipping through small spaces, easily outpacing the carriages that passed each other in a handsome, elegant trot along the road, carriages like the one carrying Mayne and Lady Violet.

His destination was Dorset House. He needed at least fifteen minutes, and when he pulled up in front, he thought he probably had it. He handed the reins of the horse, a fine youthful mare called Pepper, to one of Dorset's own stableboys.

Now it all depended on whether Lord Vere was home.

He was. He greeted Lenox, who was hot and sweaty, with some surprise and offered him a lemon ice, or a glass of water. The detective, though he was desperate for a sip of water, declined.

"Time is short," he said to Vere. They were in a drawing room, lined with oils of clouds by Constable. Yet another room new to him. Would this house never give up all its secrets! "Listen

321

to me, Corfe. I admire you and Mr. Craig for helping your sister."

"Excuse me?"

"It may still be possible to ensure that her name is not brought before the public, which I imagine to be your wish, as it is your father's. But you must tell me all."

Corfe, who was again impeccably afternoonified, in black boots and a pink-and-white striped waistcoat under his navy suit, drew himself taller for a moment.

Then his face crumpled. He was not a very bright fellow. It was best, the thought flashed through Lenox's mind, that a king or a duke be either very stupid or very brilliant. No other kind of brain would admit for the paradoxical absurdities and dignities of the position. Corfe would pull it off well; his father was perhaps just a bit too clever.

"That damnable Walters," Corfe muttered, sinking back into a chair.

Walters. He knew that he had just learned the name of the gentleman who proposed to marry Lady Violet. That was worth the price of hiring Pepper on its own.

"You do not approve of the match?" Lenox asked.

"He is not a gentleman." Sometimes silence was best. Lenox let Corfe's troubled eyes turn away. "Little more than a decent shot. What a devilish thing that he should be so handsome!"

"Mm."

"We lost a good gamekeeper out of it, worse still."

A gamekeeper! That explained it. For a gamekeeper Lady Violet Vere was going to find and sell a lost play by William Shakespeare—her family's great imagined contribution to England, its great imagined treasure.

If Walters was indeed quite so handsome, though, Lenox could see why his appeals to Lady Violet had been irresistible, given that she was already up on the shelf, a spinster at age thirty.

It was also clear why the duke had forbidden the match.

Less clear to him was why Craig and Corfe had been persuaded to conspire against their father and benefactor, respectively.

"Hard on your sister," Lenox offered.

He was keenly aware of the time, but also keenly aware that he mustn't press Lord Vere. "Yes," the heir said. "Hard on her. Listen here—how did you discover I was involved?"

He hadn't. But it had struck him as simply too unlikely that Lord Vere's fever had coincided so exactly with the period of the thefts from the duke's study, and that the painting had ended up in his room. That was the sum of it. Still, he felt a bit of pride. His instincts must be improving.

He looked out through the window, expecting at any minute the carriage bearing Mayne and Lady Violet.

"That doesn't matter now. But I would like to know how the three of you devised this plot. Your grandfather told you about the play, of course. When did Lady Violet finally decide to take action?"

Corfe looked at him. "Two weeks ago. Walters is leaving for South Africa next month, if he cannot have Violet." He shook his head. "In the end we made a choice. It's a bad fare that Craig paid for it with his life."

Lenox nodded, still dreadfully thirsty, but aware that he was about to hear the whole story at last. "Go on," he said in a measured voice.

CHAPTER FORTY-ONE

Lord Vere looked down at the drink he had in his hand, a glass of amber something—perhaps brandy. "Pater was always devilishly awkward on Violet," he said.

Pater: Lenox was returned to his schooldays, when that was what the boys called their fathers, and he realized that in many ways Corfe, never touched by the world, remained a schoolboy still.

"How so?"

"It was a long seven years before I came along, you know. Hell for her, and everyone, that she wasn't a boy. The next in line for the dukedom is a distant cousin, the Earl of Coverdale, so it would have gone out of the family, essentially. Including the secret of the portrait—and you have seen how mad that has driven my father, a sane man. But then I came. I was something of a miracle."

"I see," said Lenox.

The window had fully half of his attention. Let them have been snarled in London traffic, Mayne and Lady Violet!

"It was my sister who loved me the most. My mother is a very responsible woman, her good works, the charities, a lady of great distinction of course, and . . ." He trailed off, looking to the side, and the unsaid opened up a whole vista onto the coldness of the mother's character. "Still, it was Violet who sent me packages when I went away to school at eight. And mended my trousers when I was home on hols. Wiped my tears."

He laughed scornfully at the boy he had been, after he said this, but to Lenox it was clear that the words carried deep feeling. "A very good sister," he said quietly.

"Oh yes, good as gold. Kind to Craig, too. Made him part of the family, you know. Had him play Father Christmas for me, which he claimed to hate, but you know. Pater is a bit of a tough nut, and Craig never had a family of his own. He loved her, too. We both loved her more because we knew nobody would marry her. Finally when it came down to it, we decided to do something for her, he and I. Craig thought of the ruse of my illness and putting the painting under my bed. Not just under my bed—he was very bright, old Craig. Christ. I still can't credit it that he's gone."

"And you had known about Mr. Walters."

"Oh, Walters! Yes. Yes. It was the subject of a great deal of discussion—within these walls. It will kill Father to hear it get out, if it does. He would rather hang in the Tower ten times over."

"That is why I am amazed that your sister decided to defy him."

"She felt she had a last chance at happiness. And she is such a sensible, engaging person—but she is . . . is thirty, you know."

Lenox nodded. His tone implied that she might just as profitably have been ninety. "Of course. Was—"

But at that moment there was a loud sound outside, four horses stopping at the door. Lenox rose and excused himself, saying that he would check to see if it was Sir Richard. But that was not his intention; he knew the house fairly well by this time, and he slipped back to the stables and fetched his horse. Once Lord Vere and his sister spoke, he knew, he would be unwelcome at Dorset House.

It was all clear to him now, regardless. Only two questions remained. One would never be answered—whether she had shot Craig on purpose. The other was whether they would find the lost play.

He rode home, gratefully took a sip from the barrel of water the servants kept just outside the back door, then asked his coachman to water and feed Pepper and return her to the Wilcombe.

He went inside, dusty and tired. Graham and Lancelot were both out, as was Mrs. Huggins, who was, according to the chambermaid Clarissa, who looked terrified at her temporary elevation in station, pricing cloth.

"Cloth? For what?" asked Lenox.

"I don't right know, sir," she said, trembling.

"I'm not mad," said Lenox carefully.

"Mad, sir!" she blushed to the roots of her hair.

She was a microscopically small and delicate person, holding a broom that as she shrank back came to be about twice her height.

He sometimes forgot that the staff must think his line of work very curious. "Angry, I mean!" he clarified quickly. "I am not angry."

"Oh."

"Nor am I mad."

"No, sir," she said, but looked unsure.

"Are you the Irish one?"

Mrs. Huggins suspected everyone of being Irish, and Lenox, in a fit of insubordination not long before, had insisted that she hire an Irish maid. That had been only a few weeks before, and he barely recognized this young person.

"Yes, sir."

"Well, you're doing capitally, from all I hear," he said. This wasn't strictly a lie, since he hadn't heard anything. "Just capitally. Carry on."

"Oh, thank you, sir," she said, with impossible gratitude, and went downstairs as if there were a fire to put out there.

Lenox, for his part, went into his study, where he removed his jacket. He sat down in his chair, looking out through the windows. The shop across Hampden Lane—what had been the cobbler's until that spring—had new lettering going up in its windows.

"Chaffanbrass," he read out loud to himself.

Sounded like a butcher—he hoped not, because

of the smell. He was tired, but he began notes on the case, trying to write down all he could remember of his conversation with Corfe. Still, his eyes kept wandering to the window, the empty storefront, and he leaned back farther in his leather chair, and it was warm, and his eyes were so heavy . . .

What rest could do for a soul! When Lenox felt himself stirring half an hour or so later, lying comfortably tilted back in his thickly upholstered desk chair, he let himself linger in that half-state of sleep a little while longer, his eyes closed. He felt the coolness of the high-ceilinged room and the warmth of the day even each other out. He felt the air go in and out of his nostrils.

What a creature one was, after all, it turned out—thirsty, tired, and then to drink, to sleep, how joyful it was to be alive in a body some-times.

He slowly let his eyes open. A noise had woken him. Something to do with the front door perhaps, but he could tell, through the innumerable small specks of comprehension that every person registers without naming, that it was nothing to do with him. He let himself turn to the street, body quiet, eyes heavy still, though open now. He watched the people pass, experiencing that dispassionate, affectionate, removed sensation of one who has just woken up. He had been to the other world; it was no bad thing to sit here, between ways, for another moment.

Finally he yawned, stretched his arms, shook his head, and stood up. He retrieved his notebook from the floor and went out into the hallway.

The noise had been a telegram, it turned out.

It was from the asylum in Edinburgh, and was quite to the point.

No patient of name Belmont received here STOP Nor Irvington STOP William Wellburn

He felt a chill run through him. Wellburn was the head physician there.

As he stood there, contemplating this telegram, trying to remember Belmont more vividly in his mind, Mrs. Huggins came in.

This was odd, as she would usually have entered by the servants' door. "Good evening, Mrs. Huggins," he said.

"Good evening, Mr. Lenox. Please excuse my intrusion. I had hoped to offer you some forewarning that—"

Behind her burst through Lancelot, who looked, first, thoroughly pleased with himself, indeed was whistling, and, second, a wreck, with two swollen red eyes, a split lip, and a gash across his cheek.

"What happened?" asked Lenox.

330

"I got in a fight!" said Lancelot excitedly.

"What, with a bear?"

"It was with Lord Decimus Spate, sir," said Mrs. Huggins. "He was riding in the park. Master Lancelot called him a name, I fear."

"Decimus Spate?"

"Yes, sir."

"But he's twenty-two! He did this to a child?"

"It was a very bad name," said Mrs. Huggins. "I have spoken to Lancelot about that."

Lancelot placed himself in front of Mrs. Huggins importantly. "Here's how it was. He shoved Wutherington-Fassett out of the way while we were playing skittles in Hyde Park—reckless as you like—and I called him a pompous fool—I thought that sounded good—and he said always to make way for horses—and I said I would, but he was a horse's *ass,* so I wouldn't—and he said well didn't I think I ought to apologize—and I said I did, to horse's asses, for confusing them with him—and that was a pretty good one to get off—and he said who was I—and I said who was *he* and why was he so fat—"

"Oh, Lancelot," said Mrs. Huggins despairingly, lovingly.

Lenox sighed. It was true that Decimus Spate had begun eating twenty-two years before and permitted himself only very brief cessations of the activity since—and was very sensitive about the results.

"Then he shoved Wutherington-Fassett again—and I called him the name—and he got down from the horse—and I caught him a lovely poke in the ribs before he knew what was on—and he set upon me—but altogether, Mrs. Huggins, wouldn't you say I got the best of it? How would you rank it?"

"For shame, Master Lancelot," she said.

"I thought *you* were pricing cloth," Lenox said.

The housekeeper's brow darkened. "Is that what the Irish girl said?"

Lenox threw up his hands. "I am going to my club to dine. Put ice and raw beef on this child's face—and you'd better wire Eustacia and say he's been in a fight, but he's all right. Lancelot, you'll write a letter of apology—"

"Never!"

"—tomorrow. Good-bye."

He left in a reasonable semblance of ire. But Lenox had always hated the Spates—Decimus himself was a great lump of unthinking brutish aristocratic matter—and before he went, he whispered to Mrs. Huggins to give him something soft to eat, like Italian pudding.

He wondered, as he walked briskly down Hampden Lane, if one day he would be a father after all, and the thought filled him with such terror that he almost forgot the telegram he had in his pocket.

CHAPTER FORTY-TWO

He dined at one of his clubs, the Beargarden. Arriving there, he found that his reputation went on pinging about like a bullet in a steel drum; now he was known to be Dorset's only confidant, privy to great secrets, engaged upon important missions—every variety of thing—and found himself once more in prestige.

He sat to eat a beefsteak, string beans, mashed potatoes, and gravy with a few of the people he actually liked, younger friends, sharing a jug of house claret with them.

At about nine o'clock, when he was in the midst of a hand of cards, the porter came in and said that a Mr. Graham attended upon his leisure in the servants' waiting room. Lenox went down to the basement straightaway.

It was a convivial and comfortably furnished chamber, the servants' waiting room, where the valets bided their time, many of them playing penny hands of whist and slanging their masters to each other, usually in varying states of progressive drunkenness. You saw every type of the genus here. There was a dull, burly, fish-eyed, suspicious boulder of a man, who served the very dull, burly, fish-eyed, and suspicious Lord Varling, a fellow not past thirty and exceedingly

333

rich, who nonetheless lived his life in a state of continual ill temper. A lank, dusty chap named Pole—not below sixty-five in years—waited upon the sprightly Lucan Wells, one of the dandiest chaps in London. Half a dozen or so others were sprinkled about, none of them sober; in their midst sat Graham, legs crossed, arm along the back of the sofa, but alert. He rose when Lenox entered.

"Hello," said Lenox.

"Good evening, sir," said Graham.

"How did you find me?"

"Oh, I guessed, sir."

He said this casually, but Graham had an almost occult ability to predict where in London Lenox would be at a given moment. "You ought to guess the horses for Lancelot."

"Or Mr. Templeton, sir."

"Or Mr. Templeton! I wonder what they do with curates gone bad. Anyhow, come into the smoking room."

This was just up the front hall, a room to which members could invite their valets, or outside guests they wished to keep at arm's length. The upstairs was more restricted. As they crossed the lobby, Lenox nodded at the younger of the two doormen, who was about ninety-five.

The smoking room—a crimson-red chamber, encircled with sofas, hung with oils of various dead gentlemen—was empty. "There are two things, sir," said Graham. "First, this."

He handed Lenox a fresh copy of the *Times*, probably not more than twenty minutes from press. Lenox read its bold-faced lead article with care. Then he sighed. "It was to be expected," he said.

The *Times* reported more fully than earlier papers had that the Duke of Dorset had been cleared by an expedited coroner's report of any wrongdoing in the death of Mr. A. A. Craig, late of the Scots Guards. He would not stand trial.

No mention appeared of Lord Vere, Lady Violet, the duchess, a missing painting, or, of course, Shakespeare.

Lenox contemplated the article, which was reliable confirmation of what had seemed all but inevitable, and then told Graham about his long morning, culminating in his meeting with Corfe. The valet listened carefully, then said, "What will the young lady do, sir?"

"I cannot say."

"Are you not disturbed by her account of the night?"

Lenox looked at Graham wryly. "I am, as it happens. But what is the second piece of news?"

"Ah, yes, sir." He handed over two pages of handwritten notes. "In reference to Captain Tankin Irvington."

"Oh, thank you! That is useful. I have not told you why I asked."

Lenox explained this situation briefly to Graham, too, and the telegram he had received from Edinburgh earlier. Then he turned to the investigation Graham had done for him.

Irvington had been the only child of a prosperous seagoing family. He had cousins but no close relations. He had also had a wife: Mrs. Eliza Irvington. No issue. She had removed herself upon news of his death from the naval city of Portsmouth to Hampstead, in London.

"Was there an address for her?"

"Not in the naval archives, sir. Only a mention of Hampstead."

"No brothers, no sisters, no children, no living parents or grandparents, a cousin who is a lieutenant on a ship that is probably in the China Sea as we speak," muttered Lenox, more to himself than Graham. "His body was never even found."

The simplest identity to wipe off the face of the earth. Was it in fact Belmont's true one?

He and Graham walked home through the breezy summer evening, discussing both cases. What remained of Dorset's, of course, was the play. Lenox and Graham agreed that they would research the churchyards that evening—all those matching the geographical restrictions of the poem and dating back to at least the year 1600.

He would call on Dorset House the next morning, he thought, though he had no idea at all of the reception he would receive there.

At home they found Lancelot and Lady Jane playing checkers in the drawing room. "Look at this poor fellow!" said Lady Jane, rising and giving Lenox her hand to clasp. "Set upon by ruffians— and now losing very humiliatingly at checkers."

"I am not!" said Lancelot hotly.

"I count that nine games in a row this time."

"Have you ever won yet?" asked Lenox.

It was the wrong question—and even a hardened criminal of a twelve-year-old was still, after all, twelve. His eyes grew large and his face started to tremble.

"Oh, Charles! Shame!" said Lady Jane. "You're doing wonderfully, Lancelot. You almost won two games ago. And after the day you've had. Do you need more sherbet?"

"Yes, please," he said pitifully.

She went to the door to poke her head out for Mrs. Huggins. As soon as she was out of sight, Lancelot instantly reshaped his face into a sort of diabolical grin, and Lenox realized that he had been fooled once more.

He called to Jane to cancel the sherbet. "He's pretending!" Lenox said.

"Do be quiet, Charles," she said distractedly.

"Do," said Lancelot in a quiet voice, nodding solemnly at him.

"I'll get you for this," said Lenox.

"Get him for what?" said Lady Jane, who had come back into the room. "Leave him alone. Decimus Spate, that barrel of lard—I have half a mind to go and speak to his mother."

"You are only four years older than he!" said Lenox.

"I am a married and respectable person," said Lady Jane.

"That's true," said Lancelot.

"Shut up," said Lenox.

"Charles! You'll teach him the most ill-mannered kinds of—what would Eustacia say?"

Lady Jane waited until Lancelot's sherbet arrived. Then she asked Lenox if they might have a word in his study—she would return to finish their game, she promised Lancelot. She and Lenox crossed the hall. He had a few telegrams and numerous letters on his desk, but none of them were of immediate interest; none related to either Dorset or Belmont.

"Is everything all right?" Lenox asked her.

"I have led you up a garden path," said Jane, full of regret. "It is not Violet's fault at all, nor yours, obviously, but mine. She is engaged to be married. It's a secret."

"Oh! I see."

"Are you terribly disappointed?"

Lenox let a chivalrous amount of time pass. "Perhaps a bit. But it will be a quick recovery. We were not so very close."

She grabbed his hand, so firmly that it almost hurt. "I will find you someone."

He laughed. "Unfortunately I have very little doubt of it, knowing you."

"I promise."

"Is your aunt Moggs through her twelve and one?"

This was a recently widowed relative of Jane's, aged about seventy, and among the most unpleasant people alive; her primary pastime was sitting at the window of her cottage in Hampshire with a shotgun and firing it into the air when anyone came close, up to and including her ill-starred postman. (Lenox's question was whether her husband—whose grave must have felt a merciful place—had been dead for the twelve months and one day that a widow was required to dress in full mourning.)

"Oh, be quiet," said Lady Jane. "No, I have in mind—don't dismiss it out of hand—Miss Auburn, who will come out in the fall. She is young, but she is so lovely, Charles! And so accomplished, mature beyond her years."

It was no use at all to tell her that it was no use. In fact he had not even quite formed that knowledge into something he actively knew. It merely lived somewhere within him, forgotten. So he consented to hear more about Miss Auburn and her accomplishments, and eventually they recrossed the hall in full and fluid conversation.

CHAPTER FORTY-THREE

The Duke of Dorset was ensconced once more in his private private study. What could be more appropriate? The front hall of Dorset House was as busy as a village square on Saturday night, everyone either leaving a card (the Prime Minister's stood at the top of the gleaming sterling rack) or, in the case of a few select friends, the Earl of Cadogan for instance, accepting an escort into the library, where they could smoke and read the ironed papers while they waited to see His Grace.

Ward greeted Lenox. "He asked that you be seen straight up."

"This is quite a palaver," Lenox said, as they walked up the stairs, leaving numerous people behind them.

"Yes." He leaned confidentially close. "He has gotten me a place as the Prime Minister's second secretary. As thanks for sticking with him, he said."

"That's a coup for you, Theo," said Lenox. "Congratulations."

He had leapfrogged several intervals on his way to a seat in Parliament. Lenox was glad on his behalf. "Kind of him, yes," said Ward with satisfaction.

The duke's door was open, and Lenox caught a glimpse of him before he knew they were there. He was bent over his desk, reading intently.

Dorset looked up at their entry. "Ah, hello. Thank you, Ward. Please give us a few minutes."

"Of course, Your Grace."

Lenox sat down after the duke had gestured at a chair. There were now once again eight paintings on the wall behind him. Lenox had sent the missing one back that morning.

"All resolved, then, Your Grace," he said to Dorset. "Mostly."

The duke's handsome, middle-aged face again bore a distinctive superiority. Lenox bridled against it; he disliked the whole thing.

The duke did not respond for quite a while. When he did, it was to say, "You are now aware of several very closely guarded facts about my family."

"You ought to have hired a worse detective if you didn't wish it so."

"You are the only one I know of."

"I could find you a worse."

"Ha."

The duke was in no mood for banter. He fell silent, but his imperious stare had lost some of its power over Lenox. "May I ask where Lady Violet is?" Lenox asked.

"You took advantage of my son's open nature yesterday, Mr. Lenox."

"I thought for all our sakes that it was best I learn the full details of the matter, Your Grace. I still do not feel sure that I have them."

"What do you mean?"

Lenox shrugged. "There is a great deal of talk in all these accounts, Your Grace, of a scuffle with Mr. Craig. There is also the presence of a pistol, something I find more surprising still. Need I elaborate?"

"Perhaps you had better."

He didn't want to. So he asked again where Lady Violet was, and Mr. Walters. "I wonder if perhaps they are bound for some foreign shore together."

"In asking that question you go beyond your brief, Mr. Lenox."

"Well?" said Lenox.

He was in a hard-hearted mood, and he met the duke's stare with cold eyes.

What he suspected was this: that Craig had not been in league with Corfe and Violet at all, but that his loyalty had remained to the duke all along; and that he had died for it. How? Only those who had been in the room knew. Perhaps there had been a set-to. Perhaps Violet had shot him in cold blood when he tried to stop her from taking the painting, and she and Corfe had agreed to claim that Craig was part of it all along. Perhaps the truth lay somewhere between these possibilities.

But Lenox knew in his bones that something closer to murder than manslaughter had occurred, and he also knew that nobody would be punished for it.

"My daughter is traveling to the Continent."

"To be married?" Lenox asked.

"Stop pushing me."

"Or what?" said Lenox angrily. "Where is your loyalty to Craig, I ask you? If someone shot my valet—my friend—Graham, I would damn well push to find out who had done it."

"You are not a father."

"Nor am I a liar."

The duke stood up. "What did you say?"

"You heard me."

Lenox remained seated, and they stayed in that position, staring at each other. The duke had, on his side, the immutable social laws of their society. On his, Lenox had the truth—the truth about Lady Violet, about Shakespeare. Even about Corfe, who was dim but sharp enough to lie for his sister about Craig's involvement.

The duke at last tore his gaze away from Lenox and said, "Give yourself thirty years. Have a daughter whom no amount of money can persuade someone of her birth to marry— who is a daily shame to her mother—to both their discredit—watch her fall in love with a gamekeeper, a young woman with Plantagenet blood in her veins, with a gamekeeper!—and learn, after all of that, that she is the person who has been attempting to steal your most precious possession. Then see how you react, Charles Lenox."

"A fine speech. Craig is dead."

"Craig would have died for me."

"Presumably he would have preferred the chance to volunteer for that task rather than be volunteered for it," said Lenox. "Would you have died for him, I wonder?"

"Stay here for a moment," said the duke, and in three long strides he had left the room.

He was absent for some time. It gave Lenox a chance to examine the river through the window—it was a bright day, lovely and soft—and to contemplate the string of stupidities that had led to all this.

First was Lady Violet's attempt on the painting. (And of course, it occurred to him, if Craig had really been in league with her, she could have had all the time she wanted in the duke's study without stealing it. That ought to have told him from the start that Craig wasn't involved.)

Then came Dorset's idiotic attempt at kidnapping. The tragic attempt to steal the second painting—whoever had been in the room. Corfe's defense and alliance with his sister, though that was hardly surprising, if, as it seemed, reading between the lines, neither of them had had a very kind mother.

And finally, the system clicking irreproachably into motion to exculpate the duke and Lady Violet.

It galled Lenox that Lady Violet should get what she wanted—money, marriage—even though the week before he would have called the duke cruel in the extreme for denying it to her.

At last Dorset returned. He was clutching a white piece of paper. "Here," he said.

"What is it?"

"The codicils to my will, last updated in January."

"And?"

"You will see on the second page that upon either my death or his retirement, Craig was to receive ten thousand pounds and an extension of the lands already given him, and that his nephews' schooling was to be paid for, age eight through university. That, naturally, will still be the case. They will be set on the path toward becoming gentlemen."

"I see."

"This is how I behave to one who has earned my loyalty."

High talk, high talk. Lenox leafed through the pages, and what the duke said was true. "Generous," Lenox replied, indifferently.

"I am as unhappy as you imagine me to be relieved, Mr. Lenox. Perhaps that will give you some peace. Craig was my brother and my confidant. I hoped that we would both live out our old age in Dorset Castle. My daughter has robbed me of half of all I ever loved. Including herself."

In bitter retaliation against his own autocratic ways, however, Lenox thought. Wasn't this what Shakespeare's readers called by the name of tragedy? A man destroyed by his own qualities.

He looked at the painting of the writer—the sly, amused, sorrowful eyes.

"I am sorry about that," said Lenox, handing the pages back.

He wished he had never taken the case. "Thank you, I suppose," said Dorset.

"And your daughter? Where has she gone?"

"Corfe will accompany her to Biarritz. From there she will make her way in the world as she sees fit. I have settled a sum on her, if you want to know the crude details of the matter."

"I always do, I am afraid."

Dorset looked at him with a flash of revulsion, and Lenox realized how different their codes were—to the duke, Lenox had sullied himself; to Lenox, the duke.

"She is independent now. She is welcome to return here as a single woman. As Mrs. Walters I will not receive her."

"The blacksmith in Markethouse disapproved of his daughter's marriage, when I was a child.

On his deathbed she was the only person he wanted to see. But she could not be fetched back in time before he died."

"A fascinating anecdote," the duke said.

Lenox shrugged. "Your pleasure, Your Grace."

His Grace sat down, looking Lenox in the eye yet again, wearily, warily. "I suppose the question now is whether we shall try to find this play."

"I see no reason why we should not," said Lenox, though he felt equally tired. "When would it be convenient for you to go to Kent?"

"I can leave tomorrow morning."

Lenox stood up. "So be it. Good day, Duke."

CHAPTER FORTY-FOUR

When he left Dorset House, Lenox saw a young man in a summer suit lounging by the front steps, a foot propped back against the railing. One of Corfe's friends, from the look of him. Lenox touched his hat and went on his way, mind back on Captain Irvington, lost at sea.

"Sir," the fellow said when Lenox had gone about ten paces.

He turned back and, after a moment of what felt like an intense dislodgement from his own senses, realized that it was *Bonden,* of all people. "Bonden!" he said.

"How do you do?"

"Fairly well. You—you surprised me."

Bonden fell into step with him. They continued in the direction Lenox had been going. "I read this morning that your duke had returned. I wanted to see if his painting had followed him."

"It did."

"Yes, I saw. The matter is concluded, then?"

"It is."

"To your satisfaction?"

That was a more difficult question. "I don't know that I would say that."

"Mm."

Bonden raised his cigar again, and Lenox thought that perhaps it was this prop that allowed his astonishing concealment (for the younger man had looked the older straight in the face when he touched his hat, and Lenox would have sworn him to be no more than thirty or so). That, and the suit of clothes, and a fresh-shaven cheek.

"You spent all morning here, then?" Lenox asked.

"I often find that it pays to be careless with my time. In this instance I was curious." They turned into the park (Lenox, at least, was walking automatically toward his home), and Bonden went on. "I observe that it was the butler who died. Not the duke, or one of the duke's children."

"Yes."

"They used to sing a shanty at sea. There was always some tuneful soul who passed the third watch in song, quiet, you know, since it was after midnight, but keeping those on watch awake." Bonden tossed his cigar into the cobblestones of the street, then sang, in a quiet and surprisingly mellifluous voice, *"Same the world over, ain't it a shame—the rich what gets the pleasure, the poor what gets the blame* . . . That's the part I remember, anyway."

So, then, Bonden had sniffed out what Lenox had taken until today to piece together: that Craig's death had not been accidental.

"True too often, I fear," said Lenox.

"I wonder if you would give me an hour of your time? Not more."

They were on one of the pathways in Green Park, and before answering Lenox nodded to a gentleman he knew, Sir Thomas Clapton, and wished him a good day. Clapton was walking toward Parliament, where he was greatly concerned with foreign affairs, cane under his arm. The year before he had written a long report on currency reform that nobody had read, and with whose ideas nearly every reasonable person in England vehemently disagreed; naturally he was knighted in the next honors list, and now considered in all the papers as a wide-ranging authority.

Passing Clapton suddenly made Lenox rue every one of his decisions. Each single one. Clapton was only six years his elder! He was not very remarkably smart, not even amiable. He would be in the next cabinet.

Meanwhile, Lenox was bound for God knew where with an old sailor who wouldn't tell him anything straight, and the career he had chosen as a detective had already cut off, permanently, his path to Parliament, the other vague dream of his youth.

Without showing any of this feeling—he hoped—he turned to Bonden. "Lead the way," he said.

They boarded an omnibus bound east. They passed the trip in silence, until at last Bonden signaled, when they were in Eastcheap Street, that they should disembark.

It was an insalubrious, swarming stretch of London, families stacked too close together, pawnbrokers next to rag shops, prostitutes out in plain sight even at this early hour. Unaccompanied children ran to and fro.

They turned off Eastcheap and into Pudding Lane. This was the heart of where the Great Fire had raged in 1666, and all the buildings were of the last hundred years or so, some of them tilting oddly, jury-rigged, no doubt unsafe.

The fire had incinerated thirteen thousand buildings, Lenox knew—all slums, skirting up only toward the edge of Mayfair.

"Do you know how many people died in the fire, out of curiosity?" Bonden asked.

"I do, as a matter of fact," said Lenox. "Six."

"Ha! Yes, that's what they say up Parliament way. More like six hundred, they'll tell you here. The bodies weren't found, that's all."

Lenox was about to answer that he doubted that when they stopped. Bonden acted out his usual small performance—leaning against a building, producing his tobacco, acting busy— and Lenox followed his example.

They were opposite a small yard, mostly in disuse. In it was a lone woman. She looked up at them, without recognition, for a beat—large, faded eyes, strong cheekbones, hair in a bonnet. Then she turned back to the yard, where a small row of lettuce plants grew; she was plucking paltry leaves from them, brushing away dirt. She put what she had retrieved in her apron and then went with a small pail of water to some kind of bare-limbed tree that Lenox could have told her from this distance would never flower or fruit again.

"That is Mrs. Lila Wallace, relict of the late Alec Wallace, a carthorse driver. Two children. He was murdered seven months ago."

"Why?"

"Nobody knows."

"Money? A bar fight?"

"Not money, not a bar fight. He was shot in his own rooms."

Lenox crossed his arms. "Does she need money?"

"No, she manages."

"What point are you making, then, Mr. Bonden?"

"None at all, Mr. Lenox. I had it in mind to offer you a trade."

"What sort of trade?"

"I will teach you what I know if you help me find out who killed her husband. It is a matter of some interest to me. She is my cousin."

"She didn't recognize you."

"Nor did you."

Lenox looked across the way again. "Yes, true. But why don't you solve the case?"

"I don't have your gift."

"You!"

Bonden nodded, pipe now in his mouth, in place of the West End cigar. "I can find things; I can watch. But you can ask questions—and your name, your face, your manner, gain you admission where I could well be denied."

"This is a genuine offer?"

"It is. You know how to be active. I can teach you how to be . . . perhaps not passive, but certainly quiet. There is a great deal of power in quietness, Mr. Lenox. And not only quietness of voice but of body, of posture."

"I see."

"And together perhaps we may give my cousin some peace."

At that moment something overcame Lenox. The lesson was there, whether Bonden intended it or otherwise: that crime happened indiscriminately, or if with discrimination, then with discrimination against the poor. He must redouble his efforts. No more dukes for a while; the Yard could help him or it could not.

But there was the potential all around him to do something useful in the world, just what his father had always emphasized, and Bonden had articulated something that Lenox had known but never conceded to himself, or even considered especially.

It was that he had a gift for this. What was he thinking? He wouldn't have traded places with Sir Thomas Clapton.

"You have a bargain," Lenox said. "Thank you for taking me on as a pupil. I am full of effort, even if I am a slow fist sometimes."

Bonden nodded. "Good."

"You will have to wait two days to begin, however. Perhaps three." He didn't like to say that Lady Jane's garden party was to take place in two mornings. "I must go to Kent to see to a few remaining pieces of business."

They shook hands—and it was left to Lenox, as Bonden strode off, to determine how to return, handkerchief across his nose, to his own part of London. In any event he had his next case. He was already wondering if he and Graham had clipped anything from the newspapers about Mr. Alec Wallace, or whether the Yard had made any headway on the matter at all.

CHAPTER FORTY-FIVE

The duke's carriage was so large that it took up a lane and a half of most roads, a marked inconvenience when passing anyone other than perhaps an exceptionally thin adolescent on a donkey. Lenox would have preferred the train but had to admit, by the third church they visited, that it was a comfortable conveyance, four seats wide, well ventilated, with a compartment beneath their feet where a large slab of ice cooled the carriage, leaving a trail of water droplets in the dust behind them, fairy-tale fashion.

It was a company motley enough for Shakespeare's own enjoyment. There were the duke, Lenox, and Graham, of course, but with them as well were two learned gentlemen. One was Sir Charles Locke Eastlake, the only person other than Queen Victoria whom Dorset had told about the portrait. He was a middle-aged fellow with lank, curled brown hair who had, for reasons known only to himself and his valet, worn a heavy flannel suit and was now perspiring at rates of almost indescribable speed and volume. Lenox tired of him after, oh, five minutes of travel—he was pomposity itself—

but fortunately the near closeness of apoplexy quieted him somewhat.

That left old Duncan Jones, quiet and benevolent, whom Lenox had coaxed from the British Library with some of the story.

Dorset hadn't been happy, but Lenox had asked for and received the favor several days before, the permission to bring a friend. A duke could not go back on his word.

They had been to three of the five churches that Lenox and Graham's research had turned up: St. Wistan's, St. Aethelstan's, and St. Bartholomew's. The first churchyard had been tiny and offered no probable candidate; the second was large, but the rector informed them that nobody had been interred there until the 1790s. The last was middle-sized, and they had gone tombstone by tombstone and found nothing except a Mary Swindle, buried in 1844 beside her husband, Samuel Swindle.

This left two churches, St. John's-upon-Wold and St. James's.

They were headed now for the latter, having stopped at an inn to order food. Eastlake had drunk so much water that he looked half drunk when they were again seated in the carriage, his eyes closed. The duke, meanwhile, was equanimity itself. One would never have guessed that the week before he'd been locked in the Tower of London.

The general conversation had been only polite until now. Lenox and Jones had been seated next to each other, and talked a great deal privately.

As they had reseated themselves, though, they had ended up in opposite corners, and Lenox said, hoping to make the last few hours of this task more pleasant, "Do you believe that Shakespeare was a Catholic, Mr. Jones?"

The old Yorkshireman considered the idea carefully. He was a pleasure to have brought, Lenox was glad to observe, slow but certain in his motions, deferential to the duke but his own man, polite to Graham.

"It's a vexed question, I fear," he replied. "The—"

"OPINION IS DIVIDED."

Eastlake managed to eject this judgment before sinking back into the cushions. He wasn't a large or overweight gentleman—it was surprising that he should be quite so red—but the effort of a day out of the dim corridors of his museum seemed too much for him.

"Sir Charles is quite correct," Jones said politely. He waited a beat to see if the other man would go on, but it wasn't even clear that he was conscious. The duke looked at him with disgust. "My personal belief is that Shakespeare was irreligious. Coleridge says it well: 'Shakespeare is of no age—nor of any religion, or party, or profession. The body and substance of his works came out of the unfathomable depths of his own oceanic mind.' There is certainly a great quarrel with God running through the plays.

"On the other hand, it seems definite that John Shakespeare was Catholic, and I think it would have appealed to William in more than one way to remain a Catholic."

"How's that?" asked the duke.

"Well, Your Grace, he was mischievous, for a start. He was not Marlowe, who lost his life in a cheap tavern over spying—"

"CHRISTOPHER MARLOWE," said Eastlake forcefully.

"I am quite aware of him," said Dorset with irritation.

"He was Shakespeare's only real peer," said Jones, "but died at twenty-nine. Shakespeare's rebellions were much subtler, as befits a country boy. Marlowe had been at Cambridge."

"What was the other reason?" asked Lenox.

"Ah! Well, his father, you know, the great life force that never left Shakespeare. Evidently a man of tremendous charm. Long after his father's disgrace, William paid an immense amount of money to buy back all his father's lands in Stratford and more. And he finally obtained a coat of arms for the family, something his father had fought in vain to accomplish for many years.

It meant that they were a family of gentlemen at last."

"You think he would have been as loyal to his father's religion as to his aspirations, then," Lenox said.

"ROT," said Sir Charles.

They all looked at him expectantly.

"How so, Eastlake? Speak up," said the duke, his scorn undisguised.

"HATED HIS FATHER."

Jones tilted his head. "There may be something in what Sir Charles says. I have always thought it curious—and this is a personal theory, not an academic one," he added, though his clear blue eyes, buried in crow's-feet, sparkled, "—that Falstaff might have been based on John Shakespeare."

Probably no character was closer to the hearts of Englishmen than Falstaff, the witty, obese, drunken, zestful, devious, cowardly best friend of Prince Hal.

Indeed, it was Graham, now, who said, "Falstaff!"

The democratizing effect of their hours in the carriage could be seen—nobody thought twice about Lenox's valet interjecting. "Yes," said Jones. "To begin with there is his name—Sir John Falstaff. John! Can we consider that an accident? After William's son, Hamnet, died, he wrote his saddest play, *Hamlet*. He obviously cared about names.

"Then there is that 'Sir,' a title no character in all of Shakespeare deserves less. If John Shakespeare was a chaser after titles and coats of arms, it might be a mockery of his father, that. But what I like best of all is the name—*shake, speare; false, staff.*" He looked around hopefully. "Do you see the echo?"

"Yes," said Dorset, unexpectedly.

"Shakespeare was highly conscious of his own name. Sometimes he was called Shakeshaft. Falstaff! It seems more than a coincidence to me. And his father was a drunk, made great sums of money and lost them, beloved, loathed—a man not unlike Falstaff. Is there a more conflicted portrait in Shakespeare?"

They all glanced simultaneously at Eastlake, but he had gone as pale as Banquo's ghost and, as if sensing their gaze, finally loosened his tie. His relief was palpable. "Ah," he said. "Good God. That is better."

"It is an interesting argument," said the duke.

Jones nodded his thanks. "I have considered sometimes that Falstaff makes more direct Catholic references than almost any other character—the catechism, the *ecce signum . . .*"

He would have gone on, but at that moment the carriage drew to a stop.

And Lenox knew before he had set a second foot on the ground that this was it.

St. James's was a tiny crumbling church with a

peaceful grassy churchyard next to it, shaded by an enormous flowering oak. The sun struck the tree in different places, so that it was dark green in some, golden in others. There was a deep feeling of serenity here, of eternity. Perhaps of God.

"Sir," said Graham, and pointed.

One of the few dozen tombstones in the churchyard had recently had its dirt turned over. Dorset glanced at the grave and then broke into a hard walk. Lenox followed him. Behind them, Graham—good soul—stayed with Jones, who trailed more slowly, using a silver-capped cane.

The duke fell to his knees at the tombstone. "Mary!" he cried, and indeed the name was there on the tombstone, faint but legible: Mary Pike.

He dug with his hands, though the driver had gotten down from the box with the trowel, spade, and shovel the duke had specifically ordered brought.

After only a short time the duke brought up a dark mahogany box, battered and scored. He brushed the dirt off the top.

But why was it still here, Lenox wondered, if it had been dug up so recently?

The answer came: The duke pulled from the box, which was lined with some sort of crude tin, a single aged sheet of paper and a letter on fresh blue paper.

He studied the sheet, as Lenox looked over his shoulder.

Campion
As it hath on two occasions
beene publicly acted, by
the Right Honourable the Lord Chamberlain,
his servants
Written by Wm. Shakespere
Printed by Iames Roberts, 1599

"The authentic title page of a quarto, or the best imitation I have ever seen," Jones said softly. Both Dorset and Lenox looked back. The old scholar looked like a man gazing into the face of an angel. "Campion. A Catholic martyr. Roberts would have happily printed off five or ten copies for a playwright who had given him so much worse. He was a broad-minded man. They performed it, I would guess, for highly select audiences."

"But where is the *play?*" asked Dorset.

Lenox pointed at the letter in his hand and said, cursing himself for having told her she got the clue wrong, "Your daughter has it."

The duke looked confused; then realization dawned on him. He opened the letter.

Father,

Here is the title sheet. The remainder of the play will be yours when you receive, with her husband, at a ball of the usual sort at Dorset House,

your loving daughter,

Mrs. Isaac Walters

So the play was with Lady Violet.

All of them reacted differently. The duke looked stunned, there on his knees, unmoving. Lenox himself felt a kind of stupor. She had pieced together the clues; he had been beaten.

He gazed at the ground. Shakespeare's own hands must have turned over this earth once. Only after a moment, because of that stupor, did he appreciate the final trick of the thing, whether it was intentional or not: *pike,* Mary Pike's last name, was another word for staff; or spear.

CHAPTER FORTY-SIX

After they had all returned to the carriage—it was Graham, good fellow, who thought to smooth the earth above Mary Pike's mortal remains back into tidy order—the duke asked if they would do him the favor of a few minutes' silence.

The few minutes extended past an hour. Sir Charles Eastlake fell into a peaceful sleep, his face a less alarming color now that he had removed his tie and jacket. Jones watched the golden evening light, as old men will; Lenox read on in *Uncle Tom's Cabin*.

Occasionally he looked up and thought about *Campion*. A hundred years hence, would the play be performed on the great stages of the world, between runs of *Macbeth* and *A Midsummer Night's Dream*? It was this that they were all no doubt wondering: the immortal preciousness of what Lady Violet Walters, as she must now be called, had carried away so fecklessly, tearing a title sheet from it as if it were a common newspaper. Sublime arrogance.

Just after the carriage had stopped to let Jones off in Bloomsbury (Dorset had the grace to take each of them directly home) and the driver had opened the door, he said, "Lenox has not confided your circumstances in me, Your Grace. But I hope we may see the play. Fifteen ninety-nine! He never had a year when his genius reached a higher pitch—and if it was only performed twice, this may be the only copy, fair or foul, we have any chance of seeing."

The duke only nodded. "Thank you for your knowledge and your civility today, Mr. Jones. You have been an admirable addition to the party."

The scholar touched his hat. "Your Grace."

Now only Lenox, Graham, and the duke remained. (They had dropped Sir Charles off first; one could only imagine that it would take him weeks to recover from his bid at fashion.) Lenox was about to speak when the duke asked him abruptly if he was free to dine at White's on Monday, three days hence. Lenox said he was. The duke then tapped the carriage door with his cane.

"Take these gentlemen home," he said to the driver. "I shall walk."

They watched him go in the gloaming, spine stiff, hands clasped around the cane behind his back, his top hat adding a foot to his imposing height, his swallowtail jacket lending a formality to his passage through the throngs. Nobody glanced at him: the third man in all the land, probably; and now a witness to his own death, father-in-law of a gamekeeper, father of a murderer and her accomplice, husband to a wife indifferent on all accounts, and accidental traitor to his family's great secret pride and duty.

It was possible to have sympathy even for a duke.

"Rum day," said Lenox as the carriage stirred into motion.

"Among the rummest, sir," said Graham.

Lenox laughed. "Three years ago I thought a case such as this one would reach its conclusion and every last string would be tied off. As if I were delivering a fruitcake in brown paper on Christmas. But what do we have now? A lost play still lost, a death unpunished, a father and son who have lied to each other, a father and daughter who may never speak again. It is thoroughly unsatisfying."

"People have remarked that life is unsatisfying, sir," said Graham.

Lenox smiled. He knew his immense good fortune, and felt a guilt shadowing it—perceived it even in comments like this, which he knew were not personal. "Indeed," he said. "Indeed."

When they pulled up at Lenox's house in Hampden Lane, he saw that an arrangement of flowers was visible along every sill of his house. They hadn't been there that morning. He pointed them out to Graham.

"Peculiar, sir," said the valet.

"You see what it means?"

"No, sir."

"My mother is here. The only person whose opinion Mrs. Huggins truly cares for in my family."

Graham raised his eyebrows. "Do you think so?"

"I'll bet you Mr. Templeton's tenner."

"I shall have to respectfully decline the offer, sir. I see that the lights are on in the lower drawing room—and I smell gingerbread, Mrs. Huggins's specialty. I think you must be right."

And he was. Seated comfortably in his study were Lady Emma Lenox, along with Edmund. They both rose when Charles came in.

"Hello, Mother," he said. It was so ingrained in him not to ask a direct question of a woman that he said, first, "I hope you are doing well," before adding, more directly, "How are you? What brings you here? Am I being shipped to the colonies?"

"Where have you been all day?" his mother asked.

"Kent."

"Kent! Apples, hops, cherries, and women? For shame, Charles. And I hear you have murdered a duke, or something of the sort."

"Mother," said Edmund chidingly.

She gave Charles the kind of hug only a mother can give, in which part of her love passes into a person, truly and physically, a press of the body holding in its few seconds a history of tenderness that dates to the time when the two of you were one.

Lenox hugged her back, suddenly exhausted and feeling very, very young, where just twenty minutes before, staring at Dorset's back, he had felt old and wise.

"If you don't mind giving me a minute, I will wash and change. It has been a long day."

"Of course," said his mother.

In the hallway he met Mrs. Huggins. *"Your mother is here,"* the housekeeper hissed, forgetting all formalities.

"Yes, I know. You just saw me leave the room in which she's sitting."

"What are we supposed to *do?*"

"Do?"

"About it, sir?"

Lenox looked at her with genuine bafflement. Of all the people to pick in his family, Lancelot and his mother. After them came the cats, and then Charles a very distant sixth, probably. "I'm not sure I see it as quite the emergency you do, Mrs. Huggins. Has she tried to steal something? What's wrong?"

She looked at him with a face full of despair and betrayal and stormed away, off toward some task only she understood.

Edmund caught up with Charles in the hallway as Mrs. Huggins was going. "A quick word?" he said.

"Yes, is everything all right?"

"Of course it is. But what on earth are you doing with Thaddeus Bonden? Thomas Clapton almost fell to the ground when he saw you, Charles. You must be more careful."

Lenox was bewildered. "What?"

"Have you involved yourself in politics?"

"Politics! No. He was helping me with Dorset. Politics?"

"Oh." Edmund looked relieved. "That's all right, then."

"What does Bonden have to do with politics?"

Edmund shook his head. "I cannot say much. Only that he is our side's greatest spy against the French. If we fight a war with them again and win it, he will be the cause."

"*Bonden?* At the Dovecote?"

"Yes. Why? How did you hear of him?"

"About, I suppose. He is an expert in finding things."

"Oh, that. Right. He refuses a government salary above his naval pension."

"Good Lord."

"I'm going back to Mother. Be discreet if you wander around with him again, and don't mention what I've told you. Clapton will be comforted."

"I am so pleased to be able to comfort him," said Charles, but Edmund had never done very well with catching sarcasm, and only nodded.

Lenox went upstairs and washed. Looking into the mirror, he saw that his face was tired, sun-beaten. He realized that he had needed his mother. How did she always know?

Since his father had died, Charles and Lady Emma—who had always been closer than she and Edmund—had stuck close, but she had also transferred a great deal of her attention to her elder son. He was the baronet, and though Lenox House was hers, its ways, its history, its custodianship, its people would all slowly have to become his. It was perhaps in this that she had found consolation from her grief at being widowed—she had observed firsthand her husband discharging his duties for forty years, and nobody could be better positioned to help pass those duties between generations.

But the oceans could dry, the sky fall into darkness, Charles knew, and she would find him, one way or another.

He went downstairs, where he was immediately asked if he was going to marry Miss Auburn; he coughed into his brandy with alarm, and when he had recovered said no, not just at that moment, it had been a long day; his mother told him he mustn't be facetious; he told her not to gossip so much with Lady Jane—and all in all, to both parties, the visit had thus commenced satisfactorily.

CHAPTER FORTY-SEVEN

The two brothers and their mother stayed up late that night, talking over local matters from their hometown of Markethouse. Every name that came up was as familiar as their own; when Edmund and Charles heard that Mrs. Carter was marrying yet again they rolled their eyes at the same instant.

At long length, when the last bits of cheese, fruit, and biscuit on the tray had been eaten, when the teapot was empty and all three were yawning, and Mrs. Huggins seemed at last satisfied that she had discharged her responsibilities toward Lady Emma, Sir Edmund rose and said he ought to be getting home, and that he would drop their mother at the Savoy— where she always stayed when she didn't want to open her own London house. She added before she left that she would be by in the morning to inspect Lancelot.

"You won't like what you see," Charles warned. "Neither of you were as angelic as you seem to believe."

"I was," said Edmund.

"Ha!" said Charles.

"Charles!" said their mother. She gave him

371

a kiss on the cheek. "I wish you wouldn't tease your brother."

"Well, you may go on wishing if it pleases you," Lenox said in a grumbling way, and saw them to the door, closing it after they were in a carriage with a tremendous yawn.

Before he turned in, he decided to quickly check his desk. It was piled with notes and telegrams. He sifted through these until he saw one that attracted his attention.

It was a letter from a woman named Mrs. Anderson Withering, posted at Cowgate, Scotland. That was, if Lenox recalled correctly, the long thoroughfare that lay between the old town and the university in Edinburgh.

7 June

Dear Mr. Lenox,

Thank you for your solicitous concern about my brother. He is here at Mrs. Walsh's House for the Incurably Mad. (It is not a name I like, but offered the best care that was recommended to my husband, who sought several medical opinions.) He has a private room there and I visit him twice a week. He is a lovely companion—but as you have apparently witnessed, erratic in his behavior. He had known for some time that we were to resituate him in Scotland, and he was displeased with that. Perhaps it was this that motivated him to approach you.

The name Captain Tankin Irvington means nothing to me, and my brother has no naval background, nor has he spent any time in Australia—to answer your three questions. You are welcome to visit either him or me should you happen to be in Edinburgh.

Best wishes,
Kitty (Belmont) Withering

PS: I write this having just seen your second telegram. I was never required to sign a visitor log at Bedlam. I do not know why.

Lenox quickly dug through the rest of the letters on the desk. He checked the previous wire—the Edinburgh Asylum. He had written to the wrong institution. A creeping feeling of dread, just the initial stage of comprehension, crept up the back of his neck.

He knew he must act or he would sleep badly; he wrote out a few questions for Dr. Hansel and sent a sleepy footman out to send the telegram and pay for return post, so that Hansel could write as voluminously and as quickly as he wished.

This done, Lenox sat in his chair, holding the letter and thinking about Belmont. He fell asleep there—and it was long after two in the morning when he woke, stumbled heavily upstairs, and, a cool breeze running in from the windows, took with gratitude to his bed.

A reply from Hansel awaited him when he woke, just after seven. It was tucked under a glass of apple juice with chips of ice in it, next to his teacup. Lenox slid into a dressing gown and, picking up a piece of bacon with his fingers simultaneously, tore open the wire.

> Dear Lenox STOP received your wire and shall endeavor to answer all questions STOP in first place families have not for some seven hundred years been required to sign in STOP shame of association STOP only medical visitors and so forth STOP in second place Belmont was indeed billeted with a former member of the navy for a time STOP full name Carleton Wexford unsure rank STOP standard lunacy STOP finally Mrs Walsh an excellent home by all accounts STOP smaller and more discreet STOP in hopes this helps STOP Hansel

This was a tremendously expensive number of words, but Lenox didn't care a fig. He flattened it on the table, running over its folds with the side of his hand, and read it once more.

"Graham," he called.

The valet appeared, already dressed in his crisp gray suit, hair newly clipped. When did he find time to go to the barber? Before Lenox awoke, obviously. There was an old man who walked from house to house with scissors and mirror. "Sir?"

"Will you fetch me the naval register from the study—the big blue one on the upper shelf near the windows—and then come and join me?"

Lenox ate his eggs and pondered Belmont until Graham returned a moment later. Lenox leafed through the oversized book until he came to the name Wexford. There were two of them.

Only one he needed: "Midshipman Carleton Wexford, sometime officer of Her Majesty's ships *Isabelle, Livia, Victory, Roseanna, Julia, Victoria,* retired Her Majesty's service 1844, living Cable Street, Portsmouth."

And later Bedlam, it would appear.

Lenox saw immediately that Wexford had been on at least two ships upon which Captain Irvington had also served, the *Livia* and the *Victoria.*

"That settles it, Graham," he said.

"What's that, sir?"

Lenox sighed. "I have been made a goose of—by an inmate."

"Belmont, sir?"

"The same."

They sat and picked over the news as Lenox

picked over his eggs. Obviously Belmont had picked up Irvington's name from his bunkmate; obviously he was no more unfairly asylumed than most men at Bedlam; obviously his sister cared for him greatly.

Lenox felt very, very stupid. It was unlike him to be so credulous. He said so to Graham.

"Perhaps there is a lesson in it, sir," said Graham.

"Not to trust the passing comments of insane people? Most people learn that lesson some time before the age of twenty-six."

Graham smiled. "That sometimes there are simple, unsuspicious reasons behind a mystery, sir, I would venture. The profession you have chosen cannot always be portraits of Shakespeare."

Lenox speared a sausage moodily. "I suppose. It's not as if even that was very satisfying." He considered his lunch with the duke on Monday. "I wonder if we shall ever see that play in England again."

At that moment Lenox felt, out of absolutely nowhere, a sharp pain on his chin, like a bee sting. It took him a bewildered second to realize what had happened, and then he stood bolt upright.

"*Lancelot,*" he shouted, as the boy, with his peashooter, sped away upstairs to his hideous den.

"Shall I fetch him, sir?" Graham asked.

Lenox sat down, rubbing his face. "No. I deserve it for falling for Belmont."

"You are done with him, then?"

"I shall ask a friend in Edinburgh to verify what the letter says. But I have no doubt it will all prove out." Lenox grimaced, rubbing his chin. "It really does hurt, that little hellion."

"I can fetch ice, sir."

"Oh, sit down, bother you, pour yourself some tea." Lenox thought for a moment. "Do you know, of the numerous arguments that I have seen London make that the world is a cruel and meaningless place—murder, theft, fraud—none is more profound than that Mrs. Huggins should love that boy."

"She is childless, sir."

"And that is the child to make her regret it? No—mark my words, I will never have children, Graham. Poison my soup one supper if I ever tell you otherwise."

"Very good, sir."

"Make it some quick and painless poison, if you wouldn't mind."

"To be sure, sir."

CHAPTER FORTY-EIGHT

There was a table at White's that belonged exclusively to the duke, one of just three members accorded the honor, and was otherwise kept empty. The headwaiter led them to it—the center of the most important room at the most exclusive club in the British Empire.

By leading him here, the duke had discharged a certain duty; Lenox was a gentleman who could be respectably met in the highest echelon of London society, up to Buckingham Palace. There would be new invitations on his hall table when he returned home that afternoon, some so brazen as to be given again after an earlier withdrawal, he reflected as they looked at the menus.

They ate salmon, pheasant, mashed potatoes, and long beans, with the house popovers, light and eggy, serving as sauce-pushers, per tradition. Lenox was a member at White's, and when the check came with coffee and brandy, he offered to sign it. But the duke gave him a look somewhere between contempt and amusement, and just waved it away, unsigned.

They had spoken so far only of neutral matters. The duke reminisced about Lenox's father in kind terms, and they spoke at some length about how Edmund was managing his new responsibilities.

"Please tell him that he is welcome to call on me if he should need any advice," Dorset said, sipping his coffee black.

"It is very kind of you, Your Grace."

"Meanwhile I wonder if you would join me in nominating Ward for membership here. It is perhaps slightly above his station, but he has been loyal to me, and he is well educated and very sound."

Lenox looked down at the petit fours. "Of course," he said.

It was remarkable how rapidly the duke had returned, unstained, to his previous sphere of social activity. That night, he mentioned in passing, he would be dining with the Queen, and the next week he planned to do some stag shooting at his friend Lord Mountjoy's estate.

Lenox thought of General Pendleton.

"Tell me," Lenox said at last, "only because I am inveterately curious. Will you seek the play?"

The duke's expression flattened. When he spoke, it seemed to pain him; he did not even say his daughter's name, merely, "She has married one of my cotters."

"I know," said Lenox.

This was an ancient race of farm laborers, many of their families on the small parcels of land just as long as the dukes and earls who rented to them had been on theirs. Their dwellings, over time, had taken their names—cottages.

"You went to Harrow and Oxford. Your father was a traditionalist. You must have some comprehension of my position. Imagine your own position, but magnified a thousand times."

It was exhausting, this arrogance. He was only a man, the fellow across the table, with his lined face, his smooth gray hair, his gold ring, his cup of coffee. One day the last person who had ever loved him would die, just as was true for everyone within these convivial walls. What lay beyond this earth they none of them knew—but nobody could believe there would be dukes there.

Or perhaps they could. "I can see the difficulty, Your Grace," said Lenox. "But it is Shakespeare."

"Yes, Shakespeare," said the duke, turning his eyes to the windows. "William Shakespeare. I think it is time for that portrait to be stored in the vault at Dorset Castle, and perhaps in three or four generations someone will take it out, and read my letter. But not till then."

So *Campion* would not be coming back to England! Could that be? Lenox felt a shiver of rage—but knew he might just as profitably yell at the crashing shore as at the Duke of Dorset.

To his credit, the duke, before they left, invited him to play a few games of billiards, doubles. The message was clear: that it was a social luncheon, this one, a friendship. He was loud in his proclamations of affection for Lenox, free in his teasing, before half a dozen men who would each tell another half a dozen about it. 6+x+y.

They went to the cloakroom together and fetched their hats at a little past two o'clock. Emerging into the lobby, Lenox saw his brother.

"Edmund!"

"Oh, hello, Charles." He bowed to the duke. "Edmund Lenox, Your Grace."

The duke inclined his head in response. "A pleasure to make your acquaintance. I have been telling your brother that you ought to call upon me if you need any advice about that small estate of yours."

Only someone who had known Edmund exceedingly well over the course of many years would have discerned the anger in his voice when he said, "I will be sure to do so at the first possible chance, Your Grace. Thank you."

"Well!" The duke slapped his gloves against his palm. "I will bid you both good day."

"Good day, Your Grace," said Charles, with the peculiar consciousness that they were passing out of each other's lives. "I will write Ward's letter this evening."

"Capital." The duke looked briefly troubled. "And you will be . . . discreet."

"That goes without saying."

"My apologies. Yes. Good day, gentlemen."

The whole lobby watched him leave, that figure of greatness, and step into his gilt carriage. Charles, for his part, preferred the more modest company in which the duke had left him.

"Why are you here?" he asked Edmund.

"Lunch with the American ambassador, Streeter. Very civil fellow, you know. Lovely daughters."

"Surely you can't be trying to marry me off, too."

They had spent much of the weekend fending off Lenox's mother's suggestions, abetted by Lady Jane, of whom he ought to marry.

"No, no," said Edmund.

They turned into the card room off the lobby and ordered two cups of coffee. When it arrived, Lenox reached into his pocket. He had his little book. He finally felt, for the first time in his life, having glanced into it forty or fifty times in the past week, that he was starting to understand something about why people loved Shakespeare. He had flapped down a tiny corner above one quotation that very morning, struck at how it described his feelings for the person who had given him the book: *This earth that bears thee dead bears not alive so stout a gentleman.*

He showed the little volume to Edmund. "Did Father give you one of these when you went to school?"

Edmund looked at the title page and smiled. "No. He gave me Hesiod's *Days*. Great lot of rot about farming. Did he write in it?"

Lenox showed him the front page. "No."

Edmund looked at him queerly. "Charles, you must remember that Father always wrote at the *back* of the books he gave. It was a quirk."

"I don't remember that at all. Why?"

"He said it would be rude to speak before the author." Edmund smiled. "Excuse me for a moment, would you? I need a quick word with Chalmers there about the Irish bill, damn him. Only a moment."

Lenox watched him go, frowning—the Irish bill wouldn't come up this session—until he realized, dolt that he was, that his brother had been exercising tact, leaving him alone to look and see if his father had written in the book.

He flicked through the pages slowly.

And there, at the back, was his father's infinitely familiar handwriting, so disposable while he was alive but now so precious-seeming.

Charles,
It took me a long while to love Shakespeare. In school I preferred Donne. For a long time my main knowledge about Shakespeare was that his name was an anagram for I am a weakish speller, a trick which occasionally impressed my

schoolmates, and which now that you are going to school may impress yours.

But eventually I did love Shakespeare, for his wisdom, his wit, and above all for his clear-seeing love of his fellow man. I hope you, too, will have the pleasure of this discovery, whether it is now or much later in your life. Please know that whenever that time comes, if it does, I will be with you here, in the pages of this book, both now and then.

the proudest of all fathers, yours,
Thomas Lenox

CHAPTER FORTY-NINE

The next day, the time had finally come for Lancelot to depart.

"Well, it's flown by, hasn't it!" said Mrs. Huggins at breakfast, as she poured cream over Lancelot's porridge.

The lad was kicking steadily away at the legs of the dining table. "No," said Lenox.

"Oh, come now, Mr. Lenox!"

Lancelot, looking serious, said, "Do you think they'll believe me at school if I say I fought a duel in France with Spate?"

This was the huge brute he had argued with in the park; France where duels were still legal. "No," said Lenox.

"And you mustn't lie, of course," said Mrs. Huggins.

"Right, of course," said Lancelot, without, seemingly, any sense of irony. He looked at his cousin. "What if I just say I challenged him to a duel?"

"No," said Lenox, who was quite pleased that his lines were so easy.

"The story is interesting enough on its own," said Mrs. Huggins pacifyingly.

"Interesting!" Lenox said. "Mrs. Huggins, are you endorsing that kind of common low-down scrabble-hearted run-amok fistfight! You!"

The housekeeper went pink. "No!" she said. "Not at all!"

"It *is* a good story," said Lancelot, looking pleased. "He must weigh twenty stone."

"Yes, a regular David and Goliath story," said Lenox, "if they had both been imbeciles."

At around eleven o'clock, Edmund and Lady Jane came to say good-bye. (Graham, as usual the most intelligent of them all, had cleared off after a firm handshake before breakfast. No risk for him of getting caught in a last peashooter crossfire.) Lancelot was upstairs with Mrs. Huggins, shoving things into his trunk. Lenox's mother—who loved train stations dearly and irrationally—had gone to pick Eustacia up at Charing Cross. It had taken Charles some restraint not to mention the apple's toss.

He was entertaining Lady Jane and Edmund with the story of his misguided attempt to save Belmont; a comical story now, though for several days it had plagued him. But error could always lead to growth—and even as he and Edmund and Lady Jane laughed, he resolved that he would do better, in the future, at looking through appearances to the nuance that any plain-told story inevitably missed.

"Ed," said Charles, "did you know they give away a side of bacon to a couple in Essex every year that can prove they haven't quarreled in thirteen months?"

"Yes, I read the *Times*," said Edmund.

Lady Jane laughed. "Stout fellow."

"I bet you didn't know that they roll a tremendous wheel of cheese down a hill in Gloucester every year and the first person to catch it gets to keep it."

"Who told you that?" said Charles.

"Fotheringay-Phipps."

"A known liar."

Edmund shook his head gravely. "No, he had it on absolute eyeball account from his brother Waller, who's as honest as the day is long."

Charles acknowledged that Waller was a good source. "You should try to get it next year."

"I don't like cheese that much."

"What a thing to say," Lady Jane replied. "In my own house."

"This is my house," said Charles.

"In as good as my own house," she said, scowling at him and picking up the cane he used to knock on her wall.

"I don't! I prefer potatoes," said Edmund.

"Nobody's making you choose, you dunderhead," said Lady Jane. "In fact there is a reasonable argument to be made that cheese and potatoes are best together."

"I like plain buttered potatoes," said Charles, for one had to draw one's lines.

"I only said a reasonable argument."

The front door opened, and all three got up. Lenox's cousin Eustacia, a pretty, lively person, very small, with endless tea table conversation and endless goodwill toward the world, gave him a tight squeeze.

"You must tell me," she said, gripping him by his shoulders and looking up at him. "Has he been a bother?"

"My housekeeper isn't even willing to let him leave," said Charles.

She squeezed. "Good. I worry that he can be a bit high spirited."

"A bit, perhaps, at times," said Charles thoughtfully. "But I think he's turned out splendidly. You've done such good work with him."

"So he didn't bring his peashooter?"

"Well . . . he did bring it."

"Oh, Lancelot," she muttered. "Well, thank you anyway, Charles. He needed this."

At that moment there was a noise on the stairwell, and Lenox flinched, fully expecting to be shot one last time.

But his young cousin was looking almost bashful, if anything. He accepted a long hug from his mother, then said very polite good-byes to his cousin Edmund and to Lady Jane, each of whom tipped him. (Lenox could have told them the money would be spent on mischief, but what was the point?) Finally Mrs. Huggins enclosed him in a tight embrace, which he wriggled out of.

To Lenox's astonishment, he saw that she had tears in her eyes. "Please visit again sometime very soon, Master Lancelot," she said.

The boy looked at Lenox, whom he had been studiously ignoring until then. "Is that . . . do you think so, too, cousin Charles?"

Lenox realized that it was a sincere question. "Why, of course," he said. "You are welcome in any home I have, as long as I have one, Lancelot."

"I am?" he said, as if looking for a catch.

"Of course you are. When you are expelled from school I hope you will come directly here." All of them laughed, even Eustacia— except Lancelot, who, without warning, got his cousin into a tight squash around the mid-section, burying his head in Lenox's waistcoat. "Well, well," said Lenox, taken aback. "You know, you are family."

Lancelot let go and, refusing to look his cousin in the eyes, went outside with Lenox's own mother and waited for Eustacia—who said her own quick good-byes, for they were due on a train to Eton soon—and departed without another word.

Lenox stared after their carriage in a sort of shock. What strange creatures children were!

"That was very sweet, after all," said Lady Jane.

"Yes," he said, "it was."

He felt a vibration of happiness inside, something in between hope, sorrow, and life. He realized that he had accidentally done something *good,* having Lancelot here.

He watched the carriage all the way to the corner, where it disappeared into the great smoky city. Finally he turned back inside and checked his watch. "Blast," he said. "I'll be late. I'm going to the East End."

"You can give me a ride partway," said Lady Jane. "I'm having my tea with Duch. But open my present first."

She had brought it earlier, and it stood by the door, about the size of a footstool. "I will, thank you, though I don't know the occasion."

He unwrapped the parcel and saw, after a moment's confusion, what it was: a gleaming brass and satinwood barometer, fit for an admiral's cabin, with a delicate pendulum and beautiful workings.

"Jane!" he said, astonished.

She smiled at him. "For putting up with Lancelot. You can thank me in all the boring detail later—tell me how it works. For now I'll pop next door and get my things, then we can go. Let's meet soon, Edmund. There's much to discuss about Molly's party."

After she had left, Edmund said, "Why are you going?"

"I'm meeting Bonden and Graham. A case down there, a murder."

"Cor! What a life, Charles."

Lenox smiled at his brother, a radiant smile. "And yet here you are, in Parliament, titled, with Molly and two lovely sons. That is what I call a life."

"We'll swap for a day sometime. I have to go listen to them drone on in the Commons all afternoon."

"You have a deal. Good-bye till then."

Edmund watched as Charles walked outside to his cab. The baronet remained in the door-way, waving good-bye.

His secret, as he stood there, was that there had been no lunch with an American diplomat the day before; he had gone in case his younger brother were subject to another one of the duke's attacks.

Edmund watched Lenox and Lady Jane leave in the carriage. After a little time had passed, he buttoned his own jacket, a little more deliberately, and shut the door behind him after calling out his good-bye to Mrs. Huggins. He stood on the house's steps for some time, gazing out at the distant spires, the square countinghouses in the middle distance, the smoke rising from a hundred buildings into the clear summer sky, and wondered to which hidden, mysterious, thrilling corner, in the great city spread before him now like a world of marvels, his brother's new case would take him.

Center Point Large Print
600 Brooks Road / PO Box 1
Thorndike, ME 04986-0001 USA

(207) 568-3717

US & Canada:
1 800 929-9108
www.centerpointlargeprint.com